Truly, Madl

The Daring Daugh..... ᴅᴜᴜᴋ 1 7

By Emma V. Leech

Published by Emma V. Leech.

Copyright (c) Emma V. Leech 2023

Editing Services Magpie Literary Services

Cover Art: Victoria Cooper

ISBN No: 978-2-492133-78-7

About Me!

I started this incredible journey way back in 2010 with The Key to Erebus, but didn't summon the courage to hit publish until October 2012. For anyone who's done it, you'll know publishing your first title is a terribly scary thing! I still get butterflies on the morning a new title releases, but the terror has subsided at least. Now I just live in dread of the day my daughters are old enough to read them.

The horror! (On both sides, I suspect.)

2017 marked the year that I made my first foray into Historical Romance and the world of the Regency Romance, and my word what a year! I was delighted by the response to this series and can't wait to add more titles. Paranormal Romance readers need not despair, however, as there is much more to come there too. Writing has become an addiction and as soon as one book is over, I'm hugely excited to start the next so you can expect plenty more in the future.

As many of my works reflect, I am greatly influenced by the beautiful French countryside in which I live. I've been here in the South West since 1998, though I was born and raised in England. My three gorgeous girls are all bilingual and my husband Pat, myself, and our four cats consider ourselves very fortunate to have made such a lovely place our home.

KEEP READING TO DISCOVER MY OTHER BOOKS!

Other Works by Emma V. Leech

Daring Daughters

Daring Daughters Series

Girls Who Dare

Girls Who Dare Series

Rogues & Gentlemen

Rogues & Gentlemen Series

The Regency Romance Mysteries

The Regency Romance Mysteries Series

The French Vampire Legend

The French Vampire Legend Series

The French Fae Legend

The French Fae Legend Series

Stand Alone
The Book Lover (a paranormal novella)
The Girl is Not for Christmas (Regency Romance)

Audio Books

Don't have time to read but still need your romance fix? The wait is over…

By popular demand, get many of your favourite Emma V Leech Regency Romance books on audio as performed by the incomparable Philip Battley and Gerard Marzilli. Several titles available and more added each month!

Find them at your favourite audiobook retailer!

Acknowledgements

Thanks, of course, to my wonderful editor Kezia Cole with Magpie Literary Services

To Victoria Cooper for all your hard work, amazing artwork and, above all, your unending patience!!! Thank you so much. You are amazing!

To my BFF, PA, personal cheerleader and bringer of chocolate, Varsi Appel, for moral support, confidence boosting and for reading my work more times than I have. I love you loads!

I need to give a very special thank you to Amanda Bodemeaid from The Kent Association for the Blind, whose detailed help in developing Wrexham was invaluable and very much appreciated. For your information, Wrexham had Glaucoma. It is a hereditary condition and could be brought to the fore by a blow to the head. There is no association with madness – this lie his father's attempt to destroy his confidence – but at this period, it was not terribly unusual for blind people to end their days in asylums. If Wrexham's story touches you and you would like to make a donation, you can find them here.

https://www.kab.org.uk/

A huge thank you to all of Emma's Book Club members! You guys are the best!

I'm always so happy to hear from you so do email or message me :)

emmavleech@orange.fr

To my husband Pat and my family… For always being proud of me.

Table of Contents

Author's Note

The Duke of Sefton and his family are featured heavily in this book. Mention of the duke first appeared near the end of Girls Who Dare, when 'Mouldy Marguerite' was trying to match the duke's daughter, Constance, with Montagu.

As one series ended and another, Daring Daughters, began, I realised I had made a small but critical mistake with Sefton's family tree. Constance was given the family name Rivenhall, when it ought to have been Steyning. This has now been corrected for future purchases. Unfortunately, Amazon does not consider this a "critical error", so past books already purchased will not reflect the changes. To help alleviate any confusion I'm including a handy little family tree to guide you along the way.

Please accept my most sincere apologies for the mix-up. I hope you enjoy reading Wrexham and Emmeline's story as much as I enjoyed writing it!

Happy Reading,

xoxo

Emma

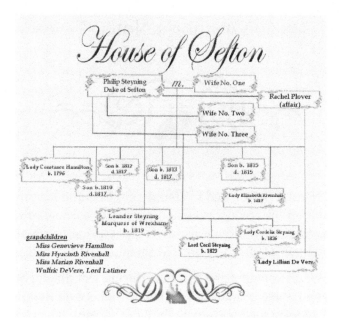

House of Sefton

Philip Steyning, Duke of Sefton — *m.* — Wife No. One

Rachel Plover (affair)

Wife No. Two

Wife No. Three

Lady Constance Hamilton b. 1796

Son b. 1812 d. 1817

Son b. 1813 d. 1817

Son b. 1815 d. 1815

Son b.1810 d.1817

Lady Elizabeth Rivenhall b. 1817

Leander Steyning Marquess of Wrexham b. 1819

Lady Cordelia Steyning b. 1826

Lord Cecil Steyning b. 1823

Lady Lillian De Vere

grandchildren

Miss Genevieve Hamilton
Miss Hyacinth Rivenhall
Miss Marian Rivenhall
Wulfric DeVere, Lord Latimer

Family Trees

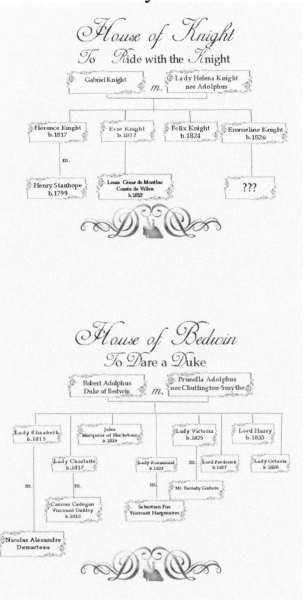

House of Knight
To Ride with the Knight

Gabriel Knight *m.* Lady Helena Knight nee Adolphus

- Florence Knight b.1817
- Evie Knight b.1822
- Felix Knight b.1824
- Emmeline Knight b.1826

Florence Knight *m.* Henry Stanhope b.1799

Evie Knight — Louis César de Montluc Comte de Villen b.1812

Emmeline Knight — ???

House of Bedwin
To Dare a Duke

Robert Adolphus Duke of Bedwin *m.* Prunella Adolphus nee Chuffington-Smythe

- Lady Elizabeth b.1815
- Jules Marquess of Blackstone b.1819
- Lady Victoria b.1825
- Lord Harry b.1833

Lady Charlotte b.1817

Lady Rosamund b.1823 *m.* Lord Frederick b.1827

Lady Octavia b.1838

Lady Elizabeth *m.* — Lady Charlotte *m.* Cassius Cadogan Viscount Oakley b.1815

m. Mr. Barnaby Godwin

m. Sebastian Fox Viscount Hargreaves

Nicolas Alexandre Demarteau

House of Hunt
To Steal a Kiss

Nathaniel Hunt **m.** Alice Hunt nee Dowding

Leo Hunt b.1815

Arabella "Bella" Hunt b.1820 m.

Lawrence Grenville Marquess of Bainbridge

House of Cavendish
To Break the Rules

Silas Anson Viscount Cavendish **m.** Aashini Anson aka: Lucia de Feria

Twins

Ashton Anson b.1816

Vivien Anson b.1816 m.

August Lane-Fox

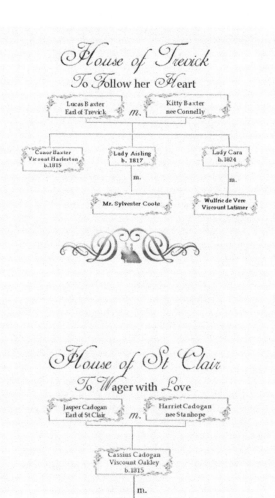

House of Trevick
To Follow her Heart

Lucas Baxter
Earl of Trevick

m.

Kitty Baxter
nee Connelly

Conor Baxter
Viscount Harleston
b.1815

Lady Aisling
b. 1817

Lady Cara
b.1824

m.

m.

Mr. Sylvester Coote

Wulfric de Vere
Viscount Latimer

House of St Clair
To Wager with Love

Jasper Cadogan
Earl of St Clair

m.

Harriet Cadogan
nee Stanhope

Cassius Cadogan
Viscount Oakley
b.1815

m.

Lady Charlotte Adolphus
b.1817

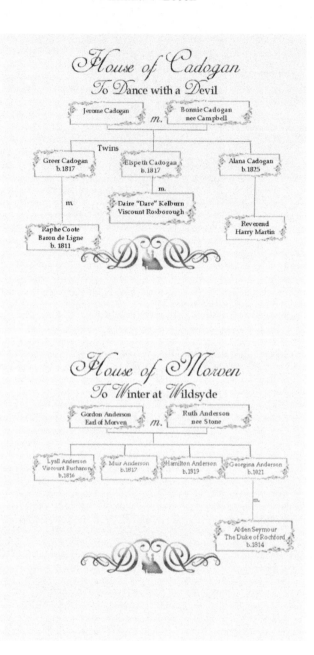

House of Cadogan
To Dance with a Devil

Jerome Cadogan m. Bonnie Cadogan nee Campbell

Twins

Greer Cadogan b.1817

Elspeth Cadogan b.1817

Alana Cadogan b.1825

m.

Daire "Dare" Kelburn Viscount Roxborough

m.

Raphe Coote Baron de Ligne b. 1811

Reverend Harry Martin

House of Morven
To Winter at Wildsyde

Gordon Anderson Earl of Morven m. Ruth Anderson nee Stone

Lysll Anderson Viscount Buchanon b.1816

Muir Anderson b.1817

Hamilton Anderson b.1819

Georgina Anderson b.1821

m.

Alden Seymour The Duke of Rochford b.1814

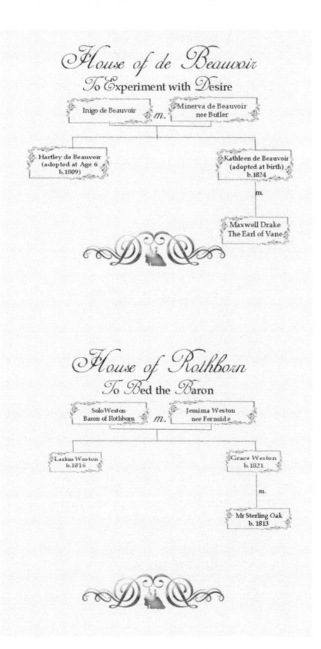

House of de Beauvoir
To Experiment with Desire

Inigo de Beauvoir   *m.*   Minerva de Beauvoir
nee Butler

Hartley de Beauvoir
(adopted at Age 6
b.1809)

Kathleen de Beauvoir
(adopted at birth)
b.1824

m.

Maxwell Drake
The Earl of Vane

House of Rothborn
To Bed the Baron

Solo Weston
Baron of Rothborn   *m.*   Jemima Weston
nee Fernside

Larkin Weston
b.1816

Grace Weston
b.1821

m.

Mr Sterling Oak
b.1813

House of Montagu
To Hunt the Hunter

Lucian Barrington
Marquess of Montagu
m.
Matilda Barrington
nee Hunt

Phillip Barrington
Earl of Ashburton
b.1816

Thomas Barrington
b.1818

Lady Catherine Barrington
(Cat)
b.1827

Lady Phoebe
(adopted 18--)
b.

m.

Maximillian Carmichael
Earl of Ellisborough

House of Ellisborough
To Dance until Dawn

Maximillian Carmichael
Earl of Ellisborough
m.
Phoebe Carmichael
nee Barrington

Jacob Carmichael
Viscount Ridley
b.1828

Rose Carmichael
b.1831

Dorothea Carmichael
b.1839

Chapter 1

Dearest Mama and Papa,

*Please forgive me. I am so dreadfully sorry for
the hurt and worry I know I am causing you,
and I know you will not understand why I
have done this, but I beg you to trust me, to
believe in me. I have good reasons for my
actions.*

*Do not come after me, or make a fuss, for you
will only risk causing a scandal. We will be
back with you very soon, I promise.*

**—Excerpt of a letter from Miss Emmeline
Knight to her parents, Lady Helena and
Mr Gabriel Knight.**

**14th February 1845, Lady St Clair's Valentine's Day Ball,
Holbrook House, Sussex.**

Emmeline sipped at her glass of orgeat and wished fervently it
was something stronger. She hadn't much of a taste for strong
liquor, but her mother swore by a medicinal tot of brandy when the
occasion arose, insisting it steadied the nerves, and Emmeline's
nerves could certainly have withstood a bit of steadying. As it was,
they were quaking like a newborn foal.

She wished she could find Cat. Speaking to that madcap
creature might give her courage, not that she was about to confide

in her. Surely even Cat would think she'd gone far too far in carrying out Lord Wrexham's plan but, all the same, it would be nice to have some company. Mostly everyone else was dancing and Alana had just left with her new husband, looking so ecstatically happy and in love with her reverend that Emmeline had almost been sick. Not because she was revolted, or jealous, or anything of the sort. She was delighted for Alana and wished her much joy. It was only that it made the contrast in their situations so obvious, because Emmeline was *not* ecstatically happy and in love, and surely one *ought* to be happy and in love before one got married?

Yet tonight, for reasons she did not wish to dwell on overmuch, she was eloping with the Marquess of Wrexham. He had recently lost his sight, which did not make him the least bit less attractive in her eyes or any less interesting. All the same, she was rushing headlong into marriage with a man she barely knew, who had a terrible reputation and was rumoured to be losing his mind. *Why?* Whenever she posed this question, her mind ran in frantic little circles, her heart raced, and her palms grew sweaty with anxiety, because there was no sensible answer. Why was *she*—quiet, well-behaved Emmeline—doing such a ridiculous and scandalous thing? Well, because in the first place she was quite obviously certifiable and, in the second, she was terrified of what might happen to him if she didn't. That was not all, however. In the third place, she had pulled that blasted dare from the hat and the horrid thing might have been written with this very circumstance in mind. There was something exceedingly spooky about that wretched hat, for *defy convention and stand up to injustice* were words that rang in her ears constantly whenever she tried to talk herself out of this madness. And as for the fourth... well, she might not be in love, but she was most certainly overwhelmingly, dreadfully, and fatally infatuated with the dratted man. In short, she was an idiot.

"Felix, what time is it, please?" she asked, grabbing her brother's arm as he sauntered past.

Felix removed her arm from his sleeve with a pained expression before she creased the fabric.

"Eight o'clock, why? Have you got to be somewhere?" he asked, a teasing glint in his eyes.

"No, of course not," Emmeline retorted, rather too sharply. She let out a breath and smiled as her brother's expression became serious. "I just wondered."

His gaze narrowed, and Emmeline's stomach lurched. Felix was just as astute as her father. Had she been anyone else, it would have been impossible to sneak anything past him, but Emmeline doubted he'd suspect his own sister of harbouring such a madcap plan... especially not after Evie's little adventure. It was a wonder their father had even allowed Emmeline out of the house after her sister's scandalous escapades. For a while she'd believed herself destined for a nunnery. Poor Papa was going to throw a fit when he discovered what she'd done. The idea made her already queasy guts roil unpleasantly.

"Are you quite well, Em? You look a bit peaked."

"Actually, no, I... I have rather a headache," Emmeline said, touching her fingers to her temple and wishing she had practised the art of lying instead of spending so many hours at the piano. It would have been a deal more use at this moment. Still, this was the perfect excuse to allow her to leave, and she did not think it would be at all difficult to conjure a real headache, as she was quite ready to cast up her accounts. "I think it's a megrim, actually. I'm afraid I ate the lemon tart at the wedding breakfast because it was so delicious."

"Well, that was daft. You know lemons always set you off! What were you thinking?"

"I wasn't thinking, I suppose," Emmeline said sheepishly, hoping her brother would just accept the excuse and play his part, though she felt wretched for telling him such whopping lies.

Felix regarded her for a long, torturous moment. "Well, that's a rotten shame. Is there anything I can do?"

"Oh, yes, be a dear and tell Mama I'm going to bed. You know the only thing that works is lying down in the dark and being quiet."

"Right you are, then. I'll play messenger. Do you want her to come up and see you?"

"Oh, no," Emmeline replied at once, shaking her head. "Don't let her miss the party. Please assure her I'm quite all right. I shall take some headache powders and you know they knock me out. I'll be asleep in no time, so there's no point."

Felix accepted this with a shrug, gave her an affectionate pat on the shoulder in sympathy, and went to find their mother. So far, so good.

Emmeline took a breath, but her lungs seemed too tight to draw in much air. For a moment, her courage failed her, and she considered changing her mind, considered really going to her room and hiding under the bedcovers. But then she remembered Wrexham, remembered the way he had looked when he had told her his family were trying to kill him. His *family!* The very people who ought to be supporting him and keeping him safe had turned upon him, and all for the sake of his wealth and title. Emmeline could hardly imagine it, but he had looked so very alone and vulnerable, and that had hurt her heart, for he was such a physically powerful man, so imposing and beautiful and... and she had wanted him so badly in that moment it had shaken her to her core. She had wanted him enough to agree to anything. Even his ridiculous proposal. Now, though....

"Oh, good heavens, Emmeline Knight, what have you gone and done? And Papa thought *Evie* was a troublemaker," she muttered to herself, and hurried out of the ballroom.

"My Lord, I—"

"Don't say it," Rex warned the man by his side.

Humboldt scowled. Not that Rex could see his scowl, having lost his sight almost three years ago, but he could feel it. He could sense the disapproval rolling off his loyal secretary in waves. Humboldt was too good, that was the trouble; too good and too honourable, and nothing like Rex.

"You can't possibly know what I was going to say."

"You were going to ask me if I was perfectly sure this was the best course of action," Rex said under his breath, for he could not be certain if anyone was close enough to hear their conversation. The sound of the orchestra was making it very difficult for him to concentrate, drowning his perceptions of the world around him. "You were going to ask me if I really wanted to drag Miss Knight into my life and rob her of the opportunity of meeting a decent man. A whole one, anyway."

"I was most certainly not going to phrase it in such a way," Humboldt replied, his indignation apparent.

"No, because you know I am an impatient brute with a vast amount of pride, which is far too easily bruised, but it doesn't make the meaning any less accurate."

"Very well. If you insist on framing my demand in such terms, so be it. And your answer?"

Rex shifted, reaching behind him to check the wall was still at his back. It wouldn't be the first time he'd felt as if it had moved to somewhere unexpected. He did not wish to answer the question, to think too deeply about what he was getting Miss Knight into. Sweet Miss Milly was far too innocent, too tenderhearted, to realise the enormity of what she was doing, but Rex wasn't. If he was any kind of gentleman, he would never have asked her, would at least have changed his mind and released her, but the truth was that he was terrified. As humiliating as it was to admit it, even to himself, he feared the future alone far more than he feared being an utter bastard. If he did not do this, did not have someone who could stay with him at all times of the day and night without causing a scandal, he was going to end up in an asylum. His father and half-brother would see it done between them, never mind if he were truly mad or not, unless they got really lucky and arranged an accident that caused him to break his neck. He was certain they'd already tried it.

No. The only way was to have someone with him, someone who could stay with him constantly, even at night, and who could be his eyes. The only person who could do that was a wife.

He still could not believe she had agreed to it. Humboldt had described the lady to him: she was undoubtedly beautiful and had a vast dowry. She must not be short of offers. Rex knew that her mother, Lady Helena, had lost much of her social standing through her marriage to Gabriel Knight. Lady Helena might be sister to the Duke of Bedwin, but Mr Knight had been born and raised in the workhouse, and even his mighty fortune could not entirely erase that stigma from his children. It made sense that Emmeline would accept his offer for the reasons he had suggested she do so, for marrying Rex would make her the Marchioness of Wrexham, a vastly wealthy and powerful woman. Every door would be open to her. Yet something nagged at him. The uneasy notion that his Miss Milly was not the kind of young woman who considered wealth and power as the most important things in her life was hard to overlook. But there could be no other reason. They hardly knew each other, and society had given him proof enough that his charms were no longer what they once were. Ida had taught him that lesson with great clarity.

Lucky for his faithless fiancée that Lord Waring had offered for her the moment the news had broken about Rex's sight. A comedown from a marchioness to a mere earl, perhaps, especially for a climber like Ida, but better that than marrying a man who needed constant attention. If he'd had any illusions about how far he'd fallen from grace, Ida's defection had shattered them. Until that moment, Rex had been the one calling the tune.

The Marquess of Wrexham had been on top of the world: popular, wealthy, powerful and skilled at most everything to which he turned his hand. He'd thought himself invulnerable, fool that he'd been. Before the accident, Ida had been doing all in her power to get him to the altar, and only Rex's determination to stay single and thwart his father's machinations had stopped it from happening. Ida had been the duke's choice, chosen for breeding and powerful connections. Anything his father wanted of him was reason enough to dig in his heels. She *had* tempted him, though, for Ida was beautiful and sophisticated, and knew all the ways to make him desire her. Oh, she had used her wiles with the greatest of skill, but in the end his hesitation had benefited her, and she'd cut him loose the moment she'd realised the kind of man she would be marrying. He'd become an invalid, in her eyes and now society had rehashed the story of his uncle's sight loss and subsequent madness, one tainted with the stigma of insanity too. She'd made no bones about it. Ida did not want to be saddled with a madman for a husband, a man who would likely breed another generation of insanity. Rex couldn't blame her.

Ida had loved to dance, visit the opera, ride for miles, and attend art exhibitions. How could he possibly do any of that? That part of his life was over, as was so much else of it. His world had shrunk down to the size of his private rooms at Buxton Hall, where his father had kept him prisoner for so long. If not for his sister and his aunt, he might be there still. And yet all Rex really wanted was to return to his own home.

Cawston Hall might become another prison of sorts but at least it was one of his own choosing, with people he trusted around him and a place he loved and knew like the back of his hand. Yet he was condemning sweet Emmeline to inhabit that prison with him. A luxurious incarceration with an ill-tempered husband who would gradually descend into madness. What a charming prospect. If only he weren't so damned stubborn, perhaps he'd take the easy way out as his father had so helpfully suggested and throw himself out of an upper-storey window. But that felt like giving up, like giving the duke what he wanted. No. Never that.

So what was his answer to Humboldt? Did he truly want to drag Miss Knight into his increasingly dangerous world, to imprison her there in order to keep him alive and out of an asylum? No. He really did not. But he would do it anyway.

Emmeline left the ballroom and made her way cautiously to the blue drawing room. With a nervous glance around her, she picked up the lamp that had been left burning to illuminate the corridor for the guests and opened the door. Moving fast, Emmeline crossed the imposing space and walked directly into the Roman room, so named for the striking paintings of famous episodes of Roman history that covered every wall, and even the ceiling. From all corners of the room, mythological figures and beasts stared, their gaze following Emmeline as she found the door to the next room, the judging eyes of ancient deities making her feel more anxious than ever. Heart thundering, she tugged open the door, walked through and gave a little shriek as she discovered someone waiting in the dark.

"It's me, Miss Knight. I beg your pardon for alarming you," Mr Humboldt said, his expression one of regret.

"Oh, that's quiet all right, Mr Humboldt. I'm a little overwrought, truth be told," she said, her hand pressed to her heart. "And it's foolish of me, for I was expecting to meet you here."

"Not in the least foolish, I assure you," Mr Humboldt said warmly. "The truth is, Miss Knight, I am glad to have this moment alone with you because… Well, there is no delicate manner of asking this so I shall put both feet in at once. Are you *quite* certain you know what you're doing?"

"Of course I'm not certain!" Emmeline said, outraged. Did he think her a complete bedlamite? "But I honestly don't see how I could not do it."

Mr Humboldt's anxious features softened. "Easily. Turn around and go back to the ballroom."

Emmeline regarded him for a long moment. "Why? Why do you say this to me? Is there something about Wrexham I ought to know? Is he tricking me? Is this all a hum? Is he a bad man?"

"No." Humboldt shook his head without hesitation. "No, he's not a bad man, and I'm afraid it's all true. He's had several *accidents* of late, which is easy enough to arrange for a blind man. He's accident prone enough with no help from anyone, because he's so determined to be independent, but of late it's become clear there have been traps laid for him, and the last one nearly did for him. If I'd not been there...." The man shook his head and rubbed a hand over his face. He looked exhausted. "But it's not your problem, and to marry a man you don't know just because you feel sorry for him—"

"*No!*" Emmeline stood a little straighter when Mr Humboldt returned her look of surprise. For she had astonished herself with the vehemence of her reaction, but the truth of her feelings gave her courage. "I am not doing this out of pity, or at least, that is only a small part of it. Wrexham is not a man who invites pity, and he would despise me for feeling it, no doubt. I have my reasons for going through with it, but my reasons are my own."

Mr Humboldt nodded, his expression grave. "Then we'd best go at once. He's waiting for us."

Emmeline nodded. Well, there was no turning back now.

Rex sat in the carriage, listening to the tick of his fob watch. They ought to be here by now. What was taking Humboldt so long? Unless Emmeline had changed her mind. The thought sent a shiver of apprehension skittering down his spine, a chill eating into his bones. Damn this bloody snow to hell. As if this journey wouldn't be challenging enough, without adding in such terrible weather. But eloping in February was hardly ideal. Still, once they got to the station, his private carriage would take them all the way to Birmingham. From there, they would take another train to Manchester, and then on to Lancaster. After that, it would become hellishly slow as there was not yet a line to take them into Scotland. Rex was dreading it. The idea of staying in rooms he did not know, where the layout would be different each time, of depending entirely on Humboldt and Miss Knight… it made him furious and frustrated and so humiliated he could weep. He sat up straighter, disgusted by his display of self-pity. Damn them all. He'd got this far. There was no way he was giving in now.

The soft tread of footsteps through snow caught his attention, making his heart pound. Too light for Humboldt… no, he was coming too, or at least a man and a woman. Rex held his breath as the door opened.

"Good evening, Lord Wrexham."

He wondered then if she could sing, for there was something so lovely, so melodious about her voice. It smoothed down his jagged edges, poured over his raw nerves like warm honey and assured him all would be well.

"You came," he said, discouraged to hear the depth of relief behind those words, wishing he had not sounded quite so desperate.

"I said I would," she replied, and he wondered at the assurance in her voice. Was she not as terrified, daunted, and thrumming with anxiety as he had been before she had arrived?

"So you did," he replied, smiling now. He reached out a hand towards her, startled by the way his heart leapt as she took it, her grip sure as she climbed into the carriage.

His future bride settled into the seat opposite him with the rustle of expensive fabric, bringing with her the scent of orange blossom. It transported Rex to the Mediterranean in an instant, to the sensation of the sun burnishing his skin, memories bright with images of a time and place when he could not tell where the sea had ended, and the sky began. His mood shifted from delight to melancholy, as he remembered he would never see such a thing again.

"My lord?"

He frowned, momentarily disorientated.

"Lord Wrexham? Have you changed your mind?" she asked, anxiety lacing her voice.

"What? No. Why the devil would I do that?" he demanded irritably, and then cursed himself as he sensed her stiffen. "Miss Knight, I... I apologise. That was... I'm rather...."

She laughed, and his ill humour faded at the discovery she could do so in the light of his rudeness.

"I think we both are... *rather,*" she said dryly.

He huffed out a laugh and nodded. "I shall do better."

"I certainly hope so, or this will be a horrifically long journey," she replied, a tart and wonderfully teasing note to her reply.

"Ah, and there is my Miss Milly, scolding me already. How delightful."

"You had best get used to it, my lord," she advised him, a glimmer of something bright and defiant illuminating her voice so he was not entirely certain she was teasing him anymore. "I'm not half so biddable as you might like to imagine."

Rex settled back against the squabs, trying to stifle a grin. He wished they did not need Humboldt and the young woman they had employed as her maidservant to travel in the carriage with them. But they must observe the proprieties, even during an elopement. Still, the journey might not be quite so horrific as he had feared after all.

Chapter 2

Lyall,

Of all the damned idiotic things to do! What in the blazes were you thinking, marrying that strumpet? How did she get her claws in you? If you were in trouble, why did you not come to me? I would have helped, surely you know that?

Lord, I want to rattle you until your teeth shake. I've half a mind to undertake that hellish journey just for the pleasure of doing so.

Explain yourself, man, for I cannot account for it.

—Excerpt of a letter from The Most Hon'ble Jules Adolphus, The Marquess of Blackstone (eldest son of Their Graces, Robert and Prunella Adolphus, The Duke and Duchess of Bedwin) to The Right Hon'ble Lyall Anderson, Viscount Buchanan (eldest son of Gordon and Ruth Anderson, Earl and Countess of Morven).

Night of the 14th of February 1845, on the road to Euston Station.

Emmeline stared out at a world that appeared dusted with icing sugar, sparkling in the moonlight. Thankfully, the snow had stopped some time ago, and the farther they got from Holbrook, the lighter the covering appeared to be. With luck, they would have a straightforward journey to the station.

Beside her, the young woman Humboldt had hired for her maidservant sat with her hands in her lap, eyes closed, looking quite unperturbed. She was a sturdy girl with thick dark hair, plaited and pinned to the nape of her neck, and was perhaps five or six years older than Emmeline. She wondered what the woman must think of her for setting off like she was. She swallowed down the sudden urge to tell the driver to stop so she could fling herself from the carriage. Her previous burst of confidence seemed to evaporate with each mile she put between herself and her family. Oh, what had she done?

"Are you well, Miss Knight?"

Wrexham's voice cut through her distraction, making her jump, and she wondered how he had known she was agitated, for he was leaning towards her, his expression one of concern.

Emmeline glanced over at Humboldt, reading in his face his willingness to stop this journey and return her home the moment she gave the word. Instead, she looked at Wrexham. His face was mostly in shadow, but the moonlight touched his high cheekbones, turning his golden hair to platinum. If only he weren't so beautiful, perhaps she could be sensible. Perhaps then she'd think of her own future, but her heart lurched as she considered telling him she wanted to go home. She couldn't do it.

"Quite well," she managed, though her voice trembled a little.

"Are you cold?" Wrexham asked, perhaps misinterpreting the quaver in her voice for shivering, though he'd been most solicitous, arranging for a hot brick for her feet and thick fur covers to keep her warm.

"No. I'm quite comfortable."

She watched his face deepen into a scowl, a formidable sight in the shadowy interior of the carriage. Emmeline wondered, rather belatedly, if she ought to be afraid of him.

"Give me your hand."

It was a demand rather than a request and she almost balked at his tone, but that was silly. Humboldt sat beside him, looking studiously out of the window. Wrexham would certainly not misbehave with an audience, though, and besides which, she trusted him to be a gentleman. He had promised her, and she had believed him.

Emmeline placed her hand in his, startled when he covered it with his own.

"Just as I thought," he grumbled. He tugged his own gloves off and then turned her hand over to undo the button at her wrist. With a swift pull, he removed the fine leather and placed it in his lap before taking her hand in his again.

"My lord!" Emmeline protested, hot with embarrassment.

"Oh, hush," he said, his tone impatient. "We're eloping. Holding hands is hardly scandalous by comparison and your fingers are icy. Why did you not say so? How can I account for your comfort and well-being if you do not tell me you're frozen to the bone?"

"But I'm not," she retorted. "I'm perfectly cosy under the blankets, it's just that my hands are always cold."

He made a sound of amusement and Emmeline tried to gather her wits as he chafed her cold hand between his, but it seemed a lost cause. His hands were warm and strong and engulfed her own and she was quite certain her heart would beat out of her chest.

"Cold hands, warm heart. It seems the old saying is true, Miss Milly."

Emmeline glared at him before remembering that was pointless. "My lord, this is most inappropriate."

He snorted. "How I love to hear you scold me, little governess."

Emmeline's stomach leapt, uncertain how she felt about his playful tone.

"Wrexham, we are not alone," she whispered, praying the maid really was sleeping, but still mortified that Humboldt was listening in.

"I'm blind, not dim-witted," he replied, though there was no animosity in his words. "I heard them get in and I am aware of Humboldt's disapproval. It burns," he added, lips quirking.

Humboldt sighed and folded his arms.

"I am a great trial to him," Wrexham whispered to her. Emmeline told her stupid heart not to be utterly charmed by the devil and avoided Humboldt's considering gaze.

"How long until we reach Euston Station?" she asked, viscerally aware of Wrexham still holding her hand. He had stopped chafing it now, and merely held it between his own, his thumb rubbing slow circles over her skin in the most distracting manner.

"Humboldt? How far have we come?" he asked.

"We are making excellent time. I believe we are approaching Wych Cross. If all goes well, I estimate we may be less than four hours away."

"How long do you think we have until you're missed?" Wrexham asked Emmeline.

She dragged her gaze reluctantly from the sight of his big hands engulfing her far smaller one and then blushed, relieved he couldn't see her. Unfortunately, Humboldt could. She put up her chin. "If all goes well, not until late tomorrow morning. I feigned a megrim. They usually knock me out, so my parents would not expect to see me much before midday."

"You suffer from such an affliction?" he asked, the concern in his voice warming her as much as his hands were doing.

"Occasionally. Lemons are my nemesis. I adore them, but they often set me off, especially if I'm tired."

"Humboldt. Inform Mrs Tweedy. No lemons."

"Yes, my lord."

"Oh, but there's no need for you to—" Emmeline began.

"Hush. Give me the other one," he demanded.

She huffed at him, torn between thanking him for his kindness and irritated at his imperiousness. "You might say please."

"Please, Miss Milly, won't you give me your cold little hand to warm?" he murmured, and with such a seductive tone she regretted opening her mouth at all. Silently, she tugged off her glove and exchanged one hand for the other. "Tuck the other one under the blanket."

"Yes, my lord," she said, not disguising the impatient edge to her voice.

Wrexham grinned at her, his white teeth glinting in the moonlight, giving his beautiful features a dangerous, feral aspect that made her shiver.

"Oh, now *that* wasn't the cold," he remarked, sounding far too pleased with himself.

Emmeline decided there was safety in silence and held her tongue.

"That was well done of you," he said after a moment. "If they don't discover you're gone until then, barring catastrophes, we ought to pull this off. Though I'm something of a magnet for accidents these days, am I not, Humboldt?"

"If my lord were a little less impatient, there would be far fewer such incidents," Humboldt replied, with the air of someone who'd repeated the refrain often and without success.

Wrexham snorted but didn't deny it.

They subsided into silence, and Emmeline shivered as Wrexham stopped warming her hand and instead began stroking the back of it, tracing intricate little patterns. She wondered if he knew he was doing it, as he wore a distracted expression. The delicate touch of his fingers seemed to set all her nerve endings to quivering, the oddest sensation rippling through her, tugging fretfully at something deep inside her that had no business getting overwrought by the mere touch of his hand.

Emmeline tugged free of his grasp. "Thank you, I'm quite warm," she said, annoyed to discover she sounded so breathless.

"Any time," Wrexham replied, and said not another word for the rest of the journey to Euston.

Matilda, the Marchioness of Montagu, moved through the crowd. Only her many years' experience at hiding her feelings kept her from screaming at the top of her voice and demanding someone find her husband. Now. *This minute.*

She could sense the excitement as word of the catastrophe— or, depending upon your point of view, the delicious gossip— circulated the room. Panic seized her lungs, and she wished for a moment that she might run and hide, that someone else might be the one to tell him. But no, that was cowardly, and she would never allow it, but the idea of being the person to break his beautiful heart was so appalling she had to blink hard and dig her nails into her palms to keep from weeping.

So she kept her head up, her expression serene, and moved purposefully with no telltale hint of anxiety or hurrying. He knew, though. The moment his silver gaze settled upon her, he knew something was terribly wrong. His expression did not change a whit. To any observer, Lucian Barrington, the Marquess of Montagu, was an exquisite block of ice, but she saw the way his shoulders stiffened, the distracted way he tugged at his cuffs.

"My lord," she said, struggling to keep her voice steady. "Might I borrow you for a moment?"

He inclined his head, coolly apologised to the men he was speaking with, and offered her his arm. Matilda's grip was too tight, and she forced herself to relax her fingers as he guided her through the ballroom.

"Cat." He spoke their daughter's pet name as an inevitability.

"Yes."

He let out a harsh breath as they exited the grand room, heading for St Clair's private library. Once they were out of sight of the guests, Lucian took her hand.

"How bad is it this time?"

"B-Bad," Matilda said, struggling not to cry. "V-Very bad."

The colour drained from his face as he shook his head, staring at her. "No. *No.*"

Matilda could barely speak, emotion clawed at her throat as she saw the devastation in his eyes and nodded, driving the blade home. "Kilbane."

For a moment, he did not move, did not even blink.

"I'll kill him."

He turned on his heel, and Matilda ran after him. "Lucian, no. *Wait!* I don't think it was his fault."

"I don't care," he said, his voice savage. "I'll make this go away."

"Darling, I don't think you can this time. There were too many witnesses, if you would only wait—"

But Lucian flung open the door to the study so hard it crashed against the bookshelves behind it.

Huddled before the fire, Cat was sobbing as Lady St Clair held her tight and stroked her hair. Lady Helena sat on her other side, offering what comfort she could. Gabriel Knight and Jasper, Lord St Clair, stood behind them. On the opposite side of the room, alone and rigid with fury and indignation, stood Lord Kilbane. His posture was defensive, arms folded, but as Lucian exploded into the room, he paled, his arms falling to his sides. For a moment, Matilda felt a rush of sympathy for him.

"Lucian!" Gabriel exclaimed, he and Jasper moving as one to intercept him, but too late.

Kilbane crashed backwards against the bookshelves with Lucian's hands about his throat.

"Son of a bitch," Lucian growled. "I warned you what I'd do if you so much as looked at her."

"Lucian, stop!" Matilda cried, for there was something in Kilbane's eyes, a flicker of something desperate and hopeless. He wasn't fighting back.

"Papa! Don't hurt him. It wasn't his fault, it was *me!* It was all me. Papa, I'm s-so s-sorry," Cat wept, and the pain behind the wrenching sobs was perhaps the only thing that could have stopped Lucian from squeezing the life out of the marquess.

Matilda covered her mouth with her hand to stifle a sob as her husband released Kilbane, who sucked in a breath and doubled over, coughing.

Cat ran into her father's arms and held on tight as Lucian embraced her. His eyes closed, emotions shutting down as they always did when he became overwrought, even now after so many years.

"Papa, I'm sorry, I'm sorry," Cat said, over and over. "I'm so, so sorry. I followed him. I made him talk to me. He was g-going away to France, and I wanted to stop him. He told me to go away, but I w-wouldn't."

Lucian said nothing, struggling to compose himself.

"It seems that Catherine tripped and Kilbane reached to steady her," Harriet said, her voice calm. "They got into something of a tangle and fell. Innocent enough in reality, but they were discovered in what appeared to be a damning position on the floor of the stables. Among the half dozen spectators was Miss Hatchet."

Harriet did not need to say anything more. Miss Hatchet was notorious for being a nasty minded gossipmonger. To have discovered the Marquess of Montagu's daughter in a compromising situation with Kilbane was manna from heaven for someone of her ilk. The story would be halfway across the county before dawn.

"I'll pay her off," Lucian said savagely. "I'll silence her... No matter how much it costs. She can live like a bloody duchess, I'll—"

"It won't work," Gabriel replied, his voice sympathetic but firm. "I'm sorry, Lucian. The news is already spreading like wildfire. The only thing to be done is for him to marry her."

"Damned if I will!" Kilbane exploded as everyone turned to stare at him.

Lucian released Cat and turned on Kilbane once more.

"You'll do whatever the hell I tell you to," he snarled, his eyes flashing dangerously. "You may rest assured I'll make a deal with the Devil himself before I resort to such a vile solution, but if I say you'll marry her, you will do as you're damned well told."

"Lucian," Matilda said desperately. "What *are* we to do?"

"We'll take her away," Lucian said, raking an unsteady hand through his hair. "We'll go abroad, an extended trip."

"It won't work, Papa," Cat said quietly, strangely calm now.

Matilda hugged her tight, fighting not to break down as the beautiful future she had envisaged for her daughter fell apart.

"It might, love. I lived on the fringes for years and look how it worked out for me," she said, striving to sound positive.

"It's not the same, Mama," Cat said, giving a weary smile. "I'm Montagu's daughter. They'll never let him forget it. Not ever."

"She's right." Gabriel nodded. "I'm sorry. I don't want to disillusion you but this needs dealing with swiftly, before the evening is over. It's the only way."

Helena was red eyed, a handkerchief pressed to her mouth, but she sent Matilda a look of such sympathy it was clear she agreed with her husband.

"Yes." Harriet nodded, her expression grim. "Much as it pains me, Tilda, love. Gabe is quite correct." She reached for Jasper's hand. He took it and squeezed.

"It will be the scandal of the decade," Jasper said to Lucian. "You've no option."

Matilda watched as her husband stalked to the fire and stared down at it. His expression was devoid of emotion now, his voice cool.

"There's always an option."

Cat slipped from her embrace and went to her father. Matilda fumbled for her handkerchief as their daughter took his hand in hers.

"Papa. It will be all right. I know… I know how badly I've let you down, but… I will make it right."

Lucian shook his head.

"We'll go away. We'll stay away if needs be. You wanted to travel, did you not? We'll see it all. France, Italy, perhaps India. We—"

"Papa," Cat said, a pleading note to her voice now. "You cannot. For one thing, you would hate it. Mama would too. Your life is here. Who would run Dern? Think of how many people depend on you. Think of Pip and Thorn. They need you here too, and I don't *want* to go. I don't want to run away in shame when I've done nothing to be ashamed of. I was foolish, yes, but not wicked."

"I can't...." Lucian said, his voice so raw and full of pain Matilda gave into the urge to weep, unable to keep the tears back any longer. "I can't let you marry that... that... damned *degenerate!* I'll kill him first."

Cat could not remember ever being so tired in all her life. All she wanted to do was to go to bed, pull the covers over her head, and pretend this day had never happened.

That was out of the question, though. She had broken her parents' hearts, when they had done nothing but love and cherish her, and as for Kilbane....

She glanced over at him. He stood in the farthest corner of the room, looking like something wild and dangerous trapped in a cage. She knew he would lash out if they provoked him, that she had backed him into a corner and the only response he knew how to give would be to make them all revile him. Somehow, she must manage this situation, must manage him. After all, she had wanted him, had she not? Now, she almost had him, or at least, was closer to it than she had ever been before. This was hardly the way she had wanted things to go, but if she came out of this the Marchioness of Kilbane, well... would that be so bad? In her heart, she believed he was a good man, a kind but damaged soul who simply did not know how to allow anyone close to him. If she was his wife, she would finally have her chance.

Not that she was a fool. This would not be the solution. He would despise her for trapping him, and getting over that would take time, but she could wait. Cat let go of her mother and went to her father's side. He was staring down at the fire, not that she thought he saw it.

Gently, she tried to make him see there was no other choice, and that she did not wish to run away. The idea of letting society shred her character to pieces as she fled made her feel physically sick. Seeing her father in such torment, being the cause of such pain, though... that was a knife in her chest.

"I can't... I can't let you marry that... that... damned *degenerate!* I'll kill him first."

"Papa, *no!*"

Her father grasped her by the shoulder, determination in his expression. "I will not allow this. You don't understand, Cat, you're a little innocent and you don't know... A man like that... No! I won't let him touch you!"

"You think I'd touch her?" Kilbane retorted, and the fury and disgust rolling off him was shocking to her. "She's just a child, for the love of everything holy!"

Everyone stared at him, their confusion evident. As humiliating as his obvious sincerity was to her, Cat felt her stomach turn as she saw him take in everyone else's response to his words, the surprise that he had anything resembling a moral. She saw the flicker of defiance and pain in his eyes before the shutters slammed down.

He gave a snort of laughter. "Oh, but I forgot. I'm so depraved I'll fuck anything."

"Mind your tongue," Gabriel snapped.

Kilbane laughed and threw up his hands, turning his back on them all.

Silence filled the room as Cat stared at him in consternation. Why did he persist in seeing her as a child? Yes, eighteen was young, but many of her friends of the same age had already wed, and he was not *much* older than she. Six years, perhaps? Hardly an unusual age gap. That he did not desire her was obviously possible. She was not so conceited that she believed every man ought to fall at her feet, though in practise, it was a rare event that they did not. Neither was she so sheltered that she had not heard the rumours about him. She knew Kilbane took lovers as and when he pleased, regardless of sex, station, or any other criteria. But his name had been connected with enough beautiful women to lead her to believe he did not think her unattractive. Was it her personality, then? She certainly annoyed him, but Cat had always believed that was because she insisted on pushing him in ways other people would not dare. That had to be good for him, though? Didn't it? Papa had said many times that he had fallen in love with her mother because she was so brave, bold enough to challenge him and tell him he was an obnoxious arse.

Cat smiled at that, despite everything. Well, she *was* her mother's daughter.

No. She would not run away from this. Marrying Kilbane had always been her goal. Yes, this happened to be the worst possible way of doing it, but beggars could not be choosers, and she was Lady Catherine Barrington. Running away was not in her nature. Silently she racked her brain, trying to figure out a way to persuade her father this was for the best, and Kilbane that he may as well get on and accept it.

Before she could, the man himself turned back to them.

"Fine," he said, his expression so grim he looked like he was agreeing to throw himself into a pit of snakes. "I'll do it, but I have conditions."

"You dare!" her father snarled, silver eyes colder than she had ever seen them.

"You believe otherwise?" Kilbane sneered.

Papa lunged for him, but St Clair and Mr Knight were ready this time and held him back.

"Hear him out, Lucian," Gabriel advised.

As neither man let go of him, her father had little option.

Kilbane inclined his head in a parody of polite thanks before he spoke again. "I'll marry her, damn you all, but it will be a marriage in name only. I decided long ago this misbegotten bloodline would die with me, and I will not be persuaded otherwise." He fixed his gaze upon Cat, his expression hard and unyielding. "Do not go harbouring any romantic notions, brat. I'm going to France just as I planned. The chances are you'll not see me again, but you'll have the protection of my name, for all the joy it may bring you. You'll be the Marchioness of Kilbane. You'll have all the wealth and power that comes with the position, the English properties are yours to do with as you please, but you will not have me. Not under any circumstances."

Cat sucked in a sharp breath. He couldn't mean it, surely.

"You condemn her to a life without a family? Without children?" her mother said, aghast.

Kilbane glanced at her, a frown tugging at his brows before he waved an impatient hand. "She can do as she pleases. I am hardly going to balk if she takes a lover. She can bed half of London for all I care, but I'll not recognise any male children. There will be no heir. Under no circumstances. I suppose if she's lucky and produces girls, I'll give them my name, much good it will do the poor devils. But any male child will be a bastard. She may take her chances."

Cat glanced at her father, who looked as if he was ready to eviscerate Kilbane the moment he was free.

"It's a fair offer." This from Mr Knight, of course, ever pragmatic.

Harriet nodded too. "It is perhaps the kindest offer he could make her in the circumstances, Tilda," she said quietly. "She'll be safe, provided for, a powerful woman, and free to live as she chooses."

Cat looked at her mother, who was calm now, and as poised and beautiful as always.

"I don't think we have any choice," she said, reaching over and taking Cat's hand. She squeezed, a silent show of support. "If Catherine does not want to leave, then she must stay, as the Marchioness of Kilbane."

Chapter 3

Dearest Aggie,

I am so desperately sorry. We both knew Cat was reckless, but I never supposed… but what is there to say? I am devastated for her, and for you, for I know your heart will break on her behalf. I am here for you both, if ever you need me. I hope you know that? I hope you know I would do anything for you.

I wanted to speak with you tonight. I almost did so a dozen times, but each time my courage failed me. It seems I'm not half so brave as I supposed where you're concerned, so I kept my tongue between my teeth and then the scandal broke and I lost my chance.

I will go back to university tomorrow and I think it may be some time before I can see you again. So, I pray you'll forgive me for pouring my heart out in a letter, for I am afraid the sight of your beautiful face will scatter my thoughts and make me tongue tied. As it is, this is the fifth time I've written this out.

Aggie, I know we have been friends forever, but I think perhaps you know my feelings run deeper than this. I have dared to believe that my affections are returned, but I cannot go on in uncertainty now you are out in society. The truth is, I am in love with you, my dearest, dreadful girl. I believe I have loved you from the first time I laid eyes on you, before I really understood what the feeling meant. The thing is, Aggie, I need to ask you not to go falling in love or marrying anyone else. You won't, will you? If you do not return my affections, I should bow out and... Drat it all. I'm not rewriting this again, but I won't bow out. At least, not without being certain you don't want me. I should not force my attentions where they were unwelcome, but... hell, I'm making a hash of this now.

Damn it, Aggie, do you love me as I love you? I am half mad with it. I think of you constantly, I shall make myself ridiculous with fretting and pacing while I wait for your reply. Do not keep me in agony, love. Tell me if there is the slightest hope you return my feelings. Tell me at once.

—Excerpt of a letter from The Right Hon'ble Frederick Adolphus, (second youngest son of Their Graces, Robert and Prunella Adolphus, The Duke and Duchess of Bedwin) to Miss Agatha de Montluc (adopted daughter of Louis César and Evie de Montluc, Comte and Comtesse de Villen).

15th February 1845, somewhere between Euston Station and Birmingham.

Emmeline smothered a yawn. She was weary to her bones but strangely alert, far too anxious to be able to fall asleep. They'd reached the train just after half past two in the morning, almost three hours ago now. Humboldt had told her the journey would take five and a half hours. Not that there would be any rest when they reached Birmingham. Wrexham was far too easily identifiable, and her father was a powerful and wealthy man, especially where the railways were concerned. Once he realised she was gone, he would find out who she was with. It might take him some time to figure it out, but he would, and then he would move heaven and earth to find her, despite her letter. She knew that.

A few weeks earlier there had been a remarkable story in the newspapers about a man who had murdered his wife with Prussic acid and then fled via the train. Someone had seen him leaving the house, and his description was sent via telegraph to the station at the end of the line. They had arrested him at Paddington station. Emmeline did not doubt her father would use this new technology to have eyes at every station in the country. So, they needed to be away from the railways as soon as possible.

"There're sandwiches and biscuits if you're hungry, Miss Knight?"

Emmeline looked up to see her new maid, Janet, regarding her with concern.

"I've some lemonade too, or some apple juice," she added.

"No lemonade," Wrexham muttered crossly.

Emmeline's stomach growled, and she pressed her hands to it with chagrin. "I could eat something," she admitted. "And perhaps a little apple juice. Wrexham, you must be famished too."

Wrexham shook his head. His posture was stiff, tight lines fanning out around his eyes. Though he was as immaculate as ever, dressed with his usual exquisite style that stopped just short of flamboyant, he looked tense and exhausted.

"Bring enough for us both, please," Emmeline said with a smile.

"What about Mr Humboldt?" Janet asked, casting the recumbent figure a dubious glance.

Emmeline smiled as a soft snore reached her ears. "I think Mr Humboldt is content enough for the moment, thank you."

Janet nodded and hurried off to fetch their sandwiches.

"I said I didn't want anything," Wrexham grumbled, folding his arms.

"I know," Emmeline said. "But you look tired and fretful and, if we add in an empty belly, you're likely to become unpleasant. So you will do me a kindness and eat something."

"My, but you're bossy."

"I am," she agreed amicably. "I did warn you."

He snorted, and then frowned, his expression fierce. Emmeline watched him as he shifted, certain he wanted to say something more.

"I dislike eating in front of people."

She nodded, unsurprised. "I know that, but I am not *people*. I am to be your wife, and your means of staying safe. Tampering with your food is an obvious way to cause you harm, is it not?"

"You have a dark turn of mind."

"I do not," she objected. "But I must be practical and not shy away from unpleasantness."

"The sight of your husband with gravy down his shirt, for example," he said, his tone bitter.

"That is hardly what I meant," she snapped. "As if I care for such things! Though, if it troubles you unduly, we shall find solutions."

"A bib?" he offered with a sneer.

"Wrexham," she said, sighing and wishing he could see himself as she did, but she did not feel equal to the task of explaining that to him. If he knew what a muddle he made of her poor brain, it would likely make things—make *him*—a great deal harder for her to manage.

"I'm sorry," he said abruptly. "I ought never to have dragged you into this. I know I ought not, I just—"

Before she could think better of it, Emmeline stood and crossed to sit beside him. Everything about him tensed, and the sense he was listening intently became unmistakeable. Gingerly, she reached over and laid her hand upon his.

"Don't be sorry," she said. "And don't make me sorry, either. I think we shall rub along quite nicely."

His lips quirked a little, giving him a boyish look that was so endearing her stupid heart lurched. Lord, but she was in a deal of trouble.

"Quite nicely," he repeated with amusement, turning his hand to capture hers.

Emmeline went to pull free, unnerved by the excitable dance her heart was performing behind her ribs, but his grip firmed, holding her fingers in place.

"Sweet Milly, what a mess you've gotten yourself into."

"I have not," she retorted, though the little voice in her head was agreeing with him enthusiastically. "I did this for very practical reasons, besides which, you clearly need someone to take you in hand, and not because you're blind," she added before he could make some self-deprecating comment.

"Oh? Why, then?"

"Because you're an absolute devil and you're going to give poor Humboldt a breakdown. How the man has borne with you all these years is beyond me."

He chuckled, and the sound did terrible things to her equilibrium. Combined with the feel of his hand holding hers, she would be a puddle at his feet long before Birmingham if she didn't have a care.

"I adore you," he said, grinning.

He was teasing her, of course. She knew that, but still, the words made her feel fluttery and daft and she very much feared she might giggle. So, instead, she frowned and tugged her hand free.

"Stuff," she replied sternly. "You're a wicked man with a glib tongue, and don't think I don't know it."

Birmingham would forever live in Emmeline's mind as a confusion of smoke and noise. Her head was pounding, her eyes gritty, and she crossed the station with the jerky, stiff-legged motion of an automaton. Her nerves leapt at every sound, and she felt certain there would be a shout of recognition from someone who worked for her father. The shrill shriek of a whistle blowing made her gasp and sidestep. She crashed into Wrexham, who was holding Humboldt's elbow as they navigated the busy platform. He muttered a curse but caught her against him, a strong arm lashed about her middle.

"I'm supposed to be the clumsy one, Miss Knight," he observed.

"I beg your pardon. I'm rather tired and the whistle startled me."

Wrexham smiled. "Rather tired, my arse. You're ready to drop. Give me your arm."

"But won't it be difficult for you—"

"Stop fussing, pet," he said, impatient now.

Too worn out to protest, Emmeline took his arm, and the three of them made their way to the waiting train. This time, Wrexham had booked the entire first-class carriage, and Emmeline fell rather than sat down. Janet bustled about, tucking the fur-lined blanket over Emmeline's knees. She was a kind and efficient young woman and Emmeline thought they ought to get on well.

"Go away," Wrexham said from beside her. He waved off both Humboldt and the blanket the man offered with a tut of annoyance. "I don't need a blanket, I'm not an infant. I just want to be left alone. Stop fussing over me! Sit at the other end of the carriage and let me speak to Miss Knight in peace."

"Yes, my lord," Humboldt said with a sigh, though he looked at Emmeline first, checking she did not mind being left alone with Wrexham.

Sadly, Emmeline did not mind a bit, though she sent Humboldt a rueful smile in the hope he might not think her forward.

"You are very rude and ungrateful," she scolded Wrexham. "Poor Humboldt had the organising of this journey, and you've done nothing but nag and worry at him since we left."

"That's what he's paid for," Wrexham groused, folding his arms.

"He is not paid to be abused," she objected. "And he is only concerned with your comfort. You might thank him, at least."

"I dislike being babied."

There was an underlying current of frustration to the words that illustrated the truth of this quite wonderfully.

"Then stop acting like one," Emmeline retorted, wondering how she dared.

Who was she to scold him? She hadn't the first idea of how difficult life must be for Wrexham. Facing things that had once been so simple and had now become so dreadfully difficult must make him wild with impatience. She braced herself for a severe set down, but it never came.

Emmeline glanced sideways at him to find his head turned her way, his expression thoughtful.

"Tell me about yourself."

She glared at him, which was pointless but made her feel better. "Oh, really. *Now?* I'm so befuddled I can hardly walk in a straight line, let alone converse. I was thinking I might try to nap."

"I know. You're getting delightfully snippy. Which is why it is the perfect time. You'll be more candid with me if you're impatient and out of sorts."

"Well, how ungentlemanly!" she exclaimed. "And did you not promise to take care of me?"

He turned more fully towards her, his hand reaching out and exploring her lap until he found hers. The bold move so startled her that she gasped. Wrexham flashed a wicked grin and grasped her hand, tugging it towards him and holding it between his, upon his thigh.

"I shall take the greatest care of you, Miss Milly. And I promise you may lay your head on my shoulder and nap to your heart's content. Just speak to me for a moment. Please. I cannot sleep when the world around me changes so rapidly. It is too… disorientating and—"

"It must be terrifying," she said, before she could think better of it.

He stiffened, and she squeezed his fingers, still scandalised by her hand resting so close to his thigh. "I only think of how I might feel. Perhaps it is different for you, but the idea of being out in the world and unable to see makes me feel vulnerable and like I want to curl up in a little ball, but you are far braver than that. I know you are."

There was a long silence.

"I'm not, though."

The stark admission made her heart hurt, knowing how it must stab at his pride to admit he was afraid.

"Yes, you are. You're here, Wrexham."

He gave a soft huff of laughter. "You'll manage me admirably, love. A clever combination of scolding and butter boat. Well done."

"As if anyone could manage you!" she retorted, disliking the faintly mocking tone she'd heard behind the comment. "No wonder Humboldt looks so worn to a thread if you seize on any compliment and turn it into an insult, or any show of care into fussing. Don't think you'll have me dancing to your tune, for I shan't. I gave you an honest compliment, expressing my admiration for you and I get sly remarks in return. Thank you very much."

She tugged her hand free, but he caught hold of it again and held on tight. "No," he said, frowning. "Forgive me. It seems you are not the only one feeling snippy."

"Well, and you have every right to be," she relented, pleased by his apology and the proof that he was not entirely without manners. "It's been a trying day."

"And I ought to let you sleep," he added with a sigh.

"It might be for the best," Emmeline said wryly. "Humboldt has placed your cane within my reach. I might use it if you provoke me again."

"You do remember you're supposed to be keeping me alive?" he replied, one eyebrow lifting.

She knew he meant for her to laugh at the remark, but it was too awful a reminder of his predicament, so her words were soft and heartfelt. "I remember."

Once again she was struck by the sense of him listening intently, as if he was trying desperately to decipher her expression and interpret her words more precisely.

"Go to sleep, Miss Milly. We've a long way to go yet."

Emmeline felt her heart tremble at the truth of that statement, though it was not the distance they needed to travel that worried her. She was to make her life with this man, and she did not know what to expect of him. Still, she laid her head on his shoulder as he had invited her to do, beguiled by the scent that drifted from his fine wool coat. He smelled of something newly green, the woody scent of freshly cut oak, and with an unusual hint of something floral. It was as extravagant and surprising as the man himself, and Emmeline drifted to sleep, dreaming of woodlands and wild, rambling roses.

Wrexham kept entirely still, or as still as he was able to with the motion of the train, but he dared not move for fear of disturbing Miss Knight. She no longer had her head on his shoulder, a feat not entirely of her own volition. He could not imagine she had been comfortable at such an awkward angle, though. When the train had jolted to a hard stop at the last station, almost throwing them both to the floor, he had held onto her instinctively and her head had slipped from his shoulder. That she had not even stirred proved how tired she was, and it was far more comfortable for her to sleep against his chest, with his arm about her. For him too. Mostly.

It had been a very long time since he had been this close to a woman. He had not wished to be, either, a mortifying fact he had assumed he'd find a blessing in the long run. That part of his life was surely over. He had assumed his condition had robbed him of his previous need for female companionship, along with his sight and the threat to his sanity. Desire had disappeared, doing just as much to damage his pride as regularly falling on his face. Not that he'd had much energy to mourn the loss of his libido, having been preoccupied with the alien and unpleasant world he'd been thrust into these past years.

When he'd considered the heir and spare he so desperately needed to secure his position, the very idea had made him anxious and gave rise to panicky sensations about being unable to perform at all. Besides, what if any children he sired inherited this cruel mix of blindness and insanity? His uncle had gone quite spectacularly mad, and various other relations had also lost their wits. His father had delighted in illustrating their ignominious ends to him in great detail, doing his level best to terrify his son into becoming a malleable creature he could control at last.

Rex had feigned indifference, out of bloody-mindedness as much as anything, but the truth was such a fate it terrified him. The idea of losing his mind and being at the mercy of people who might laugh at his insanity, who might be cruel to him, was more than he could bear. How, then, could he condemn another generation to such a humiliating and painful fate? No. He could not doom his heir to a life where blindness and madness lurked. No matter how much easier his life would be if his line were secure.

Staying alive and living his final years with some semblance of dignity had seemed the only concern, and persuading Miss Knight about the merits of a marriage of convenience, the only thing that mattered. Now, though, with his hand resting on the narrow span of her waist, he knew he'd made a gross error of judgement.

He could feel the steady rise and fall of her breathing, her body warm against his, and the knowledge that she was to be his—his *wife*—made his breath catch. Desire woke within him, renewed and stronger than ever after so long lying dormant. It was a living thing beneath his skin, thrumming urgently, and now his anxious thoughts took a new turn. His Miss Milly was marrying him for her own reasons. They had struggled through an awkward correspondence during which they had managed a bargain of sorts. She was to be his guardian, not his lover, and in return, she would be financially secure and a powerful figure in society. He had clearly defined the boundaries of their relationship, ensuring she understood there was no obligation for her to come to his bed, and he'd not considered those limits a problem, seeking only to reassure her enough to agree. Getting her acceptance was all that had mattered. Now, though....

The train once again shrieked to a halt, the stop so sudden there was a heavy thud and a curse from the seat behind them. Rex suspected Humboldt had just hit the floor.

Miss Knight awoke with a jerk, clutching at Rex in a way that pleased him far too much. He had forgotten what it felt like to be the protector. For too long, he had felt like prey. Having Emmeline Knight in his arms brought all those old instincts roaring back, pride and frustration gnashing their teeth simultaneously as the voice in his head told him he was pathetic and beyond protecting anyone, even himself. He shut the voice off and concentrated on the woman in his arms.

"It's all right. Just a stop. Did you enjoy your nap?"

There was a befuddled silence, and he tried to imagine her face, the sleepy expression she perhaps wore, blinking up at him as she got her bearings.

"Oh," she said faintly, tension thrumming through her.

He wondered at it for a moment until he remembered that her family had cosseted and protected her. Miss Knight was an innocent. She would never have been this close to a man before, certainly not in his arms. Was she afraid? Did the idea of him touching her make her nauseous? His blindness did not seem to trouble her, which made her a blessed rarity and had given him the courage to put his outrageous offer to her, but that did not mean she felt anything for him past pity and perhaps a tentative friendship.

Rex waited, unmoving, ready to release her the moment she pushed away, but she did not.

"Where are we?" she asked, sounding just as sleepy as he had imagined her to be on waking.

"I heard the porter shout Stockport," he said, resisting the urge to put his hand up and touch her face, to stroke her hair and see how soft it felt beneath his fingers.

"I've slept for hours!" she said, surprised.

"I make a comfortable pillow, apparently," he replied, his tone dry.

"Oh! I beg your pardon," She sat up at once, moving away from him and he immediately regretted teasing her, regretted the loss of contact and warmth.

"It was my pleasure," he said, striving to sound sincere, but finding the words had a sensuous tone he'd not intended. He caught her sharp intake of breath and cursed himself. The last thing he wanted was to frighten her off.

"How much farther?"

"We'll be in Manchester shortly. I believe Humboldt said the train to Lancaster is about three and a half hours."

"And then a carriage," she said with a heavy sigh. How weary she sounded. Lord, but he was a brute for putting her through this. "How long will that take?"

"A very long day, though if you cannot face it, we could stop somewhere and—"

"No. No, let us get this journey over and done. For both our sakes."

"You are indomitable, Miss Milly."

She laughed at that, and the sound reassured him she was not glaring at him with distaste or regret. "I am nothing of the sort. I'm simply desperate to be sitting quietly on something that doesn't move constantly, but the sooner we arrive at our destination, the sooner we might relax."

Wrexham considered relaxing with his wife, immediately focusing on the fact that their marriage ought to be consummated to be legal. His nerves leapt, his body the farthest thing from *relaxed* it was possible to consider. They had agreed they would simply insist that it had been consummated, if his father tried to have the marriage annulled. But now he wondered if perhaps she would consider… his body reacted immediately as anticipation stirred his blood. Wrexham cleared his throat and forced his mind to safer ground before his libido betrayed him and terrified the poor girl into running away for good. Not that she seemed the least bit missish, but rather practical and no-nonsense. He liked that, he discovered, somewhat to his surprise. He was certain he would have been foolish enough to overlook her before he'd lost his sight, too eager to chase more ephemeral pleasures, and women who were not the least bit practical. They had been illusions, he realised with a sudden burst of clarity. Miss Knight was real.

"Heavens! How tedious it must have been to travel so far before the train. When I imagine Mama and Papa coming all this way by carriage when they eloped. *Oh*…."

She gasped, and he felt certain she had covered her hand with her mouth.

"Your parents eloped?" he asked in surprise. "I never knew that. I thought they married at Beverwyck?"

There was a tense, unhappy silence.

"They did," she said, and he heard the anxiety in her voice. "But only after my uncle chased them all the way to Scotland. By the time he got there he realised he had been wrong to refuse the match and so they returned home and were married at Beverwyck with his blessing, but they were standing at the altar at Gretna Green when he caught up with them. They did the entire journey in a curricle."

"Good God. A curricle?" Rex exclaimed, uncertain whether to be delighted or daunted by this information. Her parents were clearly not to be underestimated.

"My lord, I would have your promise that you will never tell another soul about that. I ought never to have mentioned it. I can't understand why I did, only…."

"Only?" he pressed, curious when she did not finish the sentence.

"You're far too easy to confide in," she grumbled. It did not sound like a compliment, but Rex took it as one, anyway. He grinned.

"I will take it to my grave, pet. Though I am intrigued to discover eloping is a family tradition. No wonder the Knight clan is considered so *interesting*. Your sister did it in rather spectacular fashion, after all, marrying the so handsome Comte de Villen."

"I shan't discuss it," she said, sounding prim and indignant. He imagined her lips pursed to match and a confusing rush of affection and desire stole over him, so fierce it took him quite by surprise.

"Very well. Then you can tell me again how you think me as handsome as the comte instead."

She made a sound of outrage and Rex preened, delighted to have ruffled her.

"I said no such thing! If I remember correctly, I said you were a conceited coxcomb," she returned, though he could hear her smiling, feel the warmth of her amusement as though he stood bathed in sunlight. He realised in that moment how badly he wanted to stay there, in the light of her approval.

He shook his head, attempting to look grave. "Oh, no. I can't allow that. I distinctly remember reminiscing about how I'd once been a handsome fellow, beloved by all, before I fell from such heady heights, and you said… you said… 'I promise you, nothing has changed.'"

Rex grinned, waiting for her tart reply, wanting to indulge himself in more of her amusement and laughter, but the sensation faded. He frowned, wondering what he'd said wrong.

"You didn't fall, Wrexham," she said gently. "At least, not in the way you mean. Though, it was an accident, wasn't it, that lost you your sight?"

Rex stiffened, torn between anger at what sounded like pity and the desire to crawl into her lap and allow her to soothe all his hurt feelings and wounded pride.

"My lord?"

She sounded hesitant now, anxious, and he couldn't have that, so he put his indignation aside for once, reigning in the desire to lash out at anyone who dared pity him.

"It was a fall that started it," he admitted. "Some idiot fired a gun too close to me and spooked my horse. He was young and rather green and took fright. I was unseated and fell badly, hitting my head. Knocked me out cold. When I awoke, my head was exploding, my vision blurry. I just assumed it would get better, that I'd had the stuffing knocked out of me and it would take my brain a day or two to recover."

"But it didn't?"

Rex shook his head, unwilling to remember those days. He pushed the memories aside and shrugged. "No. Gradually the headache faded but my sight worsened, disappearing gradually until… well…." He shrugged, all on edge now, his pride bristling, nerves exposed, knowing he could not bear to hear the usual platitudes from her and hold his tongue.

"I am sorry that happened to you," she said, and he heard the sincerity in her voice, but no mawkish sentiment, no pity. "It must have been horrid, and disorientating, and… well, frankly, I cannot begin to imagine. How you have managed, and in the face of such adversity as your family is bringing you, well, it is remarkable,

Wrexham. *You* are remarkable. A conceited coxcomb but, all the same, a remarkable one."

And there was the sun again, breaking out from behind the clouds as he recognised a fond note behind her teasing.

Rex exhaled, completely wrong-footed, surprised, and confused and... *hopeful*, for the first time since he'd gone blind.

Chapter 4

Dearest Fred,

How can such a clever fellow as you be such a big lummox?

Of course I love you too.

You daft ha'porth.

—Excerpt of a letter from Miss Agatha de Montluc (adopted daughter of Louis César and Evie de Montluc, Comte and Comtesse de Villen) to The Right Hon'ble Frederick Adolphus, (second youngest son of Their Graces, Robert and Prunella Adolphus, The Duke and Duchess of Bedwin)

15th February 1845, Holbrook House, Sussex.

"We cannot bother Harry and Alana with this! They just got married!" Cat wailed as her mother brushed her hair. She had tried to get some sleep, but it had been impossible. Try as she might, she could not rid herself of the sight of her father's face, or the pain in his eyes. The knowledge that she had let him, and Mama down sat heavily in her chest like a burning coal. Now she was exhausted and fretful, but with only herself to blame.

"They will want to be with you, love. How do you think Alana will feel when she finds out and discovers you married without telling her?"

Cat groaned, imagining just what Alana *would* say. Both she and Harry had warned her, but… well, she'd never listened to anyone before. Why should she begin now?

"Catherine, you don't have to do this if you don't want to." Mama turned her so they faced each other, and Cat returned a sad smile. "We'll find a way. Given time, perhaps—"

"But I *do* want to, Mama. I think perhaps you understand that in a way Papa simply can't."

Her mother nodded, her expression resigned. "I do. I only hope you're right about him, Cat, but either way, you're in for a hard road."

Cat swallowed hard. "I know. But he's not the Devil, Mama. He's just—"

"Broken," her mother said with a heavy sigh. "There is something wrong with the female race, if you ask me. When one sees a man who is so obviously broken he will inevitably cause one a deal of hurt and misery, the first instinct ought to be to run as far and fast as one can, not to rush to fix the blasted fellow."

Despite everything, Cat laughed at her mother's irritation. "But where would we both be if you hadn't fixed Papa?"

Her mother laughed and nodded. "True. He is the best thing that ever happened to me, or could possibly happen. I am the luckiest of women, but I want that for you too, Cat. I want you to be happy."

"I think I will be," Cat said, though perhaps not with as much conviction as her mother might have liked. "But it will not be easy if he means to keep his word and live in France. How am I supposed to form any connection with him if he is in another country?"

"Bide your time, love. He obviously thinks you are too young to know your mind and you've a deal of growing up to do. Let him be, Cat. Enjoy your position as marchioness and make the most of it. Kilbane might take you a lifetime to figure out. There's no rush."

Cat tamped down a surge of frustration at the advice, which she suspected was sound enough. She did not want to wait. If Kilbane was her husband, she wanted to be his wife, but she knew he would not allow it. Not yet. So she must figure out a strategy to cope with him and this peculiar situation. For now, they were waiting for her father and Gabriel Knight. They had left at dawn to go to Doctor's Commons to secure a special licence.

Cat looked up at a knock on the door as Lady Helena poked her head in.

"How are you feeling?"

"Fine," Cat said with a wry smile. "Do come in."

Helena entered, looking as dashing and splendid as always in a gown of deep blue *gros de naples*. Cat had always admired Helena's poise, elegance, and inimitable sense of style.

"I have come to enquire if you are coming down for nuncheon, or if you prefer a tray in your room," Helena asked kindly.

"Oh, in my room, if I may. I'd rather not face everyone just yet," Cat replied at once, the idea making her stomach lurch.

"Of course," Helena said kindly, patting her hand.

"Does Emmeline know yet?" Cat asked. She bit her lip, wondering how many people were talking about her and relishing the scandal.

Helena shook her head. "She went to bed early last night with a migraine. I haven't had the heart to disturb her. She always feels rather fragile afterwards. She's not yet rung for her maid, so I assume she's still sleeping. I was going to check on her after seeing you."

"Oh, no. Don't," Cat pleaded, folding her arms across her stomach. "That is, let her sleep as long as she may, for I know she'll upset herself on my behalf. She's such a dear creature, and I don't want to be responsible for making her ill again."

Helena smiled at her, warmth in her eyes. "As you like, love, but you need your friends around you, and I know Em would want to be with you at such a time."

"Yes," Cat agreed. "But later. Please. Wait until she wakes up."

"Very well, I'll let her sleep a little longer. Now then, I suggest we all eat in here. We can have a picnic," Helena said with a grin, reaching out to take hold of Mama's hand. "And we always manage upsets better over large quantities of tea and cream cakes. We've overcome difficult situations before now with such tactics, haven't we, Tilda, dear? The Peculiar Ladies always triumph in the end."

"Indeed, they do," Mama replied, regarding Helena with affection.

"Then the Daring Daughters had better follow suit," Cat said, striving to smile and not to look as if she was scared out of her wits. "Send for as many cream cakes as they can carry. I believe I need them."

They reached Lancaster a little after midday to discover a carriage awaiting them. Mr Humboldt truly was efficiency personified. They did not delay, everyone eager to be away from the railways where Emmeline's father held such sway. So the carriage set off at breakneck speed, and the weary party endured the bouncing and jolting in stoic silence.

They finally allowed themselves a break when they reached Kendal. It was already mid-afternoon and there was no chance of reaching their destination before nightfall. If the weather held, there might be moonlight enough to press on. Otherwise, they would have to spend the night somewhere.

Emmeline hurried to use the necessary, holding tight to her cloak as a bitter wind tugged at it and tried to wrest her bonnet from her head. She was more than pleased to return to the warmth of the private parlour where Wrexham had already been settled. He was looking rather travel-worn and not half as immaculate as usual. Dark gold stubble glinted at his jaw and Emmeline had the near irresistible urge to touch it. She supposed she might have the right to such intimacies once they were married, but this wasn't a marriage in the usual sense. He'd been very clear about that, taking pains to reassure her he had no expectations regarding the marriage bed.

Emmeline had not known what to make of that. His reputation, before he'd lost his sight, was well documented. He'd been a wild young man, known as a libertine, so why would he not wish to consummate their marriage? Emmeline suspected it had more to do with him than it did her. Perhaps the accident that had stolen his sight had other, less obvious, implications. That was an unwelcome thought. Though he had been quite explicit in his offer to her, and whilst he had explained the possibility of losing his mind, he had reassured he was otherwise in excellent health. If he'd been afflicted with syphilis or another disease of the sort that might lead to insanity, she felt confident he would have told her so. Either way, whilst she was not about to treat his wishes with disrespect, or force an issue on which he might have strong feelings, she had every intention of doing all in her power to have the kind of marriage her parents had. Somehow, she must learn to understand him and gain his trust, and figure out how she could make this beautiful man her husband in every way, not just on paper. Otherwise, she might just run mad.

His head turned towards her as she entered the room. "Miss Knight?"

"Yes?" Emmeline wondered how he had known it was her, but was too tired to question him, only wanting to warm herself before the fire. She hurried to it, holding out her cold hands with a sigh of pleasure.

"You are eating in the parlour next door," he said.

Emmeline turned to look at him. "I'm sorry?"

"It's not complicated. You'll be served next door. Janet will stay with you for propriety." He sounded testy, and Emmeline wondered if she ought to let it go, knowing how he disliked eating in front of her.

Yet that would create distance between them, and she did not want that.

"No. Thank you. I'll stay here. It's a delightfully bright room. The other is bound to face north. It will be colder and darker."

His expression clouded. "Fine. You stay here. I'll move. It makes no difference to me."

Well, she ought to have expected that. "And leave me to eat by myself? Did you not tell the innkeeper I was your wife? Everyone will assume you despise me. No, I thank you."

He made an impatient sound. "Damn it, don't be difficult. I assure you, seeing me eat will put you off your own dinner. My manners are not what they once were."

"If banishing your fiancée to eat alone is any indication, I should say they are not," she retorted. "I refuse to marry a man who won't eat dinner with me."

He went very still, the colour draining from his complexion in a rush. For a moment, Emmeline wondered if she ought to take the words back.

"You… You would renege on our agreement?" he asked, and the anxiety in his voice made her heart ache.

Emmeline opened her mouth to deny it, to say she didn't mean it, but he spoke again before she could open her mouth.

"Fine," he said, folding his arms. "Have it your own way, but don't say you weren't warned."

"Thank you," she said politely, and moved to the place beside him.

His body vibrated with tension, and she sat with caution, too aware of his displeasure. She racked her brain for a safe topic of conversation, but could think of nothing beyond her own desire for a hot bath and a bed.

The innkeeper hurried in with a maid in tow who laid the table with jugs of ale and wine, and left cutlery and a basket of bread. The maid hurried out again.

"We've an excellent beef stew, should it please you, my lord?" the innkeeper said, looking a bit overawed at having a marquess in his midst. "Or there's—"

"I'll just have some bread and cheese. My wife may have whatever she pleases."

"Beef stew, enough for us both, please. In case his lordship changes his mind," Emmeline said, sending the inn keeper a dazzling smile.

The man hesitated, clearly torn between obeying a marquess and disrespecting his wife.

"Damn you," Rex muttered furiously. "I said—"

"My lord, we're both famished," Emmeline said gently. "I know you're cross with me, but please. I shall only fret myself to death if you don't eat something. For my sake, won't you have a proper meal?"

There was an electric silence, and Emmeline watched a muscle in his jaw leap. She thought he might be grinding his teeth.

"As my wife commands," he said finally, his tone measured as he addressed the innkeeper.

The man nodded and hurried out. The door closed, leaving them alone, and the only sound was Emmeline's heart thudding in her ears. Had she gone too far? Ought she have respected his wishes? Contradicting the Marquess of Wrexham in front of the innkeeper was dreadfully improper. Many men would have reacted very badly indeed at their wife offering such a slight to their authority in public, and they weren't even married yet. Doubts rushed in making her feel like a harridan. Her husband was a grown man who knew his own mind, but he was also assuming he knew what she would think of him, and on that he was mistaken. Besides, he was a large man who surely needed a deal of feeding. A meal of bread and cheese would do him no good and he'd be hungry again in no time.

"Are you very angry?" she asked tentatively, studying his face.

Sometimes he was exceedingly easy to read, his emotions on full display for anyone to see, but for the moment he was expressionless, only the stubborn set of his jaw indicating that his mood was less than conciliatory. He did not answer her, which was answer enough. Emmeline worried at a loose thread she'd discovered where she'd caught her cloak on a bramble thorn, twisting the bit of cotton around her fingers anxiously.

"I'm sorry, Wrexham. I can be rather overbearing, I know I can, but I'm famished and you're twice my size and you've eaten less than I have, and you know it's dreadfully silly to worry yourself over my sensibilities because you must realise by now I don't have any. I'm not the least bit sensitive. My father says I've the hide of a rhinoceros and people underestimate me because I look rather fragile. Which, of course, you cannot have done, but perhaps Humboldt has described me to you, and now I'm rambling, which is bound to make you irritable. Forgive me. I'll hold my tongue."

Emmeline's cheeks were burning now. Mortified by having annoyed him and contradicted him, her only recourse was to keep quiet and hope he calmed down. She put her hands in her lap and promised herself she would not say another word or tease him to eat anything, even if it killed her.

Beside her, Wrexham made a frustrated sound of amusement. "Diabolical girl," he said, but to her relief, the words were confused rather than furious. "I do not know what to make of you from one moment to the next. You confound me."

A rueful smile curved over her mouth as she turned to look at him, relieved to discover the hard set of his jaw had eased. "I know, but really, Wrexham, that's why I shall make this work. I'm not the least bit squeamish or sensitive. You may speak plain, and I'll not take offense. Indeed, I prefer it. My father is rather blunt, you know. He has little patience with polite nonsense, and I am used to hearing the truth, though I should prefer it if you not raise your voice. Shouting unsettles me."

He frowned. "I hope I am not such a brute."

Emmeline hurried to reassure him before he took offense again. "Oh, no. I never meant to suggest it. Indeed, you've been remarkably patient."

"Well, that's a Banbury tale if I ever heard one. I've been the very devil and you know it," he said frankly.

"Oh, no. Not in the least. Well, you were horribly rude to poor Mr Humboldt, which you ought not do, but not to me, my lord."

Wrexham sighed. "Now I see how it will be. You'll shame me into behaving myself. You really are diabolical. Positively Machiavellian."

"Well, it's about time you realised it," she replied tartly, so relieved his humour had returned to him that she dared to tease him a little.

They were interrupted by a quick knock, followed by two maids, each carrying a laden tray. They arranged a soup tureen with ladle and bowls, a large, covered dish of stew and another of creamed potatoes on the table, along with a basket of freshly sliced bread and a board with a selection of cheeses, before dipping curtseys and hurrying out again.

"Well then, Miss Termagant. What now?"

Emmeline bit her lip, wondering if he'd get all prickly again. Before she answered, she got to her feet and took hold of one end of the table. It was solid oak and weighed a ton, but she shifted it closer to him with a bit of effort.

"What the hell are you doing?" he demanded.

"The table was too far away, and it seemed easier to move that than the bench we're sharing, or, frankly, suggesting you move closer."

"I'm not that bad-tempered," he grumbled.

"Yes, you are, but with good reason. Now," she said, sitting back down and lifting the covers. "Oh, the stew is good and thick. You'll not have the least bit of trouble. Now, if I serve it in the soup bowl, that should make life easier." Emmeline put some mashed potato into the bowl first and then a large serving of the stew, added a spoon and set it in front of Wrexham before doing the same for herself.

"Here." She handed him one of the large, folded napkins provided.

Wrexham took it, but made no attempt to eat.

Emmeline's stomach made a sound of protest, and she snatched up her own spoon, too hungry to wait a moment longer. "This smells heavenly. I swear my stomach is dancing with anticipation," she said happily, digging in. "Mm-mm. Oh, it's delicious. The meat is cooked to perfection, so tender, and full of flavour. Whoever their cook is knows what they're about, I swear."

61

"All right, all right," Wrexham protested, tucking the napkin into the top of his waistcoat before carefully finding the bowl before him. "You've made your point."

"I wasn't making a point," Emmeline said, looking at him in surprise. "It really is good."

The two of them ate in silence for a while, with Emmeline concentrating on her own meal.

"Miss Knight?"

Emmeline turned to him. "Yes, my lord?"

"Might I have some more?"

She grinned at him. "You may indeed."

"I can hear you grinning, wretched girl. You know that? You sound horribly smug."

"Well, then, may that be a lesson to you," she said, attempting to sound prim and proper.

Wrexham laughed, and Emmeline's heart did an odd little jump in her chest. She paused with the ladle in mid-air and just stared at him. How she loved to hear him laugh, to know that she had made him happy, at least a little, enough to draw the merry sound from him. With some difficulty, she forced her attention back to the job at hand and set the bowl in front of him again.

"Thank you, pet," he said, such warmth in his voice that Emmeline shivered, the desire to shift closer to him, to lean into his large frame, making her nerves leap.

"I'm not a beagle," she retorted instead, retreating to the safety of bantering with him to avoid making a fool of herself. "Nor a terrier or a dachshund."

He grinned, and Emmeline smothered a sigh of despair at the effect it had on her poor, bewildered heart.

"No, I should say not," he agreed rather too readily. "Rather, a pampered little kitten, with tremendously sharp claws."

Emmeline narrowed her eyes at him. "Don't patronise me. I'm far more fearsome than a kitten, and you're a fool if you believe otherwise."

He laughed again, delighting her. "Ah, this is true. I do you a disservice. You beard the fearsome angry lion in his den, do you not... my little lioness?"

Emmeline tried hard not to preen, rather too pleased with this portrait and uncertain how to scold him for the rather flattering comparison.

"Ah, you liked that," he observed, making her flush scarlet as she wondered how on earth he could have discerned such a thing.

"A lioness is a not a displeasing image," she replied, struggling to keep her voice even. "Better than a beagle."

"I should never have imagined you as a beagle," he said, which immediately made her wonder what he *did* imagine.

"What do you think I look like?" she asked suddenly, and instantly wished to take the words back. "No, don't answer that. I should not wish you to think me vain. I'm really not."

"Then you're in the minority here," he replied gravely. "And Humboldt told me you were petite and brunette and lovely, with big green eyes, but... I should like a clearer picture, if I may?"

"Oh, you cannot possibly ask me to describe myself. I told you before I won't do it," she protested.

"Then I shall just have to imagine you," he replied, shrugging. "And besides all the lovely attributes Humboldt imbued you with, I suspect you have a turned-up nose and a stubborn tilt to your chin."

"I do *not* have a turned-up nose," she objected at once.

Wrexham burst out laughing, and Emmeline huffed at him.

"Well, perhaps I am a little vain," she admitted ruefully, which only made him laugh all the harder. "Very well, *and* stubborn."

This delighted him so much he threw his head back, apparently enjoying himself immensely. Emmeline sighed and gave in to the inevitable, gazing at him adoringly. Lord, but he was handsome, and she was smitten. Drat the man.

Chapter 5

Dearest diary,

How long it has been since I wrote anything here, and too much has happened for me to fill in the gaps.

Today is my last as Lady Catherine Barrington. By this time tomorrow, I shall be Lady Catherine St Just, The Marchioness of Kilbane.

Everyone is talking about me.

I am trying very hard to appear as if I do not care at all, and to look like Papa does, all remote elegance, but it is terribly difficult when one is constantly on the verge of tears. It is only now I truly appreciate how hard he works to keep his feelings hidden from the world.

Oh, what a blessed mess I have made of everything. But I shall come about. You just wait and see.

—Excerpt of a diary entry by Lady Catherine 'Cat' Barrington (daughter of The Most Hon'ble Lucian and Matilda

Barrington, The Marquess and Marchioness of Montagu).

15th February 1845, Holbrook House, Sussex.

Cat watched despondently as her nephew, Jacob, entered the library with one of his friends in tow. Jacob, Viscount Ridley, was the eldest son of her parents' adopted daughter Phoebe. This actually made him her cousin, for Phoebe was her Uncle Thomas' daughter. Thomas died when Phoebe was a baby, so Papa had taken Phoebe on himself. She had been a wonderful big sister to Cat, and her husband, Max, was an absolute darling. Jacob was a pain in her derriere, and the two of them usually squabbled, especially if one of his loathsome friends were with him. Now, however, she noticed the honourable Mr Peregrine Bancroft, who was actually very decent.

"Well, you've landed yourself right in the basket," Jacob said, stuffing his hands in his pockets and staring down at her.

At seventeen, he was a lanky boy with the air of a fellow who thought himself worldly wise. Cat bit back the comment brewing on her tongue as she was in enough trouble and contented herself with glowering at him.

"Oh, really, Jacob. That's just what she wants to hear. A fine comfort you are," Peregrine said crossly. He shook his head and went to sit down beside Cat, a familiarity she allowed because they'd known each other since they were in leading strings.

"As if I'd want any comfort from him," she said in disgust.

"We are sorry, though, Cat, truly. Awfully bad luck. That Miss Hatchet, of all people…." Perry sighed, shaking his head. "Wretched bad luck. Must you really marry him?"

Cat nodded, touched by his sincerity. "Yes, I must."

"You know, if it would help, I'd marry you, if you rather not marry Kilbane," he added generously, his expression filled with concern. He was a handsome fellow, sweet-natured and grave, but with a twinkle in his eye. He would make any girl a fine husband.

Cat smiled, knowing it was a genuine offer given from kindness, and not any desire to advance himself or get his hands on her dowry, or her person. "You're sweet, Perry, but no. I got myself into this, and there's no reason you should suffer. Besides, I do not believe Kilbane is half so bad as everyone makes out."

Jacob made a scathing sound, so they both glared at him until he stalked off to stare out of the window.

"I've thought much the same," Perry confided quietly. "Though he scares me half to death. Dreadfully intimidating fellow, but I know what gossip does to a fellow, and… well, his *family*." Perry sucked in air through his teeth, shaking his head, and Cat looked at him with dawning respect.

"Exactly," she said eagerly. "He never stood a chance."

"A snowball in hell had better odds," Perry added to illustrate his point.

Cat nodded, regarding Perry in a new light. She'd always liked him, finding they had a deal in common, though Perry was a much quieter, more peaceful soul. He always dressed beautifully, being something of a young dandy. Perhaps two years older than Jacob, he was turning into quite the catch. She wondered if Jacob's sister, Rose, had a tendre for him. At the age of fourteen, she was ripe to fall desperately in love with such a nice young man.

"If you ever have need of me, Cat, I'd be honoured to help you," he said, keeping his voice low so Jacob couldn't hear. "Just as a friend, you understand, and I know you have plenty of those, but… well, I'm here."

"Thank you, Perry," she said, smiling at him warmly. "Why you put up with Jacob is beyond me, but you are a dear fellow and I thank you."

Perry grew a little pink and nodded, but then the door burst open, and Lady Helena rushed in, stopping in her tracks as she realised Cat had company.

"Oh. Cat, dear," she said, her lovely complexion ashen. "Might I have a word in private?"

"Oh, of course," Perry said at once, leaping to his feet. "We were just leaving, weren't we, Jacob? Lady Catherine, Lady Helena, a pleasure. Good afternoon to you."

Perry hurried out, with Jacob sauntering along behind him.

"Helena?" Cat said, getting to her feet and rushing to her. "Whatever is the matter? Come and sit down, you look like you're about to faint."

Helena sat, her limbs stiff, and Cat noticed there was a letter crumpled in her hand.

"Have you received bad news?" Cat asked tentatively.

Helena gave a soft laugh and handed her the letter. "Only this. Did you know?" she demanded.

"Know?" Cat repeated, perplexed, as she turned her attention to the letter.

> *Dearest Mama and Papa,*
>
> *Please forgive me. I am so dreadfully sorry for the hurt and worry I know I am causing you, and I know you will not understand why I have done this, but I beg you to trust me, to believe in me. I have good reasons for my actions.*
>
> *Do not come after me, or make a fuss, for you will only risk causing a scandal. We will be back with you very soon, I promise.*

When I return, I shall be the Marchioness of Wrexham. I know this will come as an awful shock to you, but I promise you I did not do this on a whim. I know you would have allowed the match if I were certain, but the situation is more complicated than you can know, and time is of the essence. We must be married before his family can discover us and stop it.

I can only imagine how angry and upset you are, but at the risk of making things worse, I beg you will have my belongings forwarded to Cawston Hall. As you may imagine, I packed in haste and took little with me. Wrexham believes his father will come for him, will try to annul the marriage by whatever means possible. If I must stand up to a bully, I should much rather do it properly dressed. Mama, I know you will understand.

Now you know Norfolk is our destination, I don't doubt your instinct is to be there waiting for us. I beg you to give us a day or two before you come so that I may be prepared to greet you properly. I know I need not ask, but I beg you to keep this information to yourselves and tell no one.

I am sorry, so sorry, for any anxiety I am causing. I will write again as soon as I may.

Your loving daughter,

Emmeline.

"Eloped?" Cat whispered, hardly daring to comprehend what she'd just read.

"You really didn't know?"

Cat shook her head. "No! She didn't say a word to me, though she spent a lot of time with Torie whilst they were at Hart's Folly. Perhaps she might know more, but I can't begin to imagine why she eloped? And with the Marquess of Wrexham! Surely, she barely knows him. Does she?"

Helena shrugged and held out her hands, looking utterly bewildered. "I would have said not but... but now I come to think of it, he called on her and the two of them did appear rather.... Oh, what a fool I am! Why did I not see? But why? Why would she run away?"

"I don't know, but the letter says they must marry before his family discover them. The duke is a horrid man, I know. He was vile to poor Cara."

"Wrexham must believe his father will object to the match because of Gabe, the appalling old snob," Helena said furiously. "No matter Emmeline's grandfather was a duke, and her uncle, too."

"What's Wrexham like?" Cat asked anxiously.

Helena got to her feet and began pacing. "I don't know. Before he lost his sight, he was a charming rogue. A devil with the ladies, but I would have said he was an honourable sort. A fearsome sportsman, too. Losing his sight must have been devastating to him. But he's been such a recluse since it happened. He's not been seen in society for years and I do not know what manner of man he is now, but we have all heard the rumours. They say he is bound to lose his mind with his sight, as his uncle did. Surely Emmeline would not have married him out of pity? I know she is tender-hearted, but she is not a fool, and pity is no basis for a marriage."

Cat considered this. "I don't know Wrexham at all, but I have seen him. He's a very... romantic looking figure."

Helena groaned. "Lord, yes. You're quite right. Just the sort of tragic hero Emmeline would imagine herself in love with. Oh, the dreadful girl! What has she done? And her poor father...! He's going to be beside himself when he comes back to discover this, after everything Evie put him through. Oh, this has been a Valentine's Day to remember and no mistake. First you and now...." Helena collapsed into the nearest chair with none of her usual grace. "For the love of heaven, pour me a glass of brandy. A large one, and then fetch your mother, Harriet, and Prue. We must figure out how on earth to manage this before the Valentine's Day Ball becomes the most scandalous event in history."

By the time they made Gretna Green, everyone was ready to drop, and even the estimable Humboldt appeared to have reached the limits of his patience. It was close to midnight, and the famous, if unprepossessing, blacksmith's shop was nothing but a dim shape in the moonlight. There were no signs of life.

"Well, I'm not spending another second in this bloody carriage," Wrexham snapped irritably. "Wake them up, wake the damned village up for all I care, but someone had better marry us in the next ten minutes or you're going to have the very devil on your hands, Humboldt."

"Wrexham, I'm certain Mr Humboldt will do everything in his power, but I do not believe raging at him will make it happen any faster."

Wrexham's face darkened. Emmeline quailed but pressed on.

"And don't even think about starting on me or I shall refuse to marry you until you are in a better temper," she added, wondering how she dared... except she was also tired and fractious and, if she did not sleep soon, she would fall in a heap on the ground and sob like a baby.

His jaw worked for a moment but then he gave a sharp wave of his hand, dismissing Humboldt to go about his business.

Emmeline watched as Wrexham sat back against the squabs, his fists clenched.

"We are here, my lord," she said gently. "I feel confident my family cannot have discovered my absence before noon. I believe we have time. Do try not to worry so."

He made a harsh sound and ran a hand through his hair. Emmeline studied him in the lamplight. Her husband-to-be looked thoroughly disreputable, unshaven, rumpled, and travel worn. Somehow, it only made her want him more. Her stomach clenched with longing and anticipation. Unless catastrophe struck, in a very short time she would be this man's wife. *In name only,* she reminded herself with frustration. Well, not if she had anything to do with it.

"My lord," she said, aware of how her voice trembled. "My lord, there is something I wish to discuss with you."

"Very well," he replied, still terse but calmer than he was.

Emmeline swallowed, wondering how on earth to put it into words. Her cheeks burned just thinking about saying it out loud.

"I am to be your w-wife," she said, trying to ignore the way her heart was attempting to beat its way out from behind her ribs.

Wrexham's lips quirked, and an image of herself pressing her own mouth against his filled her mind, stealing her breath.

"That was the general idea, pet," he said dryly. "I should hate to think we've come all this way because of a misunderstanding."

"There is no misunderstanding!" Emmeline bit her lip, irritated at herself for snapping at him, but her nerves were all on edge and the enormity of what she had done was becoming hard to ignore. If she was to go through with this, she must tell him she did not accept his ideas of what their marriage would be.

He sat up then, tension singing through his large frame. "You've not changed your mind?"

"No!" she retorted in frustration. "Quite the opposite."

Wrexham frowned. "I don't understand."

"Wrexham." She sighed. "I… I wish to discuss our marriage. The terms of our marriage," she added for clarity.

His eyebrows pulled tighter together. "Is there something you want? More money or—"

"Oh, go to the devil!" she exploded. "Is this what you think of me? That I should wait until the last moment to blackmail you into giving me more than you have already offered. You have been more than generous, too generous, bearing in mind I asked for nothing other than to keep my dowry. Really, Wrexham, you try my patience."

"I beg your pardon," he said slowly, clearly bewildered. "I meant no offence."

"Well, you delivered it remarkably well all the same, but I was not considering the financial aspect of our marriage, more the… the…."

His face grew carefully blank, and when he spoke, his tone was neutral. "I already told you there was nothing to fear on that front, Miss Knight. I am aware of the bad bargain you have made, and that bedding a man who may fall into madness at any time is hardly a young girl's dream. Keeping me alive, or from ending my days in an asylum, is all I have asked of you, which is already far more than I have any right to expect. I should be a blackguard to importune you further by demanding my conjugal rights. You may rest easy if this is what disturbs you."

"It does disturb me," she said, thoroughly vexed. Why the stupid man should think she would not want him was beyond her. "And I wish to make it clear that—"

The door to the carriage swung open and Mr Humboldt appeared. "Well, I have made myself popular by waking the dead and soothed everyone's feelings by being very free with your purse, my lord. But if it pleases you, everything is ready. You may be married at once."

"I would have a moment to speak to his lordship—" Emmeline began but Wrexham spoke over her.

"No. We had best get this done at once. Humboldt, attend me."

Emmeline watched as Humboldt helped him from the carriage, seething that the wretched man would ignore her request to continue their conversation at such a moment. Mr Humboldt cast her an anxious glance which Emmeline was hard-pressed to meet with equanimity, but there was no point in worrying the poor fellow. Whichever way she looked at it, she must marry Wrexham now, like it or not, for in the eyes of society she was quite thoroughly ruined. The memory of Alana and Harry's recent nuptials contrasted vividly in her mind against her own as she hurried through the rain to the blacksmith's shop.

Well, she'd made her bed, now she must lie in it. Getting her husband to lie in it with her, however… that was the next hurdle.

Chapter 6

How disappointing that our mystery writer seems to have developed a character about which he or she knows nothing at all. Perhaps they come from an elevated position in life and have never experienced what it is to work for a living, for I found the blacksmith entirely unconvincing, and as for the housekeeper...

— A review of the recently published novel, "The Jewel and the Iron Key" by Anon. Review submitted to The Lady's Gazette by Miss Selina Davenport.

A wedding ceremony. 15ᵗʰ February 1845, Gretna Green.

Wrexham got through the marriage service by sheer willpower. He was utterly exhausted, his head was pounding, and his limbs were stiff from so many hours crammed in that damnable carriage. The idea of lying down flat and going to sleep was so tempting he might have made use of the cold flagstones he could feel beneath his boots if the circumstances were otherwise. Marrying Miss Knight, however, was something that deserved his full and complete attention. So he recited the words dutifully, concentrating upon their meaning and the promises he made, whilst trying to keep his mind from the conversation Humboldt had mercifully interrupted.

He supposed he could not blame her for wanting further reassurance of his intentions, but it had been a blow to an ego that had taken rather too many knocks of late. It was strange, remembering the man he had once been, so full of life and confidence. He'd truly believed himself invincible. Damned fool. It was like remembering a character he'd read in a book, one who was far removed from the man he was now. These days he lived on his nerves, always listening out for soft footsteps coming up behind him, alert for danger on all sides. He never felt able to let down his guard. Sometimes the danger was as innocuous as a rucked-up corner on a carpet, or a piece of furniture that wasn't quite where he expected it. Recently, the traps had been far more dangerous and intentional. Navigating stairs had become akin to running a gauntlet, and surfaces deliberately strewn with broken glass could appear in the most innocuous of places. It had made his existence feel like one lived upon a battlefield, where the slightest wrong turn could see him plunging headlong down a staircase or grasping the wrong end of a knife.

He'd broken a glass last week, alone in his bedroom in just his stockinged feet, and had dared not move in case he trod upon the shards. It had made him furious to have to shout for help, to wait for someone to come and clear up the broken pieces. It seemed frustration was his constant companion, forever simmering beneath his skin. Yet these past hours with Miss Knight, as wearying as they had been... he had felt more himself in her company than he had since he'd lost his sight. She had a way about her that both soothed him and gave him confidence.

His intended did not hesitate to speak her mind, nor did she flatter his ego or endeavour to treat him as an invalid or a child. He trusted her, he realised, managing creature that she was. With a sinking sensation in his gut he realised he more than trusted her: he liked her, very much, more than was good for him. So here was yet another thing he must guard himself against, for that could lead to nothing but hurt and humiliation. Their last, awful conversation had made that very clear.

Ah, well. Friends, then. It was more than he had hoped for until recently. Besides, if his libido had returned for good, there was nothing to stop him paying for a woman if he desired one. But the moment he considered the idea, he felt worse, not better, and he returned his attention to conversation around him.

"If you would sign here, my lord," Humboldt said, placing a pen in Wrexham's hand and guiding it to the page.

Wrexham signed the register and straightened, waiting as he heard Miss Knight... No, his *marchioness*, sign the register, the soft scratch of the pen upon paper tremendously loud in the quiet room. Suddenly Rex felt uncertain, not knowing what to do next. Ought he to take his wife's hand, to kiss her cheek? Perhaps it was not a romantic arrangement, but the girl had just married him, and—

Humboldt spoke, breaking into his thoughts and making him jump. "I've arranged rooms at the inn next door, but I think we'd best hurry. The landlord was not in the best of spirits."

Humboldt ushered everyone back out into the rain and along to the inn, guiding Wrexham with the same precision he gave to everything he did. All the same, Rex wished it was Emmeline upon his arm, rather than his hand upon Humboldt's elbow. He suppressed a sigh and told himself not to be so damned ungrateful. They'd got this far, which was something of a miracle.

"Here we are, my lord," Humboldt said. "This is your room. Not large, I'm afraid. The bed is in the centre, in the middle of the wall to your left is a chest of drawers. There is a pitcher of water and a bowl on top of it. I have set your toothpowder and brush to the side as usual. There are two small tables with lamps, one on either side of the bed. To the right is a window, the curtains are closed. There is a dressing table and mirror about a foot in front of the window. On either side of the bed is a small rug, thick but perfectly flat. There is a chest at the foot of the bed and your case is open upon it. I hope that will be all. Goodnight."

Rex jolted as he heard Humboldt move to the door. "Goodnight? You might remember I am without my valet, and—"

"And Lady Wrexham is content to assist you. Goodnight, my lord."

The door closed before Wrexham could say another word. He stood stiffly, listening, suddenly viscerally aware he was not alone in the room.

"Miss—*Emmeline*?" he corrected himself. They were married now. The idea sent a thrill of something he could not identity skittering down his spine.

"Yes, my lord?"

Her voice was soft, but sure. No trace of nerves. How the devil did she do it? He—once one of society's most notorious rakes— was so nervous his palms were sweating, and *she,* innocent little miss that she was, remained cool as a bloody cucumber.

"I beg your pardon," he said tightly. "I had no idea that Humboldt had arranged things this way, and—"

"I arranged it this way," she said.

Wrexham felt a little winded by that and it took him a moment to realise he was standing with his mouth open. He closed it.

"*You* arranged it?"

"Yes, my lord."

"Why?"

"Well, we just travelled all the way to Gretna Green in some haste to marry. I felt it would seem a little odd if we did not share a bedroom and, besides which, you did not allow me to finish our conversation. I will do so now."

No. No, no. Not that. He could not bear it. Not now, when he was so exhausted. In the morning, he might muster enough self-control to mask his feelings. Right at this moment, he thought that beyond him. He shook his head to deny her, but the obstinate woman kept talking.

"Wrexham, you will hear me," she said, and he detected a tremor in her voice. She was not as calm as he'd first thought. "We must consummate this marriage. If we do not, your father will do everything in his power to have it annulled. You will be vulnerable again, and I will be ruined."

For a moment, he could do nothing but stand there, the words ringing in his ears. Consummate the marriage. Of course, she was correct, and it wasn't as if he hadn't known it was a risk not to do so, but he'd assumed his previous reputation and the circumstances might be enough to....

Consummate the marriage.

Wrexham swallowed. His heart was beating in his ears.

"You...." His voice sounded odd to his own ears, thick and hoarse. He cleared his throat. "You would be willing to—"

His mind blanked at a way of ending that sentence, so he just left it hanging there.

"Yes," she said. "Yes, Wrexham, I would be willing."

"Ah."

"Unless...?"

"No! I mean... yes. Yes, I am willing—and able," he added hastily, and then felt like a twit because there was no reason she ought to think otherwise. Was there? Perhaps she had assumed.... He rubbed a hand over his face, which felt suddenly and inexplicably hot. Good God. Blushing like a virgin bride. Whatever next?

"Oh." She let out a sigh that sounded remarkably relieved. "Good. That's... good."

"It is?" Wrexham asked, stunned. For surely, she had wanted reassurance he wouldn't touch her just moments earlier and now.

79

"Yes," she replied, sounding serene and rather pleased. "Yes, it is."

Rex digested that, thoroughly confused but suddenly hopeful. She wanted to consummate the marriage. That would be wonderful if only he wasn't so bloody tired.

"Though," she began, sounding anxious. His hopes plummeted to his boots. He ought to have known better. "I confess, I'm so weary, if… if we could only wait until the morning…."

"Oh, thank God," he said with feeling. "Yes, certainly we can."

"Oh, good," she said, sounding positively cheerful. "I should love to have a bath, but I think the innkeeper might throw us into the street if I suggested such a thing now. He was rather a surly fellow."

"Was he?" Rex asked with interest.

"Yes, and he was wearing the most revolting paisley dressing gown. It was the ghastliest shade of yellow. I was dying to describe it to you, for I knew you would be horrified."

"Yellow paisley?" he said, his lip curling with distaste. "Saints preserve us."

"I know!" She laughed, the sound doing odd things to his heart. "Well, never mind that. We had best ready ourselves for bed, I suppose. If you wish for any help, you'd best instruct me quickly. I am quite prepared to sleep in my boots if it comes to it."

Wrexham opened and closed his mouth, quite at a loss. The realisation hit him in that moment. He was alone. With his *wife*. Who was willing to consummate the marriage. All at once, he was not the least bit tired and the idea of her helping him undress was making his nerves leap.

"Well, I assume you have no wish to sleep in your coat and boots," she said briskly, when he failed to answer. He heard her move closer and jumped as she put her hands upon the lapels of his coat.

"I beg your pardon," she said at once. "Forgive me, I ought to have asked."

"No, it's fine," he said, feeling ridiculous. "I just wasn't expecting…" *You,* he thought wildly. *I was not expecting you.* She had shaken him to his core.

"May I help you, Wrexham?"

He nodded, steeling himself for the touch of her hands as she pushed the coat from his shoulders.

"My friends call me Rex," he said, aware of every sound, every rustle of her skirts and the way they pressed against his legs as she got close to him. "Or at least, they used to."

She paused, and Rex held his breath, waiting. "Used to?"

"Before," he said with a shrug, listening as she walked away, he assumed to put the coat somewhere.

"Surely, they kept in touch with you?"

"Some did, but… I wasn't feeling terribly sociable."

"I'll put your watch and chain on the table beside the bed, on the right side, unless you object? May I undo your waistcoat?"

He nodded, imagining slender fingers undoing the mother-of-pearl buttons, his skin burning with anticipation. The waistcoat was a dark blue satin, almost the velvety black of the summer sky the moment before night consumed the day, or at least it was if his valet had dressed him correctly before they'd left Holbrook.

"It's understandable that you needed time to adjust to your new circumstances, but things are different now. Surely, you must get terribly bored? As I understand it, you were a physically active man, and very sociable. I see no reason you ought not return to at least some of those pleasures. Perhaps it is time to—"

"No."

He could almost hear her frowning at him and, despite his irritation with her probing into his life, the thought made him want to smile.

"Why not?"

"Because they were my friends and I do not wish to subject them to watching me turn into a—"

"A what?" she demanded, interrupting him before he could finish, a challenging note in her voice that gave him pause.

"A madman," he replied, seeing no reason not to say it. They could not hide from the truth; he had spelled the future out to her as frankly as he'd been able to. She had known what he would become.

"What manner of madness?" she asked, without missing a beat. "You have mentioned the subject several times, and that I would not need to trouble myself with your care other than ensuring that you remained in your own home and were treated with dignity, but I have heard no details. You have supplied meticulous plans for me to follow regarding your care when you can no longer make decisions for yourself, but you have never illustrated what will happen to you. Will you be delusional? Childlike? Manic? Explain to me what to expect."

Wrexham knew by now his wife was not one to shy away from difficult subjects, but all the same that bald enquiry startled him. "I do not know the precise details, only that if I follow the path my uncle trod, I shall lose my mind and end up in an asylum."

"And who told you that?" she asked, and he was uncertain if she was angry or not but there was a brittle edge to the question.

"Well, my father—"

"The father who despises you and has tried to have you killed?"

There was no missing the impatience behind the pointed remark. Rex digested this.

"It's common knowledge that my uncle lost his mind. He became paranoid and believed people were trying to kill him."

"Perhaps they were. They're trying to kill you."

Rex shook his head. "It's not the same. He wasn't the heir, he was no threat, and he also believed the furniture was alive and moved of its own accord. He gave the chairs names, like dogs, and had long conversations with a grandfather clock."

"Perhaps it seemed the furniture moved around if the family did not explicitly instruct the staff to keep things in the same place."

"He was insane!" Rex retorted, unaccountably angry now.

"Really? My friend's aunt believes in fairies. They live in her garden. Other than that, she's entirely sane."

"Your point?" he demanded.

"My point is that there are degrees of madness, and some people are not mad at all, only eccentric or misunderstood or... or perhaps there really are fairies in the garden, and only my friend's aunt has the capacity to see them."

Rex did not know what to make of that. His expression must have been one of utter bewilderment, because the next thing he knew, Emmeline took his hand in hers.

"Don't take other people's word for your future, Wrexham," she said, and with such warmth in her voice, such tenderness that his heart squeezed. A wave of emotions, so long beaten into submission, all rushed to the surface, leaving him raw and vulnerable and rather cross with her for having made it happen. "Perhaps you are correct and that will be your fate, but let us discover the truth for ourselves. You are not your uncle, you are entirely yourself, and only you can discover what you are capable of."

"Don't fool yourself into believing a fairytale, Emmeline," he warned. "This is the best you can hope for. I have seen every doctor and they all agree my sight will not return. Many thought it likely I will end up like my uncle."

"Likely, not definite," she said briskly, releasing her hold on his fingers. "And you ought not to underestimate just how good your best is."

She returned to removing his waistcoat, leaving Rex with his mind whirling, entirely wrong-footed and trying desperately not to read too much into her words. Either she was deluding herself or… or she….

"Take two paces back, please. The bed is behind you. If you would sit, I will try to get your boots off."

Rex sat, too stunned to argue. His boots were apparently rather a challenge, but she managed the job after a deal of huffing and pulling. He thought perhaps he heard a muttered curse word, too, which amused him a good deal.

"I can manage the rest," he said, too unnerved by their conversation and her nearness to allow her to help him further.

"Very well. I shall turn my back to give you privacy," she said, all prim and proper again, in contrast to her earlier forthright words. She was a puzzle, his lady wife, and one he was finding far more interesting—and challenging—than he had expected.

Rex stripped off the rest of his clothes, laying them on the end of the bed. He kept on his small clothes so as not to alarm her and was about to ask for his nightshirt when he realised he could hear her undressing. His breath caught as he imagined what was happening just a few steps from where he stood, desire hitting him so hard and fast his skin felt too tight and too hot. He ached with the need for her to touch him.

Irritated muttering reached his ears, mercifully distracting him, at least momentarily.

"Is something the matter?"

"My corset. I ought to have asked Janet to unlace me, but the poor thing looked ready to drop, and I can usually manage, but the knot... I think.... Oh, drat and bother! It's all tangled."

Rex rubbed at his mouth to hide his smirk. "Why don't you let me help? I could do this with my eyes closed before I went blind. I doubt anything has changed."

There was a taut silence.

"Very well, though you needn't sound so dreadfully smug about it."

"I beg your pardon," he replied, fighting to sound sincere when he felt more like his old self than he had believed possible.

"Well, here I am. Get on with it, then," she said, tersely, though he suspected it was nerves as much as irritation that made her waspish.

With his heart beating in his throat, Rex reached out and found her, his hands settling upon her waist. His pulse leapt as he discovered her shape, the way her narrow waist flared out into the generous swell of her hips. She was curvaceous in the best way.

"The laces are in the back," she said, sounding rather breathless.

Rex gave himself a mental shake as he realised he'd done nothing but stand with his hands upon her, unmoving.

He cleared his throat and moved to where the laces should be. Concentrating, he ran his fingers over the tangle, finding the knot at the centre and testing to see where the resistance was. Little by little, the knot slackened, and he felt a surge of triumph as it came free.

"Thank you," she said with a sigh, and went to move away but Rex held onto the laces, keeping her where she was.

"Let me loosen it for you, pet."

Rex tried his damndest to behave himself, remembering the deal they'd made, no matter her willingness to consummate the marriage. She was doing that for her own security, after all. If the marriage was annulled, she'd be ruined. No doubt she saw it as a duty that must be suffered through once and never repeated. The thought cooled his ardour more comprehensively than a dunking in ice water, so when the corset sagged he did not give into the temptation to pull her against him, to hold her and kiss the back of her neck and discover just how voluptuous his sweet little bride really was.

"Th-Thank you," she whispered.

"My pleasure."

She moved away and Rex turned back to the bed, feeling for the covers and tugging them back. He slid underneath them, shivering as the cold sheets touched him. The mattress was predictably lumpy and sagged in the middle, but suddenly Rex was so bloody tired he didn't give a damn. He closed his eyes, deciding to feign sleep to put Emmeline at ease, and discovering it took no time at all for it to become reality.

Chapter 7

Dear Bella,

How are you, Sis? Rumour has it you're as big as a house. Don't tell me it's twins again? I am uncertain the world is ready for the number of Grenvilles you seem determined to populate it with.

Anyway, it seems an age since I saw you last, and all your various brats. How many are there now? I appear to have lost count. I think I might need a bit of rusticating, and as the next addition to your brood is due in the spring, I thought I might give you the benefit of my delightful self for a few weeks from mid-May through June. There's no need to thank me, I know you'll be delighted at the prospect.

—Excerpt of a letter from Mr Leo Hunt to his sister, The Most Hon'ble Lady Arabella Grenville, Marchioness of Bainbridge (Children of Mr Nathaniel Hunt and Mrs Alice Hunt).

16th February 1845, Gretna Green.

Emmeline woke with a jolt, disorientated and bleary-eyed. The constant drumming of rain was a soothing sound, lulling her back to sleep, tempting her to ignore the fact that something about the day was most definitely unusual. The bed was deliciously warm too, though the mattress was lumpy, and her pillow remarkably hard… and breathing. The pillow was breathing.

Emmeline sat up with a squeal that startled the man sleeping beside her so that he too sat bolt upright, almost knocking their heads together.

"What? What is it?" he demanded, looking remarkably alert considering.

Emmeline clapped a hand over her mouth, feeling like a prize twit and to smother another squeal as she took in the sight of her husband's naked chest. Her *husband's*. Naked. Chest.

Good heavens.

"Nothing," she managed, the words smothered by her hand.

"What?"

"N-Nothing," she tried again, scolding herself for acting like a complete ninny. "I just… I woke up and…."

"And?" he demanded, sounding a little irritable now.

"And I'm not used to doing so in bed with a man. I forgot."

"You forgot?" he repeated, his tone offended.

Emmeline bit her lip, belatedly realising that sounded rather insulting. "I wasn't awake, I just…."

"Just?" he pressed, and she struggled to read his expression, but then noticed the way his lips twitched. The devil was laughing at her.

"I'll get used to it," she said indignantly. "I was just taken by surprise, that's all."

He gave an amused snort and reached behind him to arrange the pillows before sitting back against them. Emmeline stared, seeing no reason not to. They were married; he belonged to her now as much as she belonged to him. A woman could look upon her husband if she wished to, and… oh, she wished to. His chest was a revelation, muscular and strong, with a light scattering of golden hair, broad shoulders and powerful arms completed the picture, or at least the visible half. Emmeline wondered if he'd notice if she lit the lamp to get a better look, for the room was full of shadows, the grey daylight filtering dimly through the thin curtains.

He reached out to the bedside table, gently moving his hand over the surface to find the watch she had put there last night. He opened the casing and touched his fingers to the hands, an expression of concentration on his handsome features.

"It's not yet seven," he said with a sigh.

"I'm sorry I woke you."

"That's all right. I don't sleep late. Not these days, at least. And you, pet? Did you sleep?"

"Like the dead," she admitted.

He nodded, and an uneasy silence settled between them. Emmeline swallowed as she remembered what she'd told him last night, well demanded really. He had agreed they would consummate the marriage this morning. Lud. Well, there was no point in being missish now. It was too early to ask for a bath but there was water and… and they really ought to, well, get on with it.

"Where are you going?" he asked as she climbed out of bed.

"To have a wash."

"You're getting up?" His tone was neutral, but Emmeline wondered if he sounded disappointed.

"No," she replied quickly, praying he wouldn't ask her anything else.

Emmeline hurried behind the screen, which was patently unnecessary but made her feel better. Doing her ablutions with a man in the room—even a blind one—was an excruciating experience, especially when she knew he would be listening intently to whatever she was doing. The cold water was a shock against her warm skin and the carbolic soap not nearly so pleasant as the scented one she used at home. She had a sudden longing to be back in her own bedroom in her cosy bed, with a fire in the hearth and a maid to bring her hot chocolate and toast and jam. Scolding herself for being faint-hearted, she pulled her nightgown back on and padded back to the bed before wondering if that had been pointless. She stood beside the mattress, regarding her husband anxiously.

"Ought I take it off?" she asked in a rush before she could change her mind and flee all the way back to London. Too late now.

"Take what—"

"My nightgown," she snapped, before he could finish the question. "I don't know what is proper in these circumstances, wh-what to expect. My mother didn't know I was marrying, so…."

"Oh," he said, sitting up straighter. He frowned then, his expression one of concern. "Emmeline, do you know what it means to consummate—"

"Yes, yes, I know the mechanics of the thing," she said impatiently. "I just don't know the protocol."

"The *protocol,*" he repeated unsteadily.

"Don't you dare laugh at me," she warned.

He sobered instantly. "Forgive me, I would never… I'm sorry, Emmeline. Leave the nightgown on for the moment if you like."

"Very well," she said, mollified by his sincerity. "Shall I get back in the bed?"

"Well, it would make things easier," he said gently, but with a smile that was teasing and full of kindness, so she did not mind him poking fun at her.

Hiking up the nightgown, Emmeline climbed back onto the high mattress.

"Come, sit beside me for a bit," he suggested, holding out an arm in invitation.

Emmeline swallowed, cheeks hot with embarrassment, but moved across the bed. Gingerly, she moved into the space beside him, smothering a gasp at the feel of his bare chest against her arm. His hand rested lightly on her waist, where it had settled last night, but then there had been a thick corset between them, not just a fine piece of cotton.

"Breathe, pet," he said, and she tsked at the amusement in his voice.

"Really, it's very unfair that men know everything, and women are kept in the dark. Mama has always been very forthright about the marriage bed and the facts of life, which you probably think dreadfully shocking, but there is no substitute for experience, and I do hate not knowing what to do." Emmeline bit her lip, horrified at her outburst and wondering what on earth he must think of her. "I'm sorry. I get obstreperous when I'm nervous."

"Emmeline," he said gently. "If it makes you feel better, I'm nervous, too."

She turned to look at him, perplexed. "Don't mock me," she said crossly. "I may be sheltered by your estimation, but I am well aware of your reputation."

He shook his head. "That was before. I'm not the same man now."

She turned in his arms, frustrated by him all over again. "But you are!" Emmeline stared up at him, longing bursting to life in her chest as she took in the sight of his beautiful face. He was hers, her husband, and she intended to make him see himself as she saw him. Perhaps he was right, and this version of him would disappear bit by bit as his mind deteriorated, but she would help him fight it for as long as he was able. "You are," she said again, the words breathless and full of wanting.

He stilled, his expression intent. Emmeline gathered her nerves and reached out, taking his hand and bringing it to her cheek. His breath hitched as she pressed it to her face and turned into it, kissing his palm.

"You must help me, my lord, for now we have reached the limits of my experience."

He laughed, a startled sound of amusement that made her heart skip.

"Well, I'd best see what I can do then."

"Yes... please."

He pulled her closer and leaned in. Emmeline closed her eyes as their lips touched. His mouth was warm and far softer than she had imagined, his touch sure, brushing gently back and forth.

He pulled back, a questioning look in his eyes. "How was that?"

"Lovely," she said dreamily. "Do it again."

He grinned at her, looking so pleased her chest felt tight. Oh, this man was dangerous to her equilibrium and there was nothing she could do about it. She didn't *want* to do anything about it. If he *was* dangerous, then she was running headfirst into the melee.

He leant in again and this time she dared to put her hands on him, the feel of his skin beneath her palms both silky smooth and burning hot, making her giddy with longing. Gently, he encouraged her to lie back against the pillows and followed her down, the kiss changing by degrees as he nipped and teased at her mouth, seeking entry. She let him in, delighting in the confident slide of his tongue against hers, teasing and beguiling her, and felt the change in him. This was the Wrexham women whispered about behind fans, the one that had kept the print shops busy illustrating his shocking exploits.

The hand that had caressed her cheek so tenderly slid lower as her heart hammered and she gave a startled gasp as he cupped her breast, squeezing gently. He broke the kiss, toying with her nipple through the thin cotton of her nightgown.

"Are you well, pet?"

She nodded and then rolled her eyes. "I am. Well... that is, I am well. Yes, v-very well."

Emmeline groaned inwardly and wondered if she would always lose her wits if he touched her.

"You don't want me to stop?"

"No!" she exclaimed, rather too quickly. "No. Thank you."

He chuckled, a low, wicked sound that made her toes curl with anticipation. "Thank goodness for that, and how polite you are, pet."

"Good manners are important no matter the circumstances," she replied primly, for the sole purpose of making him laugh. She had her reward, though he was quickly distracted. Emmeline watched as he closed his eyes, his hand still caressing her breast. *He's savouring it*, she thought, *savouring me*, and she was suddenly wild to feel his hands upon her skin.

"Shall I take it off now?" she asked. "The nightgown."

His head tilted. "Do you want to?"

Emmeline hesitated, aware that most men would not want their wives to look eager for the marriage bed. Wives were supposed to endure, to allow, not enjoy; certainly not to show anything resembling desire or enthusiasm.

Her anxiety must have conveyed itself to him, for he seemed to know what troubled her without her saying a word.

"Emmeline, I would ask nothing of you. Not when you've already given up so much, but in this I must have honesty. Don't tell me what you think I want to hear, for you do us both a disservice."

"Yes," she said in a rush, already struggling to grab hold of the fabric. "Yes, I want to take it off. I want you to touch me."

He moved away to give her room, his expression carefully blank. Emmeline threw the discarded nightgown to the floor and shivered, uncertain now. "D-Do you want...?"

She did not finish the sentence, the next moment finding herself flat on her back, her vision filled with the sight of her husband braced over her. His mouth drifted over her cheek to her ear, where he nipped at the lobe and pressed a kiss to the delicate skin beneath, nuzzling gently. She shivered with pleasure, arching into his touch as his hand returned to her breast. His mouth continued on its journey until he reached the place where his hand caressed her, the hot, wet sensation engulfing her nipple, making her cry out in surprise.

"Does that feel good?" he asked, his voice husky as he lifted his head.

"No," she said frankly. "It feels dreadfully wicked. Don't stop."

He laughed, and she felt a burst of triumph at having achieved such a thing, for surely he was used to all manner of sophisticated lovers who knew what they were about.

"Ah, little love, if you think that's wicked, you have some surprises coming."

"I would be disappointed if that wasn't the case. Romantic poetry has a lot to answer for, and novels. I have very high expectations, I'll have you know. For surely people wouldn't get themselves in such trouble over love affairs if the feelings weren't spectacular?"

"Spectacular?" he repeated, one golden eyebrow quirking. "Is that what we're aiming for here?"

"I should certainly hope so. I mean, I cannot offer much in the way of experience, but I am enthusiastic," she said, emboldened by the flush cresting his cheeks, the rapid rise and fall of his chest.

"Are you?" he asked, and there was that glimmer of vulnerability beneath the beautiful, sophisticated exterior that had got her into this situation in the first place.

"Yes," she breathed, and tugged his head back to her breast. "Yes, I am."

She gasped as he resumed his attentions.

"Sweet Emmeline, how lovely you are," he murmured as he kissed his way across her body, his hand smoothing down over her belly, down her thigh, pushing her legs wide.

"My lord," she gasped as his hand coasted back up the inside of her thigh, his fingers searching through the curls between her legs.

He made a choked sound. "Rex," he corrected.

"Rex," she repeated, too giddy to care if she'd said something to amuse him. She simply lay in a happy sprawl, allowing him to do as he pleased and discovering to her delight that it pleased her too. She closed her eyes, so overwhelmed by the sensation that she did not notice the path his mouth was following until....

She cried out in surprise, eyes flying open. "Oh! *That's* the wicked surprise!" she exclaimed, hearing a muffled snort of laughter before he returned to his work, pushing her thighs wide and scandalising her to her very core. Emmeline closed her eyes again, giving herself over to him, trusting him, because she had done so from the very first. She thought perhaps she had fallen in love with him that night at the dinner party Prue had given. He had appeared so very proud and aloof, snarling and baring his teeth to keep the world at bay and disguise his uncertainty, yet he had made her laugh so, and she'd been done for.

"R-Rex, I can't," she protested, when the sensations became too much, too intense, making her feel like she might split into pieces and never be quite whole again.

He raised his head and then pressed a kiss to her inner thigh that made her shiver. "You can, you know. If you stop fighting it, there's the most delicious reward waiting for you."

"The little explosion?"

He grinned, a sight which was becoming familiar and did dreadful things to her pulse. "Yes, if you like."

"It's what Mama called it," she said, a little defensive.

"Well, and quite right she is too. I'd like you to experience it. For one thing, it will make what comes next easier."

"V-Very well, then," she said doubtfully. "But I don't know how."

"Just let it happen, that's all," he advised her, which she did not think very helpful at all, but held her tongue as he was clearly the expert here. A fact that was borne out moments later as Emmeline clutched at the bedclothes and writhed beneath him as stars exploded behind her vision.

"Oh, my," she gasped when finally the joyous waves of bliss faded, struggling to return to the real world as her blood fizzed and her mind span in giddy little circles. "Oh, my word."

"Sweet little Emmeline," he murmured, nuzzling at her belly as he moved back up the bed, prowling over her like a big cat. "I believed I had used up any good fortune remaining to me when you agreed to be my wife, but I did not realise just how lucky I was. You are quite delicious, pet."

"Am I?" she asked, wondering if he was just being kind, or if he truly meant it.

He settled himself between her legs, and Emmeline gasped as his arousal pressed against her still throbbing centre.

"You are," he whispered, nipping at her earlobe.

He pressed his hips closer, and Emmeline could not help the sound that escaped her as pleasure spiked through her blood again. She slid her hands down his back, revelling in the powerful muscle beneath her palms and reaching for the waistband of his small clothes. More than anything, she wanted them gone, wanted nothing between them. She had not until this moment realised how elemental the need to have him inside her, how ferocious the carnal desire for a man could be. Suddenly, all those ill-fated love affairs she had read about were a deal easier to understand.

"Do you want me, Emmeline?" he asked, his voice dark and wicked.

She almost laughed, for surely that was obvious enough, but before she could answer, there was a heavy pounding at the door.

"My lord?"

Rex jolted, turning his head towards the door, and scowling. "The devil take you, Humboldt. Go away!"

"I beg your pardon, I would dearly love to do so, but Mr Carter is here. He left some hours after we did and has had a rather trying journey."

"Well, and what of it? Why is he here?"

"It appears Mr Thompson has betrayed us. He sold the information of our plans to your father. Carter has gone above and beyond to warn us, my lord, but it appears your father will meet Emmeline's parents today and he has sent Lord Cecil to detain you. He is not far behind Carter and has several, er... *bully boys* in his company."

"Damn him!" Rex growled, quite plainly furious.

"I quite agree, my lord, but I think it would be prudent to leave as soon as possible. Once we are settled at Cawston Hall, we'll be far more secure."

"Very well. Have the carriage made ready," he snapped, rolling off Emmeline and flinging the covers aside in one angry motion.

Emmeline heard Humboldt's footsteps retreat and dithered for a moment, uncertain what to do. The lovely spell had been broken and the man beside her seemed a more daunting incarnation of Wrexham than the one who had kissed her with such tenderness and made her feel so wonderful.

"Wrexham?" she asked, too anxious to call him Rex, as he had suggested just moments earlier when everything had seemed so hopeful.

"My half-brother will enjoy this. He loathes me. Damn him to hell. I thought we might have more time."

"But there is nothing he can do, my lord," Emmeline said. "We are married."

"He doesn't need to do anything but hold us up. My father will have the marriage overturned on the grounds that I am mentally unstable," he said, his voice cool.

"But that isn't true," Emmeline objected. "Anyone can see you are perfectly sane."

"The truth is rarely a commodity that troubles my father. He will bribe and bully and bend the world and everyone in it as he sees fit."

"He won't bribe or bully me," she said fiercely, disgusted at the idea. "I won't let him hurt you. We'll find our own people to dismiss anyone who says you are anything but sane."

Wrexham smiled, though it was not a happy expression. "You'd best get dressed, pet. We need to leave. If you would be so good as to hand me a clean shirt, I would be obliged."

Emmeline slipped from the bed, shivering as her feet touched the cold floor. She had been so full of hope, and now worry slithered beneath her skin. She did not know Lord Cecil or what he was capable of, but the idea of his own brother coming mob-handed to stop Wrexham was horrifying. Plus, Wrexham was obviously concerned, as was Humboldt. Quickly, she went to Wrexham's case at the foot of the bed and found him a clean shirt.

"Here," she said, handing it to him.

He took it, and Emmeline went to move away but he reached out, grasping her arm. "Emmeline?"

"Yes?"

"I'm sorry. I wish—"

She smiled and covered his hand with her own. "So do I," she said quietly, and hurried away to find her things.

Chapter 8

Dear Perry,

I wish I'd had the chance to speak to you before you left Holbrook. I know your brother used to spend a lot of time with Lord Wrexham before he disappeared from society. Can you tell me what you know about him? It is an odd demand, I know, and I cannot tell you why I am asking, but I am putting my trust in you to hold your tongue and mention it to no one. I have always found you to be honourable and decent, and Cat said you've been very kind to her since the business with Kilbane. I pray I may rely upon that kindness and discretion myself. Please reply with all haste, the matter is urgent.

—Excerpt of a letter from Mr Felix Knight (Son of Lady Helena and Mr Gabriel Knight) to The Right Hon'ble Peregrine Bancroft.

16th February 1845, Holbrook House.

"Emmeline said we must trust her," Helena repeated, though it wearied her to keep harping on so, but Gabriel was fit to be tied and she could hardly blame him.

"What did I do?" he demanded, throwing up his hands. "To be given such obstinate, wilful, dreadful girls?"

"You married me," Helena said, giving him an odd look because that must have been obvious, surely? "I raced you from London to Brighton in a curricle and then eloped to Gretna Green with you. You cannot have believed I'd produce biddable little china dolls, Gabe."

Gabe made a choked sound and rubbed a weary hand over his face. "No," he said dryly. "Only I was not quite as prepared for them as I might have believed. I thought Florence marrying one of my best friends was bad enough, but then Evie gave me weeks of terror, and now... *now* Emmeline! I cannot believe it. Of all of them, I thought I'd be able to see her happily settled with the minimum of drama, but no."

"Evie and Florence are both very happily married and settled," Helena pointed out.

"To men they knew, at least!" Gabe retorted, dragging a hand through his thick hair and making it even more disordered than it had been. He sat down with a groan and Helena went to him, sitting on the arm of the chair and smoothing down his unruly locks. "There's no sign of them anywhere. The likelihood is they've gone straight to Gretna Green, but they managed it before anyone was looking for them and quietly enough that they've drawn no attention to themselves. Someone meticulously planned their journey and paid everyone involved to keep their mouths shut. I should never have let you persuade me not to go after them," he growled.

"Emmeline would not have done this without good reason," Helena said, holding onto that belief with her fingertips because the truth was, she was worried sick, too. "Besides which, it was too late. You said so yourself. By the time we discovered them gone, they were beyond our reach. Chasing after them would have only added to fuel to the inevitable scandal. Our daughter has made her

101

decision and we must respect that and pray she has done it for the right reasons.

"Emmeline is a romantic," Gabe said, his voice betraying the fact he'd had no sleep since he'd come home to discover Emmeline missing. "She'll think it all a wonderful adventure until reality hits."

"No!" Helena rose angrily.

"No?" Gabe said, his dark eyebrows going up. "Think about the men she's been sweet on over the past couple of years. How did they turn out?"

Helena waved this away. "That's different. They fitted her romantic ideal, but when they discovered Emmeline is rather blunt and provocative, and not the sweet little ninny they were looking for, they did not behave how she imagined they would. They either ran away or scolded her for being too forward and outspoken. They disappointed her badly, that much is true. Yet the first time she met Wrexham he was dreadfully rude to her, but I believe she handled him with her usual no-nonsense manner, and he did not shrink from the challenge nor revile her for it. Indeed, from what I can gather, he rather encouraged her."

"Oh, he encouraged her, all right," Gabe said darkly. "The man was a libertine, Helena. Just because he's lost his sight does not mean the rest of him doesn't work the same way. He's seduced our daughter into running away with him and I'm going to bloody murder him."

He got up, pacing to the window and glowering outside.

"Nonsense," Helena retorted. "Emmeline herself told us his family were the problem, that they would stop the match. No doubt it's that awful father of his, the blasted snob. Oh, I could wring his neck."

"Well, now's your chance," Gabe said, his tone grim. "The miserable old sod is here."

"What?" Helena sprang to her feet, hurrying to stand beside her husband. "Oh, no. Gabe, he must have discovered their plan. You don't think—"

"I don't know, but we're about to find out."

"Gabe, don't tell him anything. Don't tell him where they are going," Helena said, suddenly panicked as she grasped his arm, reassured by the hard muscle beneath his sleeve. Her husband returned a level look, which made her blush. "I beg your pardon. Of course, you wouldn't. I'm a little overwrought. Oh, Gabe, whatever shall we say?"

Gabe took her hand and raised it to his lips. "Don't fret, my lady. We shall handle this as we handle everything life throws at us."

"Beautifully?" Helena suggested, wondering if there would ever come a day when this man did not make her heart quiver like she was still a lovestruck girl.

"Together," Gabe replied softly, and Helena did not care a whit if the first sight the Duke of Sefton got of them was of her gazing at her husband as if he'd hung the moon. As far as she was concerned, he had.

Once the butler had left them alone, the duke lounged back upon the elegant silk covered sofa like a fat toad on a cushion. Helena repressed a shudder; the image was all too compelling. A man in his sixties, he might once have been handsome, but had long ago gone to seed. His life had been one of indulgence in all things. A greedy man with a love of power, Helena had long pitied his children for their misfortune in having him for a father. No amount of money or title could make up for his vindictive nature, or his need to control everyone and everything around him.

"Well, it seems Lady St Clair's ball will go down in history as the most eventful since the Duchess of Richmond's in 1815," the duke remarked.

Helena denied herself the pleasure of rolling her eyes. "What is the purpose of your visit, your grace?" she demanded, seeing no reason to beat around the bush.

His thick white eyebrows rose, small, glittering blue eyes looking Helena up and down in a way that made her skin crawl. "The purpose? The purpose is to commiserate and apologise, my dear. That boy of mine has gone too far and your lovely daughter will be ruined if we do not act swiftly."

"Act? In what way?" Gabe demanded. "They'll be long married by now."

Sefton shrugged. "Nothing that can't be undone, and if we are careful, there is no reason for anyone to be the wiser. We can put the whole affair behind us. I imagine you have kept the news quiet yourselves."

"Naturally," Helena said, hard pressed to keep the loathing from her voice. "But why should we do so?"

"Because Wrexham ain't right in the head, that's why. You know the gossip as well as anyone so there's no need to pretend otherwise. He'll go the way of his uncle soon enough, the truth is it has already begun. He's got a wild temper, and he's paranoid to boot, accusing the staff of everything from attempting to poison him to tripping him down the stairs. None of it's true. All anyone has tried to do is keep him safe. I did my best to keep him at home and out of harm's way, not that I was thanked for it. Society accused me of being a cruel parent and of keeping him a prisoner when all I tried to do is to stop him harming himself and others. If only the Duchess of Bedwin had not invited him to that fateful dinner. That's where he met her, of course. That's where he got his claws into her."

"Really, Sefton. His claws, indeed. You sound like a bad Gothic novel," Helena said in disgust, though his words had her heart beating frantically. "And I might remind you that her grace invited Wrexham on your request, though how you had the temerity to ask her is beyond me."

"Something I regret to this day," Sefton said with a mournful sigh. "I was tired, is the truth of it. Tired of being painted a monster. I thought if everyone saw the truth, they might understand. As luck would have it, it was one of his better days and he was merely drunk and disagreeable, rather than dangerously unhinged. But his mood turns with the wind, and when he's in a black temper, it's stygian indeed."

"That's enough," Gabe said, with enough force that Helena jumped a little in surprise, for he'd been remarkably quiet until then. "I've had enough of the amateur dramatics. I think it is time someone spoke the plain truth and I've never heard a word from your mouth that hasn't been twisted into a knot to suit whatever scheme you've got your fingers in. You've hated Wrexham since he was a boy and the idea that he'll inherit everything when you do us all a favour and shuffle off makes you wild."

"Gabe!" Helena whispered faintly, for even she would have refrained from putting it quite so baldly.

"Watch your mouth," Sefton growled. "You forget to whom you speak."

"I forget nothing," Gabe replied darkly, holding the duke's gaze. "*Nothing.*," Helena watched with interest as the duke's colour rose.

"That's as maybe," Sefton replied coolly. "But this is a mesalliance that will cause us all nothing but trouble."

"Ah, and now we get to it. You don't want your bloodline sullied, is that it?"

"No, I don't, and why should I? A common-born bastard as grandfather to a future duke? I think not!"

He was angry now, and Helena could see that he'd taken off the gloves. There was to be no more beating about the bush.

"Happily, I don't reckon Wrexham has it in him to sire a brat any longer. That side of his nature disappeared along with his sight. I'll be amazed if he can even consummate the marriage, which suits me fine. Cecil will provide me with an heir in due course, but it will leave your daughter in a difficult position, eh?"

"You dare to threaten Emmeline?" Gabe said, rising to his feet.

"Not a dare, it's a promise," Sefton said in disgust. "You help me find that boy and get the marriage dissolved, and I'll hold my tongue. No one will know your daughter is no better than she ought to be. She'll be untouched by the scandal, and I'll get Wrexham back under control, where he can do no one any harm."

Gabe lunged before Helena could stop him, grabbing hold of the duke's lapels and hauling the man's considerable bulk to his feet. There was the ominous sound of seams tearing.

"You listen here, and you listen good," Gabe said, his voice quiet and angrier than Helena had ever heard it. "I had my doubts when I heard the news, but I ought to have known better. If Emmeline married Wrexham, it was for good reason, and I reckon I've got a fair idea what that reason was, having listened to you spewing lies since the moment you arrived. I know a shyster when I see one. If our daughter decided to stand by Wrexham, then it's because she's judged him worthy. Emmeline is no fool, Sefton, and I promise you, neither am I. You've got it in for Wrexham and I can guess why. You and I both know you've made some disastrous investments of late. Short of ready funds, are you, your grace? Might be nice to declare your son unfit and take control of his fortune, mightn't it? He was always a canny one, even as a lad. He was one of the first to invest in the railways. Reckoned it was worth a punt. A pretty penny that investment has made him by now, though, eh? He's worth a damned fortune and you know it."

The duke said nothing, not that Helena needed confirmation, never having doubted Gabe when it came to finance.

Gabe looked down at the duke, who was at least a foot shorter than he was, his expression one of disgust. "I'll do everything in my power to keep you from annulling this marriage, Sefton, and I'll make sure anyone who cares to listen knows you're up the River Tick without a paddle. And an awful lot of people listen to me, your grace, so I suggest you think twice about making an enemy of me."

"It's you who ought to think on, *Mister* Knight," Sefton exploded, his colour high and his eyes bulging so furiously Helena wondered if he might suffer an apoplexy. "You're nothing but a jumped-up barrow boy, and don't think we all know it! I'll see you shunned in society, you see if I don't."

"The devil you will," Helena said, her crisp voice cutting through the toxic atmosphere. "Gabriel, put it down before you catch something. One never knows where such a creature has been, always scuttling about in the filth."

"You dare!" Sefton choked out, so outraged he seemed hardly able to breathe.

Helena stalked to the door and snatched it open. "His grace is leaving," she said in carrying tones. "Please escort him to the door *at once.*"

The butler and two burly footmen arrived with pleasing efficiency. Really, she must congratulate Harriet on her excellent staff. The duke took a moment to straighten his waistcoat and settle his lapels, which were looking sadly mauled, Helena noticed with satisfaction.

"You'll regret this," he sneered, looking at them both with contempt before he slithered out of the room like the snake he was.

The door closed behind him and there was a taut silence before Helena smothered a sob and ran into her husband's arms.

"Oh, Gabe," Helena said, her voice trembling with emotion. "I'm so very proud of you, but... whatever shall we do?"

Chapter 9

Dear Felix,

Dashed sorry I missed you before I left. I would have stayed longer had I known but my father demanded I attend some dull family affair and I can never bring myself to refuse him.

No need to give me details, old man. If you're asking, I know there's a good reason. Always liked Wrexham as it happens. He was very decent to me, nicer than my brothers ever were, not that it's a difficult thing to accomplish. I know he had a reputation as a troublemaker and petticoat chaser. To be honest, though, the petticoats chased him as far I ever saw, and any trouble usually stemmed from him sticking his oar in when someone else was getting bullied or if he felt the need to even the odds, if you get my drift.

In my opinion he's a good sort and I was never sorrier to hear what happened to him. I called on him a few times at Buxton Hall, but I was always told he wasn't at home, which I knew wasn't true. I was never certain if he didn't want to see me, or if his family were keeping me out. So, I don't know, is the truthful answer. I heard he took losing his sight hard, and it affected his mind, but I don't put much faith in gossip. If ever I get to speak to him, I shall decide for myself.

I don't know if this has helped or not, but I am at your service if you need me. You might remind Lady Catherine of that fact, too. I should be pleased to be counted as a friend if ever she requires one.

—Excerpt of a letter from The Right Hon'ble Peregrine Bancroft to Mr Felix Knight (Son of Lady Helena and Mr Gabriel Knight).

16th February 1845, Holbrook House.

The carriage took them at breakneck speed to Carlisle, where they arrived just in the nick of time to catch the train to Newcastle. The speed and frantic nature of the journey left Emmeline with a headache, her stomach churning unpleasantly after an hour of being jostled and jolted over difficult roads. The train hardly soothed her and by the time they reached York the headache had intensified and the oddly shaped bright shapes dancing before her eyes told her it was only going to get worse. Yet she held her tongue and endured, too aware of how white and tense Wrexham was and how badly they needed to reach his home before his half-brother caught up with them.

They were forced to wait an interminable two hours at York for the next train, which at least meant Emmeline could sit still and keep quiet, closing her eyes against the sudden glare of a day that was overcast yet far too bright for her suddenly sensitive eyes. Just breathe, she told herself sternly, concentrating on each breath in and out as the pain intensified.

Finally, they were moving again, and Emmeline drew on every reserve of strength and determination to keep herself upright and not to be sick as the megrim worsened and her stomach roiled. The desire to remove her own head and set it aside might not be a reasonable one, but she longed for it all the same as the carriage rocked and jolted and the brakes screeched. At each stop, whistles blew, and excited passengers chattered and sometimes screamed with alarm, as many of them were travelling for the first time at speeds they found difficult to comprehend.

Her father's foresight in investing so heavily in progress meant Emmeline had long since become accustomed to such a mode of transport, so she was not alarmed. She could have cheerfully murdered anyone who spoke above a whisper, however, let alone squealed, screamed or made any other disturbance. By the time they reached their journey's end at Scunthorpe, and were reduced to taking another carriage, she had reached the end of her endurance. It was almost six in the evening and the light was fading, a day which had been merely overcast becoming colder as a chill wind whipped up and the first drops of rain pattered heavily upon the flagstones where they waited.

Emmeline swallowed, trying hard to still her rebellious stomach. She sucked in a deep breath and let it go again, slowly, raising her face to the cold air and sighing with relief as the rain wet her skin.

"Lady Wrexham?"

Humboldt's voice seemed a long way off and Emmeline struggled to focus upon it.

"Humboldt, what is it?" Wrexham demanded, his voice sharp with concern.

"My lady, are you quite…?"

Emmeline was vaguely aware of a commotion, of Wrexham's furious voice issuing orders, but she was far too tired to discover what the trouble was, and instead closed her eyes.

Wrexham sat beside Emmeline's bed and cursed himself for the hundredth time. She had been asleep for hours, obviously exhausted. Damn him for a heartless brute. She'd been his wife for barely a day and already she was sick with fatigue after the strain he'd put upon her. A megrim, the doctor had told him, a fact that had struck Wrexham hard as he'd known well enough she suffered from the affliction. She'd told him herself just hours previously.

He ought to have known something was wrong when she became so quiet, but he had assumed…. Well, in truth he had wondered if she was regretting her decision and had been too anxious to hear something to confirm his fears to enquire. Damned coward. And this was the result. But why, why had she said nothing?

The fire in the hearth crackled and snapped, and Wrexham was glad he'd had it built up before sending the servants away. The room was warm now and his feet had stopped feeling like blocks of ice. Emmeline had collapsed in the middle of a freezing rainstorm which had soaked them all to the skin. A maid had taken her clothes and his boots away to dry and promised to return them good as new. Wrexham had not allowed Humboldt to fuss over him and take the rest of his wet things, however. A sense of deserving the discomfort for having treated his wife so badly making him refuse.

He sat up as the sound of bedcovers rustling reached him and he heard a sigh.

"Emmeline?"

"Wrexham?

"Are you well, pet?" he asked, prepared to hear her rail at him for being an utter bastard.

There was a brief silence. "I think so, yes, but… where are we?" she asked, sounding fragile and confused, which only made him more furious with himself. Emmeline was never fragile, and only ever sounded entirely sure of herself.

"We're in Scunthorpe, the best inn I could find close to the railway."

"Oh, I'm so sorry. Did I—?"

"You fainted," he said, realising too late it had sounded like an accusation.

"I *never* faint," she said, sounding indignant at the idea.

"Well, you've never been dragged from one end of the country and back again by an unfeeling brute either, I'd wager."

She sighed. "Don't be silly. It wasn't your fault in the least, and I'm perfectly well now. Though a little thirsty."

"There's water beside the bed, and I'm not being *silly.*" He heard water pouring into a glass and rustling as she sat back against the pillows. Scowling, he knew he must apologise. He'd been trying to do so, but he was so damned angry with himself and everything else it was hard to find the right words. He took a breath and tried again. "I apologise, Emmeline. It was entirely my fault."

"No," she said evenly, and he had the distinct impression she was vexed with him now. "It wasn't, and you look as though you ought to have been sleeping too. You're obviously exhausted and... is that coat wet? It looks dreadfully crumpled."

His temper lit. "I don't give a damn about the blasted coat! I'm perfectly well, and why else are you here if not for me?" he demanded in frustration, dragging a hand through his hair.

"And now you've messed your hair up," she said reprovingly.

"Never mind my bloody hair!" he snapped, unable to help himself. "Why didn't you say anything? Why didn't you tell me you were ill? Did you think I wouldn't care? Did you think I wouldn't ensure your comfort?"

There was an impatient sigh which was so much more in character his anxiety ratcheted down a notch. "No, Wrexham. I knew if I told you we would halt our journey and you would find the most comfortable inn you could and a doctor to attend me, and would insist I rest for as long as I needed. Which is exactly what you have done. *That's* why I didn't tell you."

"But you were sick, in pain, and I didn't know. I ought to have asked, I know I ought to have. I knew you were quiet but... but I thought. Well, never mind what I thought, but you cannot keep me in the dark like that. I spend a deal too much time there as it is."

"I'm sorry, Wrexham, but I am very aware of how urgent it is we reach Cawston Hall before Lord Cecil catches up with us. I did not want to risk slowing us down."

Wrexham digested this. "I understand that, pet, and I thank you for it, but Emmeline, you need to understand. There are many things I cannot do for myself, and I'm going to make a poor excuse for a husband, but I can ensure that you have everything you need. Please. *Please,* don't take that away from me."

"Wrexham," she said softly, something that sounded horribly like pity in her voice. He stood abruptly, turning away from her and walking to what he hoped was the window. A low, hard object hit him hard in the shin and he stumbled, reaching out and finding nothing but air. He staggered sideways and crashed into more furniture, as something toppled and smashed. The scent of a flowery yet chemical liquid spilling reached his nose, and he instantly recognised the smell of laudanum. The bottle the doctor had left for Emmeline.

"Damnation!" he roared, frustration and anger and regret churning inside him.

"Wrexham!" She was there suddenly, before him, sliding her hands into his. "Rex, it's all right," she said, sounding so damn sympathetic he wanted to scream or to weep and he wasn't certain which way it was going to go.

"Don't pity me!" he snarled, snatching his hands away.

"I don't pity you, you impossible man!" Wrexham jolted as she smacked his chest, not with any real heat, but the irritation behind the gesture was obvious enough.

Before he could think of an adequate retort, she took his hand and placed it upon her breast, holding it there, which shut him up very effectively. Her maid must have helped her undress, for he remembered the feel of her nightgown and the soft body beneath it. For a moment he couldn't think, let alone speak, stunned by the feel of her full, round flesh beneath his palm, the hard little pebble of her nipple as it grew taut beneath his touch.

"Emmeline," he said, suddenly breathless.

"We have unfinished business, you and I," she said firmly, no longer appearing the least bit fragile.

"B-But you're sick," he said, because he was damned if he would compound his ill treatment of her by taking advantage.

"I'm feeling rather better now."

"You don't have to—" he began, only to have the words cut off as she pressed her mouth to his. He groaned, wrapping his arms around her and pulling her close, desire sweeping through his blood like a spark hitting gunpowder. He kissed her deeper, harder, gratified by her willingness, that she remembered the way of it, and responded eagerly.

He broke the kiss, feeling dazed and overwhelmed with need and hope.

"I won't let your father annul our marriage, Wrexham," she said, sounding very sure of herself. "You're my husband, and I like being Lady Wrexham. We're in this together now, you and I, and I won't let them beat us."

Hope fizzled out as he realised what she was saying, because of course it was her position she needed to secure, that was what she wanted. Not him. He was a title, a means to an end, not a man.

But he had known that, he told himself. It didn't matter. He hadn't expected more, and it was foolish to expect it. Cruel, even, when he remembered the fate that awaited him. She was a kind-hearted creature, and it would be hard enough on her to watch a friend deteriorate into lunacy. He told himself he was selfish to wish she might love him, for that would be wicked of him, to wish for her to mourn the loss of him, but the protest seemed hollow and unconvincing. He shook the feeling off. He could please her, at least, he knew that now, and it wasn't like she didn't enjoy his touch. She'd come for him eagerly enough this morning, so… so they may as well enjoy each other for as long as they may.

Perhaps she would not allow him the liberty of touching her again. It was what they'd agreed, but for now, in this moment, she was his and he wanted her. He wanted her badly.

Emmeline stared up at her husband, her heart beating in her ears. She still could not believe she had done such a shameless thing. Only he had looked so defeated, so angry, yet so lost, and she could not bear it. She had mis-stepped before, allowing him to hear the aching sadness in her voice, which he would naturally interpret as pity. Emmeline did not pity him. She was in awe of him, she longed for his touch and was desperate to know every single thing about him. Her feelings for him seemed increasingly complex and tangled, ranging from physical need and protectiveness, to love and frustration, admiration and fascination, with the occasional powerful desire to shake him for being an absolute idiot.

"I won't let your father annul our marriage, Wrexham. You're my husband, and I like being Lady Wrexham. We're in this together now, you and I, and I won't let them beat us," she said, praying he could hear the truth behind her words, and all the things she was not quite brave enough to say out loud.

She still did not know this man who was her husband, and whilst she trusted him with her body, and felt instinctively that he was good and kind and honourable, there was a part of her that remained cautious. He had never promised her fidelity, after all. Indeed, he had never expected to bed her at all. She presumed he had a mistress, or perhaps a string of mistresses, and if there was to be anything real between them, she would ask him to put an end to that. She did not want to share him. If that was not what he wanted, however....

As ever, the difficulty of her situation came home to her with unpleasant clarity, but she was here now. She was his wife, in his arms, and when he kissed her, nothing else mattered.

He tugged at her nightgown, raising it up over her head and Emmeline moved, lifting her arms so he could pull it free. She stood, shivering, her earlier fatigue and the foggy sensation she endured after a migraine, chased away by nerves and anticipation.

"I wish I could see you," he said, his voice low, almost angry.

"You've an imagination have you not, my lord?" she asked him, wondering when she had become so very bold as she moved closer, pressing against him and sucking in a breath at the cold touch of his waistcoat buttons against her skin.

"Yes," he said, the word little more than a rasp of breath against her cheek as he buried his face against her neck. He breathed in deeply, and she had the sense that he was revelling in the scent of her as much as the feel of her beneath his hands as they roamed over her, making her shiver harder still. "God, Emmeline, your skin is so soft, so fine."

She opened her mouth to reply, but he stole the words with a kiss, demanding entry this time and only taking more when she gave what he asked for. His obvious desire for her was like adding fuel to a blaze and her blood heated, making its own demands. Her fingers went to his damp coat, and she pushed it from his shoulders, uncaring when it fell in an untidy heap on the floor. They were rumpled enough from such an unceasing journey, so what did it matter? She began next on his waistcoat buttons, clumsy in her haste to strip him. He laughed softly and removed his cravat as she undid the last buttons and then he shrugged off the waistcoat.

Emmeline watched with her heart thudding as he tugged his shirt free of his trousers and pulled it over his head, dropping it carelessly to the floor. She dared to press her hands to his chest, stunned anew by the feel of him, smooth skin and hard muscle, the glint of gold in the wiry hair that trailed down his abdomen.

"You are quite magnificent, my lord," she whispered, feeling his body react to the words, a new thrill of tension tightening his muscles.

"You think so?" he asked, a thread of uncertainty audible though he smiled at her words, and her heart wept for this man who had been so confident, so young and brash and powerful before fate had stepped in.

"False modesty doesn't become you," she scolded him, though she knew it was nothing of the sort. "You know very well how fine you are, else you would not have enjoyed such a successful career as a libertine."

"Ancient history," he murmured, his expression one of concentration as he moved his hands over her, cupping her breasts and squeezing gently.

Emmeline gasped, finding it hard to keep her mind on the conversation.

"I don't see why," she remarked, her gaze falling to the hard shape visible behind the placket of his trousers. "Everything seems to be in correct working order. Not that I'm complaining. I want you to myself."

There was a brief, stunned silence and then he gave a sharp bark of laughter. "You confound me. Do you know that, Miss Milly?"

"You can't call me that any longer. We're married."

"Ah, pet, you'll always be Miss Milly to me," he murmured, nuzzling her neck and trailing kisses to the sensitive place beneath her ear. "You want me to yourself, then?"

"Yes," she said firmly. "I've never been terribly good at sharing. It comes of being the youngest," she added breathlessly, gasping as his hand slid between her legs, caressing.

"If you want me to yourself, it's only fair I ask the same in return," he said, and he sounded amused, yet Emmeline had become sensitive to his moods, to the inflection in his voice, and more than anything his expression.

Now and then he was unguarded, perhaps forgetting she could see what was written upon his face, as now. He wanted that, she thought, her heart skipping. He wanted her to himself.

"Yes," she said, without hesitation.

"But our agreement. I said you could—"

"I don't want to. I only want you," she said, with as much certainty as she could, before pressing her mouth to his.

The words seemed to light a fire inside of him and he reached for her, hefting her into his arms. Emmeline squealed, wrapping her legs about his waist, rather scandalised by the intimate position.

"Where's the bed?" he demanded.

Looking around, she calculated quickly. "Turn to your right, yes, now three steps, one more…."

His legs hit the bed, and he grinned, dropping her onto the mattress. Emmeline huffed at his expression, wriggling fully onto the mattress, secretly delighted by the smug look on his beautiful face. His hands fell to his waistband, and he undid the buttons with nimble fingers. Her mouth went dry at the thought of those clever hands upon her, and Emmeline swallowed, anticipation building.

He had not given her the privilege of looking at him on their wedding night, or morning, as it had been. There had not been time before they'd been so rudely interrupted, and she knew they could not linger now. If Lord Cecil guessed they were returning to Cawston Hall, he might be close behind them. This was important though, and not only to cement their marriage in law. Wrexham didn't trust her. Not entirely. Not yet, and she needed to change that to have a chance of creating a future with him.

A dark voice nagged at her, reminding her he didn't have a future, but she refused to listen. Perhaps she was foolish, perhaps she was living in a fantasy, but she didn't care. She would not give up on Wrexham until it was obvious his mind was gone for good. Perhaps not even then, for the emotions filling her heart were too powerful, overwhelming her and underscoring what she already suspected. She loved him as much as she desired and admired him, and she would fight for him, no matter what it cost her.

Wrexham pushed the trousers and smallclothes down in one smooth movement, before kicking them aside, and Emmeline's breath caught. Narrow hips followed elegantly into muscular thighs and that most male part of him jutted forward, demanding her attention. He leaned down, hands seeking the bed, coasting over her body to place her on the mattress before he climbed carefully over her.

"Touch me," he said, his voice soft.

Emmeline obeyed happily, reaching up to cup his face. "How handsome you are," she said in wonder, stroking the prickle of the beard he'd not had the time to shave.

"It's scratchy. I'm sorry, love."

"I'm not," she replied. "You look like a wicked pirate. I rather like it."

"Ah, Miss Milly has a taste for fantasy," he murmured.

"Perhaps I do," she retorted. "I shall pretend you are a ruthless buccaneer who has kidnapped me for his own nefarious purposes."

Watching the surprise on his face was worth every moment of pain and discomfort she had endured on their journey and Emmeline grinned.

"I've shocked you."

"You needn't sound so pleased about it, wicked girl," he said, shaking his head and then sucking in a sharp breath as Emmeline's hand closed around his erect flesh.

"Well, you *did* say I was wicked. I thought I might as well act the part."

He groaned, and the sound darted to the place where he had pleasured her yesterday, making her ache, her insides molten, her skin crying out for his hands upon her.

"Teach me how," she whispered, for he had gone still, his eyes tight shut as his breathing grew uneven.

Silently, he reached down and wrapped his hand about hers, showing her the way of it. Emmeline paid attention, both to the instruction and to his reaction to her caresses. Every shiver, every sound he made was a lesson in how he liked to be touched and she paid close attention, determined to learn everything she could. He leaned down, seeking her mouth and she kissed him, wondering at the way it felt to have such power over this beautiful man.

"No more," he said, gently taking her hand and pressing it into the mattress. "I want you now. I want to be inside you."

The words made her blush and quiver with anticipation.

"Yes," she said, a startled sound torn from her as he pressed close, the heat and hardness of him in exactly the right place.

Emmeline sighed and tilted her hips to meet his. Suddenly, he moved away, and she watched as Wrexham sat back on his heels. Emmeline pushed up onto her elbows, wondering what he was about and regretting the loss of his weight and his heat as his big hands arranged her, pushing her thighs wide. He shifted farther back and ducked his head, and she gave a little shriek, part shock, part delight as his tongue swept over her. She collapsed onto the pillows, ready to experience the marvellous sensations he'd shown her yesterday. To her regret, he was in no mood to linger this time and only toyed for long enough to ensure the way was prepared for him. He returned to his place between her thighs and Emmeline's breath caught as she felt him nudge his way into her body. How strange, she thought wildly, how intimate and close, and....

She cried out as he pushed inside, sheathing himself inside her in one swift movement.

"I'm sorry," he gritted out, holding still now. "Forgive me, pet. It will get better, I promise. I'll make it better."

"I know," she said, relaxing at his words, trusting him as she breathed through the shock of it and the discomfort gave way to other sensations.

She wrapped her arms around him, delighting in how solid he was, how strong, his frame enveloping hers in the best way. Slowly, he moved, and Emmeline gripped his arms hard as the sensation shifted from discomfort to a peculiar acceptance.

"Oh," she said as he eased inside her once more, her body becoming accustomed to his presence. *"Oh."*

"Is that good, pet?"

Emmeline gave a little cry and wrapped her legs tighter around him. "Y-Yes," she said, eyes wide now as she relaxed into the pleasure of it.

Wrexham sighed and kissed her again and Emmeline lost herself in the moment, in him, her husband, this extraordinary man she was determined to know inside and out.

"So sweet," he whispered, touching her with such reverence she felt loved and cherished, no matter if that were an illusion.

She did not know what went on in his well-guarded heart, but in this moment there was tenderness and a genuine desire to please her and that was enough for now. She wanted more, she wanted everything, every piece of his heart, but she could wait. He raised his hand to her mouth and traced the shape of her lips and Emmeline kissed his fingers, nipping at the pads. He smiled at her.

"Open your mouth," he told her, and when she did slid a finger past her lips. Instinctively, she closed her mouth over it and sucked and Wrexham's breath hitched.

"Lord, I shall remember that," he said, his lips quirking as he withdrew his hand and slid it down her body, moving to seek the place between her thighs that had yielded so dramatically to his tongue yesterday. He teased her with the slick finger, touching lightly as he loved her, carefully stoking the fire he had lit until she was hot and restless, almost frantic with need.

"Wrexham," she pleaded.

"I know, pet," he soothed, his voice like dark silk. "Be patient. You'll have your way, for I cannot last much longer. You feel too good, so good, and my control is unravelling."

That pleased her more than she cared to consider, the idea of a man like this losing control because of her. Though she knew herself to be pretty—not that her husband could see her—but she had never considered herself the kind of woman that men lost their wits over. With Wrexham, though, the way he touched her, the things he said… he made her feel desirable, powerful, and more at home in her own skin than she ever had before.

The touch of his hand on that tiny nub of flesh became firmer, more insistent, and then he ducked his head and closed his mouth over her breast, suckling hard. Emmeline threw her head back as the climax hit hard and fast, stealing any semblance of control. She cried out, the shocking sound ringing in her ears but not stopping her from shouting again, unable to stop the raw cry of pleasure as it tore from her. Her body seemed no longer her own, but his, under his control as he sent her spiralling into the sweet, bright dark where little explosions glittered against a black velvet sky.

"Christ," Wrexham murmured and sucked in a breath, his body growing taut, and he jerked away from her. His sudden withdrawal made her exclaim with shock and disappointment, swiftly followed by fascination as he took himself in hand. Emmeline watched with rapt attention as his powerful frame spasmed. He let out a coarse exclamation that shocked her but was immediately forgotten with the sudden splash of heat over her belly as he spilled his seed upon her skin, making her gasp.

He didn't move for a moment, his breathing harsh and uneven, his beautiful skin flushed and damp. Emmeline simply stared, drinking in the sight of him.

"I'm sorry," he said, gruff now. "I… I ought to have warned you. Are you horribly shocked?"

Emmeline tried to smother her bark of laughter, but was not entirely successful. "N-Not at all shocked," she managed.

His eyebrows drew together. "Are you laughing at me?"

"No! No," she said firmly. "It's only… I wasn't shocked in the least, Wrexham. I… liked watching you."

She bit her lip at the obvious surprise she saw on his face.

"I beg your pardon, my lord. I'm not what you expected, am I?" she asked, suddenly concerned she had been too honest. She was supposed to be an innocent girl. She was *supposed* to be horrified by such intimacies, though how that did anyone any good she had never understood.

"Indeed, you are not," he said, and her heart thudded anxiously when she could not read his tone. "You are a constant surprise, Miss Milly."

"I'm sorry," she offered..

He frowned at that. "Whyever would you be sorry? I'm not."

"You're not?" Her lips quirked upwards as he shook his head.

"Marrying you was the most sensible decision I ever made in my life. How on earth did I persuade you into it? You're quite marvellous, you know."

"Am I?" she asked shyly, delighted by his words.

He leaned closer, and she met him halfway, sighing as he pressed a soft kiss to her mouth.

"Quite, quite marvellous," he murmured against her mouth. "Thank you."

"You're welcome?" she replied uncertainly.

He laughed and sat back. "I'm honoured, pet. You've no idea how much, but though I deeply regret it, we'd best get cleaned up. We'll need to be on our way. That is… if you're feeling well enough?"

Emmeline could not help the laugh that escaped her. "Oh, I feel *very* well, my lord," she said, rather glad he could not see how much she was smirking. "Very well indeed."

Chapter 10

Dearest Pip,

How I wish you were here today. I need your steady presence, your kindness, and even your scolding would be welcome. That must show you what a sorry state I am in. I don't know why it is you are keeping away, but if it is because you fear you have let mama and papa down, please know that I understand.

You will hear soon enough what a monumental fix I have got myself into, and there's no one to blame but myself. Please don't get on your high horse and come back hell bent on vengeance, for you must take your frustration out on me. By the time you read this, I shall be the Marchioness of Kilbane.

I can almost hear your shout of horror, but it truly was not his fault. Even Papa has accepted that much. I pursued him and... well, never mind the details, suffice to say we were seen in an innocent but outwardly compromising position. So our fates are sealed.

If you want the truth, I am not entirely displeased, for I have had every intention of marrying Kilbane, though I did not expect it so quickly or in such a manner. What I cannot bear is the heartbreak in Papa's eyes, the sorrow in Mama's. I wish you would come back so at least they might have something to take their minds from their wayward daughter.

I miss you.

—Excerpt of a letter from Lady Catherine 'Cat' Barrington to her older brother The Right Hon'ble Philip Barrington, Earl of Ashburton. (Children of The Most Hon'ble Lucian and Matilda Barrington, Marquess and Marchioness of Montagu).

16th February 1845, Holbrook House.

Cat glanced at the dark, glowering figure beside her and shivered. Kilbane had never seemed more aloof, or less approachable and yet here they stood, side by side as Harry Martin pronounced them man and wife. Only the vicar looked more unhappy about it than her husband. Behind them, she could hear the soft sound of weeping. Either her mother, or Aggie, or Alana, or all three of them. She sighed inwardly, guilt sitting heavy in her chest, because the truth of the matter was—if not for the pain she'd inflicted—she wasn't sorry.

Feeling rather as though she was living in a peculiar dream, Cat signed the register and suddenly it was done.

"Right. That's that," Kilbane said to her, for all the world as if he'd just settled a debt, which was exactly how he was viewing it as far as she could tell. "I'll have my man of business contact you.

He'll give you access to funds, addresses to the properties, et cetera. All being well, we need not see each other again."

Cat's cheeks flamed as she realised he wasn't even going to stay to make a show of their wedding night. Everyone would know that their marriage was a sham.

"Might I have a word with Lord Kilbane in private?" she managed, though her voice sounded shaky and most unlike herself.

Her parents glanced at each other, and everyone shifted uneasily but no one actually spoke.

"You've got the title you coveted, you've got funds enough to live like an empress if you so desire. As a married lady, the world will open its doors to you. There's nothing to say," Kilbane replied, his voice brooking no argument, but then he did not know his wife very well yet.

"Nonetheless. If I am to be abandoned so summarily, I demand five minutes of your time. Might you spare me that much?" she asked crisply, drawing deep on reserves she well knew she was going to need in the years to come.

Clearly irritated, Kilbane made a sharp motion, which appeared to be a concession.

"If you would all leave us, please," Cat said turning to face the small assembly that included her parents, her brother Thomas—white-faced with impotent rage—Lord and Lady St Clair, Aggie, and Alana, and of course the Reverend Martin.

"Cat," her father began, but she took his hands before he could say whatever it was he wished.

"It's all right, Papa. You heard Lord Kilbane. He is leaving at once, but I must say my piece. I know this entire debacle is my own fault, but I have that right."

Her father swallowed down the words he dearly wanted to speak and leaned in, kissing her forehead.

"We'll be just outside," he told her, his silver eyes settling on his new son-in-law. His expression made Cat shiver and wonder for the first time how many of the less complimentary stories about her Papa and his ruthless nature might be true.

Once everyone was gone, Cat turned back to face her husband. His expression was not encouraging, those strange violet eyes flat and cold, that beautiful, dissolute mouth set in a hard line.

"Well?" he demanded, folding his arms.

"Might you at least stay the night?" she asked tentatively. "N-Not with me, but… at least so people might think—"

"They already *think*," he replied, sneering. "That's why we are in this bloody mess."

"It's humiliating."

"I warned you," he growled. "I told you to stay away."

"I know!" she exclaimed, throwing her hands up in frustration. "I know it was and I'm sorry."

"No, you're not."

Cat's breath caught at the look in his eyes.

"You think me a halfwit, do you? You think I don't know that you're plotting and planning? You still think you can reform me, that there's some happy ending to be found at the end of this debacle. *Don't* you?"

Cat jumped at the fierce demand, her cheeks flaming.

He snorted. "Well, you can't, and there's not."

"Why?" she exclaimed, throwing caution to the wind and stalking towards him. "Why not? Are you really so wicked and dissipated as that? Don't you want anything for yourself? Won't you even let me be a friend… a companion to you?"

"Why won't you just leave me be?" he exploded, the sound of his anger making her jolt with shock. It vibrated through her, undermining her composure.

"Because I don't believe it's really what you want," she managed, though her voice trembled, and her eyes burned. She would not cry, she told herself. Under no circumstances would he see her cry.

"Holy God, why did your father not lock you up until he'd found a suitable husband?" he demanded, looking so bewildered she almost laughed.

"Because you can't keep the things you love in a cage and expect them to thrive. He knows it and so do I. I'm not trying to put you in a cage either, my lord. I never meant to trap you, I promise you I did not, but won't you give me a chance? Just a chance, a small place in your life. I do not ask for much."

He made a sound of disgust. "Ah, yes, a small place in my life, which would satisfy you for precisely ten minutes, after which time you would gently insinuate yourself into the cracks and crevices of my world, taking root and taking over and always bloody well there. No! I won't have it."

"Am I such a horrific prospect?" she asked tightly.

Kilbane looked at her, his expression hard. "If you'd wanted a man who would write sonnets to your beauty and offer you his heart on a platter, you have made rather a devastating mistake."

"That is hardly what I asked," she retorted angrily.

Cat walked away to the window and looked out. It was raining, which seemed fitting for her mood and the occasion. Wasn't rain on your wedding day supposed to be lucky? No doubt a lie they told despondent brides to make them feel better. She took a deep breath and let it out again. Anger would get her nowhere, she must try to find some small shred of hope, some tiny bit of leverage, and then he would discover how right he was. For she would insinuate her way into his world, by stealth if she must, but she would find a way, like ivy getting a hold upon the foundation stone of a castle, she would invade by degrees. If she were patient, if she came to understand him, one day she might know how to reach his heart. One day, he might give her a chance. "So, you're going to France, then?"

"Yes."

She nodded. "Very well. I will let you go, and I will make no fuss about it."

"How very good of you," he said dryly. "Do you actually think you could stop me?"

"No, but my father could," she replied, turning to face him.

Kilbane went very still.

"I could make your life very difficult indeed, if I chose to."

His face darkened, and it took everything she had not to flinch, not to gasp and take a step back.

"Don't," he warned her. "Don't play games with me, child. You won't enjoy losing."

Cat put up her chin, heart thundering. "I am *not* a child, and I don't play games with you. I offer you a trade. A peaceful life in return for one small concession."

"One fucking concession!" he exclaimed, laughing bitterly. "Good God, you've got a title, houses, money enough to buy a small country. What the devil else do you want?"

"Your address," she said, hating that her voice sounded so breathless and afraid. "I want to always know where you are, s-so that I might write to you."

"So you might descend upon my household and play lady of the manor, you mean," he said in disgust.

Cat shook her head. Her hands were tight little fists now as she fought to keep calm. She was shaking with emotion, with frustration and hurt and disappointment, but she had known it would be hard. She *had* known. "I give you my word of honour, that I will never do so. I will never seek you out. If we ever see each other again, it will be at your instigation. Not mine. I swear it."

"You lie," he said, his gaze upon her so intent she felt he was looking into her soul, into the recesses of her mind where she had hidden her dreams of him.

"I am a Barrington," she said coldly, meeting his gaze, refusing to let him intimidate her. "I do not give my word and then break it."

"You will leave me be, never seek me out, if I allow you to write to me?"

Cat nodded, her throat so tight she could barely swallow.

"I won't read them," he said, watching her. "I'll throw them directly onto the fire."

"That is your right," she said.

I won't cry. I won't cry. I won't cry.

There was a taut silence, and all Cat could hear was her own heart beating, the stupid thing still battering itself against her ribs although it had broken into pieces.

"Very well. A deal," he said, holding out his hand to her.

Cat moved towards him on legs that did not seem equipped to carry her. She placed her hand in his.

"A deal," she agreed, holding his gaze.

He looked away first and let go of her hand, walking to the door without another word. Cat held her breath as he grasped the doorknob and then paused.

"Good luck to you, Lady Kilbane."

"Goodbye, my lord."

And then he was gone.

16th February 1845, between Scunthorpe and Lincoln.

The following day's journey was just as frenetic and uncomfortable as every other mile they had travelled, but Emmeline hardly noticed the discomfort. She alternated between daydreaming about the way it had felt to be in her husband's arms, and gazing at him with what she knew must be a moonstruck expression. She suspected Humboldt and Janet had guessed what had transpired between them, which was mortifying, but then she was newly married and surely every bride had to endure such minor embarrassments.

What made the journey pass far quicker than it might have, was Wrexham's mood. He seemed… happy. Despite the tedium of being stuck in a carriage that was ill-suited to his long legs, despite the jolting and jostling and the difficulties of the interminable journey, he was polite to Humboldt, unfailingly solicitous to Emmeline, and even held his tongue when the carriage got temporarily bogged down and they had to wait for a neighbouring farmer to help pull them out again.

When they finally reached Lincoln and found a place to spend the night, it was late and long past dinnertime. Wrexham was free with his money, paying generously to ensure they all got a hot meal and when Emmeline traipsed wearily up the stairs to their room, she found servants hurrying back and forth, filling a large copper tub with hot water.

"Oh," she said, so happy at the prospect of soaking her aching limbs that she felt almost tearful.

"Anything wrong, pet?" Wrexham asked as Humboldt guided him into the room.

"No! Not in the least. A hot bath! Thank you for thinking of it, my lord."

He smiled at her words. "Well, you didn't get one in Gretna Green like I promised, as we had to leave with such haste, and only cold water this morning. I thought you deserved a bit of luxury. You've been an absolute Trojan. Hasn't she, Humboldt?"

Mr Humboldt nodded, giving Emmeline an approving smile. "Indeed, Lady Wrexham has borne the difficulties of the journey with grace and fortitude."

"There, you see, pet, you've even impressed Humboldt, and that doesn't happen often, I might tell you."

Humboldt coloured and muttered something about Lady Wrexham not needing to trouble herself about what he might think. Emmeline hid a smile.

"Thank you, Humboldt, you are most gracious. We can manage now, however. I'm sure you'll be looking forward to getting some rest."

"If you're sure, my lady. My lord, I will arrange for someone to shave you in the morning, if that suits? Until then, I'll bid you both goodnight."

Wrexham stilled, listening as Humboldt went out. "You... You're sure you don't mind acting as valet? Usually, I travel with him, of course, but there wasn't room in the carriage, and I needed Humboldt, so—"

Emmeline moved towards him, taking his hand. "I don't mind in the least. The truth is that I have waited all day for the time I might have you all to myself."

Wrexham bowed his head, his eyebrows drawing together. "Emmeline. You don't need to do that."

"Do what?" she asked, confused.

He shrugged, reaching up a hand to squeeze the back of his neck. "Be... I don't know... caring, wifely. I don't know how else to put it," he said, suddenly tense.

"I don't have to care for you?" she repeated, uncertain what he meant. "I don't understand."

"Just… don't pretend," he said, his expression fierce. "This morning was wonderful, a gift I had not expected you to give, but I'd rather not—"

"You think I was playacting?" she said, dumbstruck. "To what end?"

"I don't know," he said in frustration. "It just seems so—"

"So *what*?" "Too good to be true!" he exclaimed. "I have been reliving this morning in my mind all day and longing to be alone with you, but I don't want to act the fool, Emmeline. I feel foolish often enough without that. Don't you make a fool of me too."

"What is wrong with you?" she demanded, putting her hands on her hips, for if she didn't, she might be tempted to throw things at him. "And don't tell me you're blind, for that doesn't make you a blithering idiot. Pretending indeed. As if I could! You think I was pretending when I—"

Emmeline snapped her mouth shut, blushing as she realised there was no power on earth that would make her describe the little explosion and her noisy reaction to it out loud.

Wrexham cocked his head. "When you what?"

"You know very well what, you dreadful man. Honestly, just when I was feeling in charity with you for your care of me, you must open your mouth and spoil it. Mama was right, men are perfectly ridiculous over the most peculiar things."

"It was not a ridiculous thing to think," he persisted. "I know you married me for status and wealth, I had no expectation of anything more than that. To discover you being so… so…. It's disconcerting, is all. And, as wonderful as it is, I don't want to read too much into it."

Emmeline made a sound of frustrated fury, which made his eyebrows go up.

"Did you just growl?" he asked incredulously.

"Yes," she said, cross with him for spoiling the mood, furious with the world for having hurt him so deeply he did not trust anyone, angry with herself for not having realised how badly his confidence had been shaken, and on the verge of tears for him because he could not believe she had been in earnest.

Yet, she did not think he would believe her reassurances if she wept and hugged him and swore to him it was true. He might still believe her to be playacting if she denied she had married him for status and wealth and had done it instead for her own sake, because she was a besotted fool who could deny him nothing.

"How fierce you are, pet," he said, smiling a little.

There was such affection in the expression she almost gave in and ran to him, hoping he would take her in his arms again and become her wicked pirate once more.

"Don't speak to me," she said instead.

He frowned. "You're angry with me."

"How perspicacious you are tonight, my lord," she said tartly. "Or perhaps I am merely an excellent actress practising her skills. I open at Drury Lane the week after next, you know."

"Emmeline," he began, his voice conciliatory.

"Don't you *Emmeline* me," she said, her temper rising. "You insult me and yourself and then expect me to act as if you've said nothing of note. I have spent all day longing to be alone with you and now I wish you to Timbuktu, you great oaf."

"Well, I didn't think—"

"Ah, the first sensible thing you've said since Humboldt left the room. Indeed, you did not think. If you had, you might have thought about suggesting to your new wife that she was the kind of woman who could give herself over to you as fully as she did in your bed this morning and then accept claims that she was merely playacting with equanimity."

"I did not mean it that way!" he protested, his colour rising. "You cannot blame me for being sceptical in the circumstances."

"What circumstances?" she demanded, folding her arms.

"Oh, come now," he said, and she could hear the anger in his voice now. "Don't play games. You know very well. It was hardly a romantic offer of marriage, now was it?"

"No," she said, and suddenly her chest was tight, and it was hard to breathe, let alone speak. "No, it wasn't the least bit romantic, and yet here I am, despite every notion of good sense that told me I ought to run a mile, because I was horribly infatuated with you, and I would have done anything you asked, you great l-lummox!" Emmeline snapped her mouth shut as her voice quavered and tears pricked at her eyes.

There was an electric silence.

"Emmeline?" he said, his voice soft. "You... You don't mean it?"

Emmeline smothered the desire to scream and stamp her foot and instead contented herself with one final exclamation. "Oh, go to the devil, Wrexham!"

Chapter 11

My Lady,

Please allow me to congratulate you on your recent nuptials and introduce myself. I am Lord Kilbane's man of business. If I understand correctly, you will take charge of the properties that come with the marquisate. This, I must assure you, is most welcome news and a great weight from my mind. It is a very long time since the properties had anything resembling a chatelaine. Please accept my heartfelt thanks and be assured of my willingness to aid you in whatever capacity I may. I am at your service.

Yrs etc,

—Excerpt of a letter from Mr Archibald Bright to The Most Hon'ble Lady Catherine 'Cat' St Just, Marchioness of Kilbane (daughter of The Most Hon'ble Lucian and Matilda Barrington, Marquess and Marchioness of Montagu).

16th February 1845, between Scunthorpe and Lincoln.

Wrexham felt behind him for the thick wooden post of the four-poster bed and moved until he could sit down on the mattress.

He felt oddly winded, and utterly confused and… a smile tugged uncertainly at the corner of his mouth. She was furious with him. Why that pleased him quite so much was a mystery. Except, she would not be so furious if she *were* playacting. If she had been using her wiles, hoping to control him and bend him to her will, she would have cajoled and flattered and pleaded her innocence. Instead, he felt very lucky not to have been beaten about the head with the nearest heavy object. He would have deserved it, too.

Emmeline Knight was sweet and honest and trustworthy. It's why he had chosen her, because she was too kind for her own good and probably the only woman alive prepared to sacrifice her own happiness to keep him safe. He'd told himself she was doing it for her own reasons, for security and status and wealth, because it had made him feel less guilty, but he never could swallow that story. It simply did not fit. His Miss Milly did not have an avaricious bone in her body and didn't give a snap of her fingers for his title. Instead, she had been *horribly infatuated* with him and ready to *do anything he asked.*

He sucked in a shaky breath. Of course, she had also called him a blithering idiot, a great lummox, and wished him to Timbuktu, or the devil. He didn't think she was fussy at this point. Wrexham shook his head. He had assumed his blindness and the likelihood of his imminent descent into madness would be enough to put off any woman who wasn't in it for money or status. It had been so clear to him that this manner of woman was his only option, but trusting such a creature with his future had always made his blood run cold. Anyone with such mercenary priorities would surely have no qualms about locking him up in an asylum the moment he became hard to deal with. Yet, he had known at once Emmeline would not do that. He had felt instinctively that here was a woman who would keep her word, no matter what.

He had persisted in viewing her in the same light though, a woman who was marrying for practical reasons, not romantic ones. Not that he had blamed her for it but now he needed to rethink. He rubbed a hand over his face to hide his smile, not wanting to provoke her into railing at him again, because no matter how gratifying the knowledge that he had not entirely lost his appeal, he had just put his bloody foot in it and ruined everything.

There was a soft knock at the door and Wrexham heard her maid enter, no doubt to help Emmeline undress for her bath. Aware he was in disgrace, Wrexham busied himself by taking his coat off and then yanking off his own boots, an endeavour which left him hot and irritable. He sorely missed his valet, who was a loyal fellow and had stuck by him, despite the change in Wrexham's circumstances. Lennox could have found himself a place with most any wealthy man of fashion, having been a source of envy for Wrexham's erstwhile friends when Rex had still been amongst the best dressed and most sought-after bachelors of the *ton*.

Wrexham settled himself against what felt like a mountain of pillows piled before the bedhead and closed his eyes with a sigh. He was about to set his mind to the thorny problem of what to do about his wife so that she might deign to speak to him again instead of committing murder, when he heard it. The soft sound of water sloshing as Emmeline stepped into the bath.

She was naked. In the bath. Right in front of him.

His eyes snapped open, and he cursed fate all over again for stealing his sight. Except, it occurred to him then that if he hadn't gone blind, Emmeline wouldn't be here. He waited for his brain to do the usual calculation and dismiss this argument as irrelevant, because nothing could make up for losing his sight. Except it wasn't irrelevant. *She* was not irrelevant, and not easily dismissed. He liked her very much, liked her all the more for the way she had torn him off a strip and not been shy in speaking her mind.

"Thank you, Janet. You may go now. I can manage the rest," his wife said, sounding perfectly calm, whereas Wrexham was feeling decidedly agitated.

"Are you sure, my lady?"

"Quite sure. You must be tired too. I am quite capable of getting myself to bed."

"Thank you, my lady. I've left your nightgown by the fire to warm, and the towels are right there."

"Oh, pass me my soap before you go."

"Such a pretty scent," Janet said with a sigh, having apparently lifted the soap to her nose.

"It is, yes. There's a lovely little shop on Bond Street that sells all manner of soaps and lotions, with the loveliest perfumes, but this is my favourite. Thank you, Janet, and goodnight."

Wrexham heard the maid leave the room, the door closing behind her, and then it began. The tormenting sound of water moving, caressing his wife's silken skin. The delicate scent of orange blossom reached his nose, tantalising his senses. Rex imagined the soap in her hand, and the way she might rub it against her body, smoothing the subsequent bubbles over her splendid breasts until her skin was slick and wet. He swallowed a groan and shifted on the bed, his trousers suddenly feeling too snug.

Hell and damnation. He wanted her, and she was right there, and he'd been a complete pillock and bollocksed everything up. She was right. He *was* a blithering idiot.

"Emmeline," he said cautiously, alert for the sound of flying missiles.

There was a brief but pointed silence.

"Yes, my lord?"

Oh, that was a discouraging tone.

"I'm sorry, pet."

She snorted, which was even less encouraging, but still made him smile. "I imagine you are."

"It's me that's doing the imagining," he admitted, his voice hoarse. "I'm driving myself to distraction by picturing everything you're doing."

The sloshing stopped and Rex waited, every fibre of his being tuned to the woman in the bath.

"And what are you imagining?" she asked, and there was a breathless quality to the question that gave him hope.

"The way the hot water has given your body a rosy flush, the way your lovely skin must glisten in the candlelight, and—" Rex cleared his throat as his pulse accelerated. "—and your hands smoothing the soap over your body, your breasts."

"Perhaps you have clairvoyant tendencies," she remarked lightly.

He swallowed. "You're doing it now?"

"Yes," she replied, her voice little more than a whisper. "What else should I do, my lord?"

Rex felt suddenly giddy with longing, but he kept his head, sucking in a breath to steady himself. "Soap your arms, from wrist to shoulder and back again."

He sat up on the bed, listening as he pictured her doing just as he had instructed.

"Now what?" she asked.

"Are you quite sure you have washed your breasts thoroughly?" he asked, unable to keep the smile from his voice.

"Quite sure," she replied, momentarily dashing his hopes until she added, "But one can never be too clean."

Rex sat up, moving so he was sitting on the edge of the mattress, one hand on the post at the end of the bed, imagining the slide of her hands over the soft mounds, the way the soap would make the skin slippery, her touch making her nipples grow taut. He swallowed.

"There," she said. "All clean. What now?"

"Your stomach," he said, aware the quality of his voice was becoming strained, not to mention his trousers where his arousal pressed hopefully against the fabric, eager for her attention. "And then down, down to that sweet little patch of curls between your legs, the place where I put my mouth on you."

He smiled as he heard her breath catch.

"You liked that, didn't you?" There was a long pause, and he imagined the blush that stained her cheeks, the effort it would take her to speak her desires out loud. "Emmeline? Or was I mistaken?"

She sighed. "You know very well you were not."

"Then you liked it?"

"Yes," she said, enunciating the word carefully.

Wrexham grinned.

"Tell me you liked it."

"I just did!" she objected.

He tsked, shaking his head. "No, no. Tell me properly. You promised to obey me in all things, did you not?"

"I'm still cross with you," she muttered.

"I know, and with good reason, but I will make it up to you, and that is a promise."

"Yes, I liked it," she said, sounding a little impatient.

Wrexham struggled to hide his smile. "I'm not sure I believe you. That did not sound the least bit convincing. Are you at least doing as I asked?"

"Yes." Her voice sounded rather strained now and he couldn't stand it a moment longer.

Wrexham stood and made his way to the foot of the bed, listening to the water splashing to orient himself.

"There is a chair to your right, but nothing directly between you and the bath," she said, and he heard the anticipation in her voice. "Four steps."

"Thank you, pet. Much as I'd wish to join you, I'd rather not fall in face first. Though perhaps I deserve to." He moved cautiously, taking four steps and then kneeling, reaching out to discover the edge of the bath. "Good evening, my lady. Might I attend you?"

He jolted as a pair of warm lips pressed firmly against his. Emmeline's body, warm and wet, was suddenly against him, soaking his shirt. Water ran down his back as she wrapped her arms about his neck. Wrexham groaned, desire rushing through his veins, setting fires under his skin and making him feel more alive, more joyful than he could ever remember.

"Get in," she demanded, tugging his sodden shirt from his trousers.

"Is there room?" he asked, remembering how small the tubs most inns provided usually were.

"We'll make room," she said, such a determined note to her voice he laughed.

Between them, they stripped him, and Emmeline stood, guiding him so he could step safely into the bath. He sat with a sigh of pleasure as the warm water surrounded him. The tub was a decent size, but it was going to be deliciously snug for two. He held his hands up to her.

"Come along then, pet. Don't torment me by making me wait."

She took his hands, stepping carefully as she placed her feet on either side of his hips. Wrexham felt her move, her hands resting on his shoulders as she knelt. The breath seemed to leave his lungs in a rush as she sat, finding the perfect place with his cock nestled against her sex. He reached for her, pulling her against him for a kiss and startled when she resisted.

"Oh, no you don't," she said, batting his hands away, and he heard the laughter in her voice. "You are still in disgrace."

"You won't kiss me?" he asked, torn between frustration and amusement that she thought to punish him. He reached for her anyway, but once again, she pushed his hands from her lush curves.

"Not until you're clean," she said, using the prickly governess voice he was coming to adore.

"Yes, Miss Milly," he replied gravely. "Just as you say."

He sat still, meek as a lamb, with his hands resting on the edge of the bath, but with his heart crashing about in his chest as she reached for the soap. The warm, damp air, redolent with orange blossom filled his senses until he was giddy with longing, drunk with wanting her. Emmeline's body, so warm and so close, was an intoxicating temptation, but she had made her rules and he wanted her to trust him. So he behaved himself, though the ache in his loins when what he wanted was mere inches away was almost more than he could bear. Yet, then the torment began in earnest, as her hands soaped his chest and shoulders, gliding over his body with such care and attention, the longing he felt transformed into something else, something far more dangerous and powerful than mere desire. She touched him like it meant something, like he was precious to her, necessary to her, and Wrexham told himself he was being ridiculous when his throat grew tight. But he could remember no one ever caring for him in such a way.

There had been women, of course there had, and some had professed themselves in love with him, but their love had always seemed to come with conditions, with a price attached, with expectations of what they believed he owed them. He had assumed Emmeline would be the same. Sweeter, perhaps less demanding, but the same.

Her slick hand coasted down his torso and sought the place that ached for her attention, wrapping her fingers around him and moving just as he had shown her.

"Oh, God." He closed his eyes, tilting his head back. Wrexham felt the touch of her lips against his throat, pressing soft little kisses up and up until she nuzzled at his jaw and his patience snapped. "Emmeline," he murmured, taking her in his arms and kissing her.

This time she let him have his way, which was just as well, for he did not know what he might do otherwise. Perhaps beg. His hands dropped to grasp her bottom, delighting in the plump, soft flesh and lifting her, desperate to be inside her.

"We can... in the bath?" she asked sceptically, making him laugh.

"Yes, love. We can wherever you like. In a carriage, upon a table, in the garden, whenever and wherever you desire."

"I didn't realise," she said breathlessly as she guided him inside. "Like this?" she asked, sitting down and making him groan at the feel of her around him, hot and tight and sinfully good.

"Yes. Like that. God, you're perfect, sweet Milly. So utterly perfect."

She let out a little sigh that sounded amused and pleased and Wrexham's heart soared. This was beyond anything he had imagined possible, beyond his wildest dreams of what his life might look like now. He'd believed everything had been taken from him with his sight, that he had been condemned to exist in the darkness until he went mad, but now.... If this was possible, if she could really care for him, what else might there be?

Wrexham was lost, overwhelmed with the feel of his wife in his arms, of the pleasure she gave him so willingly, so generously. He'd so richly deserved her anger, but she had not only forgiven him but shown him such tenderness, so that when she found her peak, the climax coming upon her, he was beyond control. He held her close, holding on for dear life as her body tightened around him and his own release shook him to his marrow. The cry that tore from his throat was raw and fierce and probably shocked her, but he couldn't help it, couldn't hold back.

Any thoughts of withdrawing were beyond him as the pleasure overwhelmed him, leaving him boneless and sated and happier than he could ever remember.

Emmeline collapsed against him, breathing hard, her head resting on his shoulder as he stroked her hair.

"That was even better than the first time," she observed faintly.

Wrexham grinned, not above feeling smug about it, until he realised what he'd done.

"The devil take me," he whispered, his heart growing cold.

Emmeline sat up. "What? What is it?"

"I was so carried away I neglected to… take precautions," he said, raking a hand through his hair.

"Precautions?"

"Against getting you with child."

"Oh? *Oh,*" she said, as she understood. "You don't want a child? That's why you withdrew the first time?"

He nodded.

She said nothing, and he wished he could see her face, so that he might read her thoughts.

"What?"

"Nothing. Only… Why?"

"You think I would inflict this fate on a child?"

There was a stony silence, and his heart sank at the possibility he'd said something wrong again. Emmeline moved, clearly trying to get up. Wrexham clamped his hands about her waist.

"No. Stop. Don't go. What did I say?"

"I just hadn't realised your life was such a horrific ordeal."

There was a note to her voice he ought to heed, but frustration gnawed at him. This interlude had been exquisite, a gift he'd not believed possible, but that did not mean his life was a pleasant one.

"Well, it's not exactly fun," he said, the words rather sharper than he'd intended. "I don't enjoy being a prisoner, or being treated like a bloody invalid."

"I should think not. There's not the least thing wrong with you, other than your sight and a tendency to talk utter rubbish. I know things have been difficult, probably far worse than I know, but all the same, Wrexham. You are astonishing, and capable of so much more than you give yourself credit for."

"And you think that's basis enough for siring a child who will inherit the condition?"

"Wrexham," she said, and she was losing her temper now, that much was evident from her tone and the way her body had become stiff and unyielding. "How many siblings do you have?"

"Four legitimate, another seven bastards. Well, to my knowledge. There may be more. The duke is not shy in that regard."

Her breath caught. "Good heavens. He really is an appalling human being."

"No argument here, pet, but what's your point?"

"Are they older or younger than you?"

He frowned, wondering what she was getting at. "Six older, the rest younger, though not by much."

"And have any of them lost their sight?"

"No," he said with a sigh. "But that doesn't mean—"

"And how many siblings, illegitimate or otherwise, does your father have and how many children do they have between them?"

This took him a while to calculate, for the ins and outs of the late duke's affairs were legion and his progeny extensive. "Perhaps fifty in all."

"And only your uncle lost his sight?"

"That proves nothing!" he said crossly.

"It proves it is not a certainty, and if you had not fallen and struck your head, you may not have ever succumbed, either. We will never know. I do know one thing though, and it's that life is uncertain, Wrexham. There are no guarantees for any of us. Some children never live to take a breath, others die in infancy. You cannot be certain what is in store for anyone, not yourself, or me, or any children we may have. But I will always believe in the best possible outcome and live in hope. If you do not look for happiness, for the opportunity of happiness, you will never recognise it when it arrives."

"A sweet sentiment, pet, but in my position, a harder one to believe in."

"Even now? Even after... never mind," she said, getting to her feet before he could stop her again.

Wrexham scowled, irritated. That wasn't fair. She wasn't being fair. How could she understand what he had lost, how difficult his life was? Yes, this evening had been wonderful, astonishing even, more than he had dared hope for but it did not mean his life would suddenly become sunshine and roses. But she would see that for herself soon enough. She was deceiving herself if she believed they could live a normal life and it would only lead to resentment and disappointment. Far better that he put her straight now, and then they could find some measure of contentment until….

He pushed thoughts of the future away. They were too grim, too horrifying to dwell upon and he felt a sudden surge of fury with Emmeline for putting him in this mood when everything had been so perfect mere moments before.

Wrexham stood, wondering if she was angry enough to leave him to his own devices, but he ought to have known better.

"Here," she said, her voice crisp as she pressed a towel into his hands.

He dried his torso and wrapped the towel around his middle.

"Give me your hand."

Wrexham did as she told him, taking four careful steps to the bed.

"I've laid your nightshirt on the end of the bed. The jug and basin is on the left bedside table, your tooth powder and brush and a glass of water to the right. I believe I laid it out as Humboldt did."

"Thank you," he said, wishing she could understand how galling it was to be reliant on her when he was cross and out of sorts. But she never would understand that. How could she?

Once he'd finished readying himself for bed, he climbed in, viscerally aware of her warm body just inches from his own. The desire to reach for her, to hold her against him and take comfort from her nearness was an ache in his chest, but his stubborn pride would not let him breach the distance between them. Instead, he turned on his side and tried to sleep.

Chapter 12

My lady,

Forgive me if I am presumptuous, but society has always tongue enough for two sets of teeth. Is it true you will be taking up residence at Connaught Place? If so, I shall be the first to welcome you, as we shall be neighbours.

Yrs etc,

—Excerpt of a letter from The Right Hon'ble Peregrine Bancroft to The Most Hon'ble Lady Catherine 'Cat' St Just, Marchioness of Kilbane (daughter of The Most Hon'ble Lucian and Matilda Barrington, Marquess and Marchioness of Montagu).

17th February 1845, Boston, Lincolnshire.

The next morning was dismal, and Emmeline walked to the carriage with a heavy heart, and with a chill wind buffeting rain into her face. Doubt nagged at her as she wondered if she'd been in the wrong last night. She'd not slept well, her mind turning their conversation over and over and becoming increasingly uncertain. She thought perhaps Wrexham had also slept little.

Certainly, his mood was far from that of yesterday, and the light-hearted, good-natured fellow she had enjoyed being with so much had been replaced with someone who glowered and snapped, and became surly at the least provocation. Though, Emmeline had to admit, some people seemed to go out of their way to provoke him.

They stopped briefly to change horses and get something to eat when they reached Boston. Humboldt, who had borne the brunt of Wrexham's bad mood for most of the morning, had become increasingly vexed and was obviously at the end of his tether. Indeed, everyone was beyond weary and sick to death of being crammed together in a carriage that had seemed determined from the start to seek out every rut and pothole from Gretna Green to Kings Lynn. It was perhaps for this reason that Humboldt neglected to instruct Wrexham to duck beneath the lintel as they entered the coaching inn.

Wrexham staggered back, uttered an oath that made a lady inside give a gasp of horror, and then tore Humboldt off a strip for having allowed him to brain himself.

"For the love of God! Are you trying to kill me, too? Is my father paying you to finish the job he couldn't manage himself, you incompetent fool?"

Emmeline itched to step between them and tell Wrexham off for being such a bad-tempered devil, but then she saw the lump rising on his forehead and could feel nothing but compassion. How it must vex him. A man who had once fenced and boxed and been skilled with the ribbons and on horseback, reduced to relying on others to guide him into a building. Sympathy rose in her chest, and she almost went to him, wanting to take care of him and see to his comfort, but then she remembered how he disliked being babied and held her tongue.

It only grew worse when they reached the private parlour. They were getting closer to home here, and it had not taken long for someone to recognise Wrexham. Soon enough, word had spread that the blind marquess was among them. The innkeeper's wife, a Mrs Enderby, hurried in and cast Wrexham an awed and rather anxious glance, before addressing Mr Humboldt.

"Does he want gammon? Or should I prepare some milk toast?"

Emmeline's mouth dropped open, staggered that the woman could look at a vital man like her husband and see an invalid in need of nursery food. Though he sat on the far side of the table from her, Emmeline was rivetingly aware of the fury vibrating through him.

"Damn the stupid bi—"

Before he could finish the eviscerating comment and make himself exceedingly unpopular in the busy pub, Emmeline spoke.

"Lord Wrexham is blind, Madam, not insane nor infirm. Frankly, I wonder at your own eyesight if you cannot see he is in the prime of good health. In the future, I suggest you address your questions to him directly. As for myself, I should be content with the gammon. My lord?"

Wrexham's hand lay upon the table, his fist clenched so tightly that his knuckles were white.

"Fine," he growled. "I will endeavour not to drool over the table. Bring an unopened bottle of your best port at once. I might warn you there's nothing wrong with my mouth, either. I can tell if you've watered it down, so don't bother trying it."

The lady flushed scarlet, bobbed a curtsey, and hurried out again.

"I am quite capable of speaking for myself," Wrexham snapped, the moment the door closed.

Emmeline started. "I am aware of that," she said evenly. "I am also aware that you have a foul mouth when you're in as great a tweague as you are now. The woman was ignorant, but not malicious. She did not need a big brute of a nobleman ripping her to shreds. Humboldt has endured quite enough of your wretched temper as it is."

"Er… if you'll excuse me for a moment. I think I might check on Janet. The men in these places… Best be sure she's… excuse me," Humboldt said again and rushed out.

"There, now you've scared him off," Emmeline said in exasperation. "Why he bears it, I cannot imagine."

"I told you before. Because I pay him a sizeable wage to bear it," Wrexham retorted, folding his arms. "I don't pay for incompetence. If he can't do his job, he should suffer the consequences."

"I begin to think there is not enough money in the world to make your company worthwhile!" Emmeline cried, so furious with this obnoxious, supercilious man who was so far removed from the person she had believed Wrexham to be that she felt close to tears.

"Well, if that is the case, don't let me stop you. Leave. Do as you please, see if I care. Go to the Devil!"

Emmeline gasped, beyond shocked that he should speak to her so. Unsteadily, she got to her feet, uncertain if he meant it, but knowing she could not bear to be in the same room with him a moment longer. The chair screeched against the flagstones as she stumbled, pushing it out of her way. Before she took a step, Wrexham stood.

"Wait. Emmeline. Don't… Don't go."

She hesitated, daring to look back at him. His face was pale, colour cresting his high cheekbones.

"I didn't mean it," he said, sounding so wretched her heart went out to him, despite everything.

"Neither did I," she said, and ran to him, throwing her arms about his waist and holding on tight.

He laughed unsteadily. "You didn't say anything, pet," he said, and Emmeline let out a breath of relief as his arms closed around her. This was what she had needed, had missed so badly since last night.

"I did," she said, her voice muffled as she buried her face against his chest. "Last night. I was presumptuous and bossy, and I'm terribly sorry."

There was a thoughtful silence. "I'm not. I need someone to push me, to challenge me when I'm behaving like a spoiled brat. I know well enough that I'm capable of doing so."

"No, Wrexham, never that. But it broke my heart to hear you speak of your life as if it were an ordeal to be endured. We can do better than that, you and me. I promise you we can."

He smiled and bent to kiss the top of her head. "I would like to believe that, Emmeline, but you don't understand. You cannot understand what it is like to be treated like a silly child, as if I don't have a brain in my head, like I am a piece of furniture to be moved from here to there with no say in the matter."

She swallowed down the desire to lose her temper again, instead speaking calmly, in the hope he might listen. "My lord, it may have escaped your notice, but I am a woman, and this is the way of things for every female in England. We are possessions. Women do not even exist in law once we marry. We belong to our fathers or our husbands, with little or no control over our lives or even our bodies. I understand your frustration better than you may imagine. I am exceedingly lucky in my father, who is more enlightened than most men, but that does not mean that I am free to do as I please, when the world frowns upon me for setting a foot out of line."

He frowned, reflecting upon this apparently new observation. "I confess I have never considered it that way, but I am a man, Emmeline, and I have been used to organising my world as I see fit. That may be a privilege, but it was mine, and it has been taken from me."

Emmeline squeezed him tighter and raised her head, looking up at him. "Then let us take it back again."

He sought her face, stroking her cheek. She turned into it, pressing a kiss to his palm.

"You would stay? Even after today, after everything I said? I'm a bad-tempered brute, pet. I can't deny it, can't pretend that I'm anything else. I want to promise I will never speak to you so again, but the truth is—"

"The truth is, you've had a very stressful few days, your new wife has provoked you dreadfully, and I suspect you've a nasty headache, going upon the size of that bump."

"You'd not be wrong," he said ruefully.

"Poor Rex," she said softly, going up on her toes to press a kiss to his mouth.

"Lord, Milly, love. I have missed you," he said, holding her tighter. "I've been cursing myself for a fool all day."

"Then you were in good company. Could we forgive each other and start over?"

"On one condition," he said, his voice low.

"Oh?" Emmeline looked up at him, wondering if he would chastise her some more, or make her promise never to scold him so again.

"Kiss me."

Emmeline sighed happily and had no trouble whatsoever in acceding to his demand.

If Mrs Enderby had harboured any misgivings about the Marquess of Wrexham's character, it must have reassured her he was little changed after walking in upon him enthusiastically embracing his new wife. Emmeline had been mortified whilst Wrexham, apparently restored to good humour, thought it dreadfully amusing. The lady hurriedly set down the bottle of port and two glasses and rushed out again.

"Well, you've done it now, Milly, love. The innkeeper and his wife are at the heart of most village gossip. Word will go around in no time now, and everyone will believe it was a love match. I can't say I'm sorry, either. I've no doubt the speculation among the *ton* will be less than complimentary to either of us otherwise."

Emmeline huffed, unable to reply as the flustered innkeeper's wife returned with a maid in tow, carrying their dinner. Avoiding the woman's eye, Emmeline concentrated on arranging herself on the bench beside her husband and waited for the serving staff to leave.

"Is there gossip?" she asked once they were alone again.

"Not yet, according to Humboldt. Obviously, your family will have kept it quiet, as would my father, in the hope he could have the thing annulled with no fuss. That will change once he discovers it's too late."

"What do you mean?"

His expression became grave, and he reached out a hand. Emmeline took it, assuming that was what he wished, and he covered it with his other hand, holding it in his lap.

"Milly, love. The duke is a contemptible excuse for a human being. I'm afraid he will not hold back. I have no doubt he'll spread gossip that I'm a simpleton, out of my wits, and you've taken advantage of me. I would not put it past him to paint you as an adventuress who married me for my wealth and title."

"Yes, and everyone will believe it, I don't doubt," Emmeline said, suddenly nauseated by the thought of everyone gossiping about her and what she'd done.

It wasn't a surprise, of course, she had known she would create a great scandal, but she had not really considered that everyone would believe her to be a fortune hunter, or at least a title hunter. Everyone knew her father was one of the richest men in the country and her dowry was considerable. But they'd believe she wanted to be a marchioness, without question.

Wrexham squeezed her hand. "No one who knows you will believe it for a moment," he said, his voice soothing.

Emmeline smiled ruefully, knowing he was doing his best to calm her. "You thought it," she pointed out, though with no malice, for she knew why he'd believed it, and that said more about his own insecurities than it did about her.

"I did," he admitted. "Though it never rang true. From the start I knew you were special, pet. It didn't take long to discover I was luckier than any man had a right to be."

He lifted her hand to his mouth and kissed her fingers. Emmeline sighed, leaning into him.

"I'm glad, and I'm so glad I married you."

He turned towards her, his thumb stroking over her palm in the most distracting manner. "Do you mean it?"

Emmeline bit back the desire to chastise him for asking, aware that his confidence was a fragile thing. Yet he did not like being babied, and he seemed to enjoy her rather sharp tongue.

"Wrexham, I am not in the habit of telling lies. If I say something, I mean it. You are quite conceited enough without me getting into the habit of flattering you for no good reason. You'll become quite unbearable if I do."

He grinned at her, such a pleased, boyish expression that her heart lurched, and she felt the ridiculous urge to sob.

"Well, that told me," he said, sounding amused. "And just so you know, I'm awfully glad I married you, too."

Unable to answer, for her throat was too tight, Emmeline got over the difficulty by kissing him until she felt hot and flustered instead of sentimental and weepy.

"Now, then. Will you allow me to cut the meat for you, or are you going to get all huffy about it?" she asked, returning to her no-nonsense voice before things got out of hand.

Wrexham's revelation about marital relations being possible in carriages and gardens and baths had put all sorts of wicked notions into her head, and her husband did ridiculous things to her equilibrium.

"I wouldn't dare," he remarked, his voice mild before adding, somewhat diffidently: "You don't mind?"

"You're being daft again. Whyever would I mind? How you manage everything is a wonder. Truly, Wrexham, I'm so impressed at how adept you've become in such a short time, and no, I am not flattering you, so don't even think about suggesting it."

She darted a glance at him to see a fond expression on his face, and occupied herself at once with cutting up the gammon for him before she got herself in a silly state and ravished him on the spot.

They arrived at Cawston Hall long after dark, which was a disappointment to Emmeline as she longed to see it in the daylight.

"Tell me about it?" she asked, as the carriage turned onto what she had been told was an impressive driveway that ran for miles up to the house.

"Cawston Hall is mentioned in the Doomsday book," he said with evident pride. "Though the original house was torn down and rebuilt at the beginning of the seventeenth century. It is one of the finest examples of a Jacobean mansion in the country."

"His lordship has extensively modernised the property though, my lady," Humboldt said, and Emmeline noted the satisfaction the man took in telling her this. He, too, was proud of Wrexham and of all he'd achieved. Bearing in mind how difficult her husband could be to work for, that spoke volumes about the man he was at heart. "When Cawston Hall became his, he was only sixteen, but at once set about rebuilding the west wing, which was in a poor state of repair. He installed a new kitchen and laundry room, a brewhouse and game larders. His lordship also modernised much of the main house as well as building a new dairy and—"

"Thank you, Humboldt," Wrexham said wryly. "I already apologised for my bad behaviour, there's no need to make me feel worse by pouring the butter boat over me."

"My lord!" Humboldt said, indignant at the suggestion.

"Oh, Mr Humboldt," Emmeline hurried to interject. "Please, pay him no mind. Lord Wrexham is teasing you, I'm afraid. I have discovered he finds compliments hard to bear and so makes a fuss rather than accept them."

"Ah, you have me all figured out, pet," Wrexham said, a quirk to his lips that boded ill, but Emmeline ignored it and gave a little sniff, putting up her chin.

"Indeed, I have."

"We'll see," he said, laughing softly.

Emmeline did not spare him a second glance though, for dark it may be, but the staff had been informed of the return of their master and his new wife. Cawston Hall was lit up in the darkness, golden light blazing from its many windows. The magnificent red brick building glowed in the light of the many torches that illuminated the driveway and the front of the house, where a daunting number of servants gathered to receive them.

"When were you last here, Wrexham?" Emmeline asked them as the carriage slowed.

"Two years ago. I convalesced here after the fall, hoping I'd get better. When I didn't, I went abroad to seek treatment, but everyone told me the same thing. Amaurosis. No cure, nothing to be done. When I returned, my father asked to see me. Fool that I was, I went."

"And he didn't let you leave again?"

Wrexham's face darkened, his expression harsh in the lamplight. "No. He banished my staff, all except Humboldt, and I was entirely isolated. If not for my aunt and sister, I might be there still. They helped me escape him. We feared if I returned here at once, he'd come for me, so I stayed in a hotel for a while, and then with Aunt Lucy for Christmas, where I was fortunate enough to meet you again."

The carriage door opened then, a footman setting the steps in place for them, and Emmeline did not have the chance to answer, which was likely for the best. If ever the duke crossed her path, she was going to have a few choice words for him. Instead, she climbed out and was immediately engulfed in an excess of feminine flounces and bows.

"Oh! I'm so happy to meet you at last!"

Emmeline staggered back, looking into wide, expressive eyes the same indigo blue as her husband's. Indeed, she was so very like him there was only one explanation.

"Lady Cordelia," Emmeline said, smiling warmly at her. "I am delighted to make your acquaintance."

"Oh, call me Delia, everyone does," the young woman said, grinning at her, the expression so like Wrexham's that Emmeline felt at once at home in her company.

"I should be glad to," Emmeline replied.

"And you are Rex's Miss Milly," Delia said, almost bouncing upon the spot. "Oh, you have no idea how I have prayed for a woman like you to find him, for he is the very best of brothers.

Well, except for when he's being exceedingly aggravating," she added, flashing a smile which dimpled her cheeks.

Emmeline laughed, enchanted by her. She was a beautiful woman, no more than twenty years old. Her hair was a darker gold than Rex's and she was petite and curvaceous, and clearly a bundle of energy.

"We shall be a merry party now, for Aunt Lucy is here too. Between us, we shall heave to, repel boarders, and give no quarter to keep Rex out of trouble," she declared stoutly.

"Delia, for heaven's sake, take a breath. My poor wife has enough to cope with dealing with me. She doesn't need a lunatic sister to contend with too. She does not need to know of your peculiar fascination for pirates at this early stage."

"Rex!" Delia said, running to hug her big brother tightly, apparently not the least bit offended by his remarks. "I've been so worried. Oh, you cannot know. Father confronted me and went on and on, trying to discover what I knew. It was awful. You know how he gets, but I didn't tell him anything. Not a word."

Wrexham hugged his sister back, his expression fond. "You did me proud. I'm so grateful, and so sorry you had to endure it."

Delia blushed, smiling at him. "That's all right. Anything for you, Rex, though I'd rather not have to do it again, if it's all the same to you."

"I wouldn't ask it of you," he assured her. "Now, then. Could we get Emmeline indoors before she freezes to death? She's had quite the ordeal these past days."

"I can imagine. Rex is a horrid travelling companion," she said frankly, slipping her arm through Emmeline's. "But first you must meet the staff, then I shall show you to your room to freshen up before dinner. Aunt Lucy will be in fits, for she's so excited to meet you, but she must wait. Come along, I'll introduce you to Mrs Tweedy, she's a marvellous housekeeper, and of course you must meet Bunting. Such a dear fellow. He's butler here and has lived here, man and boy. If you want to know anything about the family history, ask Bunting, he's a mine of information. After that there's...."

Emmeline let Delia carry her along, doing her best to remember names and faces but feeling thoroughly overwhelmed. By the time Delia had shown her to her room, which was astonishingly lavish in shades of deep wine-red and gold, her head was spinning.

With Janet's help, Emmeline washed and changed and was just having the last adjustment made to her coiffure when there was a knock at the connecting door.

It opened to reveal Wrexham, looking splendid, having shaved and had time to spend over his appearance. Emmeline's heart did its usual little skip in her chest, and she sighed. Perhaps they had not married for love, but there was no doubting that this man held her heart in his hands now. She hoped he'd treat it carefully, for she was in a bad way.

"My lord," she said, getting to her feet. "How handsome you look."

"Thank you, pet," he said, and she counted it a victory that he refrained from making any scathing, self-deprecating comments. "Though I've no doubt you put me to shame. What are you wearing?"

Emmeline hesitated, unused to having to describe herself and relieved that her mother had sent her belongings as she'd asked. "Well, the gown is one I've looked forward to wearing, for it is especially lovely. It is a light green silk, striped with emerald green velvet. Here...." She moved towards him and took his hand, stroking it over the fabric of her skirts so he could feel the slick silk and the soft nap of the velvet. "There is white satin underdress, and the sleeves are rows and rows of Honiton lace, which gives it a lot of movement. The effect is beautiful."

"Beautiful," he repeated, his voice low as his hand moved to her waist, drawing her closer.

The moment stretched out, with Emmeline's nerves leaping, his hand burning through the fabric of her gown and sending heat radiating outwards as everything feminine in her quivered with anticipation.

"My lord, your aunt is waiting for us," she said, remembering that his Aunt Lucy must be getting impatient by now. Emmeline felt rather winded.

He didn't move for a long moment, his expression considering. "So she is," he said softly, and released her, holding out his arm. "Shall we?"

"I should be glad to," she replied with a smile.

"Now, then," Wrexham said, reaching out his right hand to touch the chest of drawers beside him. He moved past it, trailing his hand over the surface and then walking unerringly to the door. Emmeline watched, deeply impressed, as he found the door handle and opened it. "I'm afraid you must guide me to the top of the stairs. I can do it from my room, but I am not used to exiting through her ladyship's apartments."

"You've memorised the house," she said in awe, wondering if she could be prouder of him.

He laughed at that and shook his head. "Lord, no. The place is immense, but sections of it, yes. My rooms, and from them to and inside the main saloon, the small parlour, the dining room, my study. That's all."

"That's all!" she exclaimed, staring at him. "That's astonishing, and you can move within those spaces with confidence?"

He pulled a face. "It's not foolproof. It relies on the staff keeping everything in exactly the same place. Here they are well trained and do their best, but mistakes happen, both theirs and mine. But I am reasonably safe to move about here."

"But not at Buxton Hall," she guessed.

Wrexham let out a harsh breath. "No. My father ensured the staff moved two or three crucial pieces of furniture in each room every day. Not all of them, just enough to completely disorientate me."

"Why, the despicable pig!"

"Now, now, Miss Milly," he said, giving a bark of laughter. "I never can get used to how fierce you are. Such language!"

She glowered. "I shall say it to his face if he dares set foot in this house, you see if I don't."

Wrexham drew her to a halt and reached out a hand, as if seeking her face. Emmeline took it and pressed it to her cheek, her breath catching as he lowered his head and brushed a soft kiss to her lips.

"Thank you," he whispered. "But I would never ask that of you."

"You don't need to ask," she retorted, cross and flustered all at once. "And I should like to see you try to stop me."

He grinned at her, apparently pleased, and allowed her to guide him down the stairs.

Chapter 13

My Lord,

I don't doubt you are regretting the concession you offered me, and yes, I sat down and wrote this barely an hour after you left me. I apologise if it disturbs you, but then you will likely throw it directly on the fire, or better yet, have a servant do it for you, but I am writing all the same. There is nothing else for me to do. I gave you my word I would not follow you, no matter how badly I want to.

First, I wish to apologise. You were not entirely correct in assuming I wasn't sorry to have trapped you. Yes, I wanted to be Lady Kilbane, I cannot deny it, but I never meant to do it this way. You will think me a fool, I know, but I hoped that one day you would choose me. I knew it was a forlorn hope, and I know most people believe me to be reckless and irresponsible, and it is true enough. I am tenacious and patient when I must be, however. I am like my father in that respect. Please believe me when I tell you, I would never have wished to take your choices away from you, and I deeply regret having done so.

I cannot help but wish you had given me a chance, though. I know you think me young and naive and foolish, and perhaps you are correct, but I feel I understand you. I cannot help but believe this is why you despise me so, because you do not wish to be understood. There is the world, and then there is Lord Kilbane, and that is the way you prefer it. You have become accustomed to being an outsider, to being reviled, and there is comfort in familiarity. Trying for anything more makes you vulnerable, it gives others power over you, and you do not want that.

I have no power over you, my lord. I am your wife, and I am in your hands. There is no risk here. If you ever change your mind. I shall be waiting for you.

—Excerpt of a letter from The Most Hon'ble Lady Catherine 'Cat' St Just, Marchioness of Kilbane (daughter of The Most Hon'ble Lucian and Matilda Barrington, Marquess and Marchioness of Montagu) to her husband, Ciarán St Just, Marquess of Kilbane.

17th February 1845, Cawston Hall, Cawston, Norfolk.

Lady Lucinda Steyning was an elegant woman in her early fifties, tall and slender, and with piercing blue eyes of a shade lighter than her niece and nephew. The resemblance was marked, however. She shared Wrexham's high cheekbones, fair hair, and remarkable looks. Though she must have been an extraordinarily lovely young woman, she was still stunning, shining with confidence and an air of vibrancy that made one suspect she was plotting mischief. Yet she had never married. Emmeline admitted herself intrigued, but was far too polite to ask questions.

"Rex, you wicked boy. You know very well I've been sat upon thorns these past days and still you make me wait. Surely you might have left off primping and preening for a few moments to come and see me?"

"Sadly, no, Aunt," Wrexham said, shaking his head and adopting a sorrowful expression. "For I am a shallow and frivolous creature, as you well know."

"Scapegrace," the lady said, shaking her head as she walked to him and took his free hand. "Embrace me, you horrid boy."

Wrexham laughed and did as he was told until Lady Lucinda straightened and turned her attention to Emmeline.

"So, your wife," she said, her expression unreadable.

Emmeline quailed inwardly, instinct telling her Aunt Lucy was no pushover and was exceedingly protective of her nephew. However, she was disinclined to be pushed around either, or intimidated. "I am delighted to make your acquaintance, my lady. Wrexham speaks most fondly of you."

"I did nothing of the sort," Wrexham retorted. "I said you were a frightful old bat and not to be trusted."

"Wrexham!" Emmeline muttered, mortified. She turned back to his aunt. "Indeed, he did not. My husband is teasing me, I'm afraid. It seems to delight him to do so."

Lady Lucinda looked from Emmeline to Wrexham and back again.

"Is she glaring at me, aunt?" Wrexham asked, clearly hellbent on being a devil. "No, don't answer, I know she is. I can feel it. Such a glower she has, I swear it could etch glass."

Emmeline blushed, uncertain what to say but as ever she could never resist a tart remark. "If that were true, there would be no windows remaining in your travelling carriage, my lord, only a small pile of sand."

"Oh, Rex, were you beastly on the horrid journey to Scotland?" Delia asked, her expression one of concern. "And I begged and begged you to be patient."

"I *was* patient," he said, folding his arms. "I was saintly and impeccably behaved for the entire journey. A perfect gentleman."

"Ha!" Emmeline said in outrage, unable to hold her tongue despite his aunt's unnerving gaze. "You were a perfect *nuisance*. Poor Humboldt could have murdered you five times over, you provoked him so, and I'd not have lifted a finger to help you."

"There, you see, Aunt? You see how she scolds me."

"I do see," his aunt replied, and Emmeline's heart dropped at the cool comment. "And I'm relieved to discover you've married a woman with wit enough to keep up with you. Well done."

"Knew you'd like her," Wrexham said, smirking as Emmeline sighed in relief.

"Welcome to Cawston Hall," Lady Lucinda said, her expression warm as she held out her hand to Emmeline. "Not that it is my place to welcome you, but we are so pleased to see you. That brute of a brother of mine needs thwarting, and Delia and I are not up to the job alone. Delia is in a precarious position as his daughter, and the duke knows too many of my secrets. You, though, you have spirit. I can see it in those green eyes of yours. You're very like your beautiful mama, aren't you?"

"Thank you, my lady. I consider that a great compliment," Emmeline replied sincerely.

"I wish you could see her, Rex. You'd be exceedingly smug."

"Describe her to me," Wrexham asked, suddenly intent. "I asked Humboldt, but you know what he is for keeping things brief."

Emmeline fidgeted as Delia and Aunt Lucy looked her up and down.

"Oh, Rex, she is beautiful," Delia said with a sigh. "Her hair is thick and lustrous, a dark chestnut, but it sparks bronze in the firelight, and her skin is fair, smooth as cream."

"I must agree, she is quite lovely," Aunt Lucy said in a considering tone. "An excellent figure, slender but not skinny. A classically proportioned face, straight nose, and rather an imperious slant to her eyebrows that gives her character, but it's her eyes. Don't you agree, Delia?"

"Yes!" Delia replied enthusiastically. "She has the most extraordinary eyes, such a vivid green. I've never seen such a colour."

"Ah, you've not met Bedwin and his sister, then. She's very like them," Aunt Lucy said.

"And is she blushing scarlet?" Wrexham asked them with amusement.

"Yes, the poor dear." Aunt Lucy chuckled. "Now, we had better go into dinner. Cook has delayed and delayed it and she'll be beside herself by now."

Emmeline let out a sigh of relief, both that the critique of her assets was over, and that she could eat. "I'm famished," she admitted to Wrexham, taking his arm.

He patted her hand and smiled. "Fear not, pet. Our cook is a wonder. You'll be well fed, I promise. But... Emmeline?"

She turned to him, waiting as he lifted his hand to brush the back of his fingers against her cheek, then trailed his finger down the bridge of her nose. "You were right, it isn't turned up at all."

Emmeline laughed and reached up to kiss him.

"I told you so. Now, for heaven's sake, take me into dinner before I faint from hunger."

⌂ ⌂ ⌂

18th February 1845, Cawston Hall, Cawston, Norfolk.

Emmeline blinked sleepily as the mattress shifted beneath her.

"Wrexham?" she said, reaching a hand out to the place beside her where her husband had been.

"Here," he said, his voice low as he found her hand and squeezed it before letting go. "Go back to sleep."

Emmeline stared blearily at the clock on the bedside table. "It's barely six in the morning! Where are you going at this hour? Come back to bed."

"I'd like that more than anything," he said wistfully. "But I suspect either Cecil or my father will come crashing in upon us at any moment and I'm damned if I'll greet them in my nightshirt. I'm going to take a bath and get dressed."

Emmeline let out a groan of protest. "I dislike that man more intensely with every day that passes."

"You'll get no argument here, pet, but you don't need to get up just yet. Go back to sleep. I'll have Janet bring you some breakfast in an hour, how's that?"

In the dim light, she saw him walk around the bed, tying the sash on his dressing gown as he went. He stood beside her, and Emmeline stared up at him.

"No, if he's coming, I'm going to be right beside you," she said, dragging her unwilling limbs into a sitting position. She stifled a yawn and heard Wrexham chuckle.

"Stubborn little thing, aren't you?"

"I'm not little, and you don't know the half of it," she retorted.

Wrexham bent, and she moved towards him, touching his face with her hand before their lips met. "I'm beginning to, my lady," he said with quiet amusement. "At least take your breakfast in bed, for my sake. Then I shan't feel so guilty for waking you."

"Very well. If it pleases you."

"It does. I shall have it sent up."

With a sigh, Emmeline rearranged the pillows and sat back against them while Wrexham walked through his dressing room to the lavish bathing room, which had both hot and cold running water. A short time later, she heard the muffled sounds of Wrexham speaking to Lennox, his valet, and closed her eyes until Janet arrived with her breakfast on a tray.

"It looks like it will be a fine day, my lady. The rain has gone, and the skies are clear. We may even see some sunshine," Janet said, and set the tray before her.

Emmeline gazed upon the simple repast of hot chocolate, toasted crumpets, and a dish each of butter and jam with pleasure.

"Cook asked that you let her know your preferences as soon as you are able, but I assured her this would suit you for this morning. I hope that's correct?"

"Perfectly," Emmeline said happily, slathering a crumpet with butter. "And if I haven't said so, you've managed the past few days marvellously, Janet. I know it's been terribly trying for you, what with us being new to each other and that awful journey, but you've been an absolute wonder. Truly."

Janet went a becoming shade of pink. "Thanks ever so, my lady. Truth be told, I've enjoyed it. I'd never left London before Mr Humboldt came and fetched me. When I realised it was an elopement, well, I thought it were dreadfully romantic, like, and I've never dressed a marchioness before, and what with you being such a beauty. Reckon I've died and gone to heaven, I have."

Emmeline added a large dollop of jam to the crumpet and shot Janet a grin. "You flatter me, but we'll get along famously, I think."

Janet nodded, and then her face fell.

Emmeline paused with the crumpet suspended in mid-air. "What is it?"

"I… I don't like to say, my lady."

"Nonsense, Janet. Anything you say is between you and me. No one else will know of it. You have my word."

"Even his lordship?" she asked sceptically, wringing her hands together.

Emmeline set the crumpet down, anxiety in her heart. "Janet. Whatever is the matter?"

Janet hurried to the side of the bed and lowered the voice. "I don't want you to think me ungrateful, this is the best job I ever had, or could dream of having, but… the people here, my lady. Not all of them, but one or two." The woman looked over her shoulder as if she were afraid of someone listening. "I ought not say. It's only been one night, and I was that tired I hardly knew where I was, only—"

She clamped her mouth shut again, her fingers pressed to her lips. Emmeline could see the anxiety shining in the woman's eyes.

"Janet, something has clearly upset you. These past days you've been level-headed and entirely sensible. I do not believe you would get yourself in a tizzy over nothing."

"Thank you, my lady," she said in a rush. "And I don't think I would, neither, it's just I got a bad feeling about this place. Leastways, some of the folk what work here."

"Who?" Emmeline demanded, but before Janet could answer, there was a tremendous crash and a bellow of rage from the bathing room. "Rex!" Emmeline exclaimed, shoving the breakfast tray aside and leaping from the bed.

Rushing across the room, Emmeline hurried through the dressing room and flung open the door to the bathing room, to find

Rex sprawled naked on the floor, blood pouring from a gash on his forehead.

"Rex!" she exclaimed, kneeling beside him. "What happened?"

"I slipped, but… the bath," he said, ashen faced. "There's something in it."

Emmeline reached for a towel and handed it to him, aware he would not wish to be seen in such a position if his valet returned. She helped him to his feet, and then turned to look at the large claw-foot tub, and screamed.

"Emmeline!" Wrexham exclaimed as she ran back to him, burying her face against his chest. "What? What is it?"

Emmeline shook her head, unable to breathe, let alone speak. Her body shook with fear, with horror at what someone had done. Janet was right. There was something very wrong in this house.

"My God, you're trembling," Wrexham said, furiously.

"I'm fine," she managed, pulling herself together. "It's just the shock, that's all. I don't know how anyone could do anything so unspeakable."

Wrexham went very still. "What's in the bath, Emmeline?"

Emmeline took a deep breath and told her rebellious stomach to behave itself. Someone had tried to put the fear of God into them, and she would not oblige them by casting up her accounts.

"Eyeballs," she said succinctly. "Dozens of them. They're floating all over the surface of the bath. The water is all bloody too. I pray to God they're from a butcher's shop."

Wrexham took an involuntary step back, his expression appalled, and then his face set in hard lines, rage lighting his eyes.

"Emmeline, go back to the bedroom, pet. I'll deal with this."

"Wrexham, you're bleeding," Emmeline protested, snatching up a small towel and pressing it to his forehead.

He took the towel from her. "Never mind that, I hit my head when I fell. Just... go to the bedroom. Please, love."

Emmeline nodded, not wanting to leave him, but suspecting he needed to take control of the situation to steady himself. "Very well."

Keeping her gaze averted from the horrific contents of the bathtub, Emmeline left the room. The moment the door closed behind her, she heard Wrexham bellowing for his valet.

From that moment on, the morning went from bad to worse, for Wrexham was fit to be tied. Emmeline had once heard her father turn the air blue and bellow himself hoarse when he'd hit a difficult situation when a supplier had let him down, endangering one of his largest railway projects. He'd had nothing on Wrexham. The entire house was in uproar, the staff skittering about like Satan himself had come to bear them off to the fiery inferno.

Wrexham reduced his valet to tears, and demanded that every member of staff present themselves in his study, one after the other, and interrogated each one in turn. He began with the upper staff and a procession of weeping maids and red-faced footmen exited his study over the course of the next hour. With every person who failed to give him satisfactory answers, his temper rose until Emmeline feared he'd murder someone, or one of the staff would snap and murder him.

On seeing a burly fellow who looked as if he could carry an ox on his shoulders leave the study teary-eyed, Emmeline decided enough was enough. She knocked and waited, entering the room after hearing the terse demand to, "Come in, damn you."

He was standing in the far corner of the room with his back to her. His posture was stiff, his shoulders rigid, and her heart went out to him despite the havoc he'd caused.

"My lord," she said placidly.

"Emmeline," he said in surprise. "I beg your pardon. I would not have spoken so harshly had I known."

"Really? You have turned everyone else into a quivering wreck, whether or not they deserved it. I see no reason to leave me out."

"Because I know very well, you did not have a hand in this ghastly affair," he said impatiently.

"And do you think everyone on the estate is in your father's pocket?"

"No!" He raked a hand through his hair, scowling at her. "Of course not. But it's obvious at least one person is, and I mean to discover who."

"By setting them all against you? Did it never occur to you that this is exactly what your father had in mind?"

"He has in mind to put me in my grave but, if he can't manage it, he'll settle for making me believe I'm losing my damned mind."

"I know that," she said, going to him and slipping her hands around his waist.

He sighed and pulled her into his arms, burying his face in her hair. "I'm sorry. I told you I was a bad-tempered brute. I did not mean to prove it to you so quickly or so thoroughly."

"Never mind that. I am not the least bit impressed by large men shouting the odds. You're very like my father, I think and it's all a lot of hot air. The trouble is the staff might not know it."

"It's hardly the first time I've shouted the house down," he muttered ruefully.

"Yes, but is it the first time you've questioned them all about a specific incident? Is it the first time you have treated each one of them with suspicion?"

He hesitated, and Emmeline knew she was right. "My lord, you must speak to them. All of them, at once. You must apologise and—"

"Apologise!" he said, his head coming up. "Damned if I will. I'm the Marquess of bloody Wrexham, if I go around apologising every time I—"

"Behave like an ignorant arse?" she suggested.

His expression darkened further, but Emmeline pressed on.

"Wrexham, put your pride to one side, or do you intend to act like the duke?"

"Take that back!" he said, letting go of her. "You do not know, can have no understanding of what a cruel, spiteful—"

Emmeline held on to him, not about to let him divert her with his indignation. "I never said you *were* acting like it, but the staff might believe like father like son if you carry on like this. Those who have been loyal to you might doubt you, might become willing to take a bribe…"

"A bribe?"

"Wrexham. If your father did this, think what he has achieved. He has upset and infuriated you and set the entire house upon its ears. I should think he's well pleased with himself, and all for the price of a three dozen pigs' eyes, which is what Cook assures me they are. If you undermine the trust between you and your staff, you play directly into his hands."

To his credit, he was listening, though his brow remained furrowed. "But someone betrayed me. Someone who had access to my private quarters."

"I know, darling," she said unsteadily, hearing the pain and frustration behind the words. "And I promise you, we will find out who did it, but that will be a great deal easier if the staff are on your side."

There was a brief, taut silence.

"Hell and damnation!"

"I know," she said sympathetically.

"I dislike apologising," he grumbled, scowling furiously.

"It's awful," she agreed. "But just think how much practise you've had the past few days. You're quite the expert now."

For a moment, she wondered if it was too soon to tease him, as his expression did not ease, but then his lips quirked.

"Wretch," he muttered, pulling her back into his arms.

She let out a breath, relieved, and laid her head on his cheek. "Do you promise to be calm now?"

He drew in a deep breath and released it. "Fine," he said, terse but resigned. "I'll do my best, and… I'll apologise," he said, sounding as if the words had been dragged from him under protest.

"I'm so proud of you," Emmeline said, hugging him tighter.

"I'm only glad you're too short to pat me on the head," he griped, but she heard the amused tone and was not disturbed by his grumbling.

"Well, now you are behaving like a rational human being, I think you ought to speak to Janet. I would have suggested it sooner had you not been thundering about the house like Hades come to drag us all into the darkness."

"If I were Hades, I'd only take you, Persephone, and none of this six months of the year nonsense, either. You're not getting rid of me now."

Emmeline preened, rather delighted. "I should have insisted upon it, but never mind flirting with me. Will you be kind to poor Janet? You've scared her out of her wits with your behaviour this morning, and it's taken me ages to persuade her to tell me what she overheard last night. And, I might add, she was only so terrified because she knew I'd tell you and you'd want to speak to her."

"Of course, I'll be kind to her. I'm not a monster!"

Emmeline regarded him silently until her stillness conveyed the message. He huffed out a breath.

"Now," he amended, rolling his eyes. "I'm not a monster *now.*"

Emmeline kissed him for his honesty and went to fetch her maid.

18th February 1845, Beverwyck, London.

Fred handed his dripping hat to a footman with an apologetic smile before stripping off his gloves. His heart was beating too fast, excitement thrumming under his skin in joyful anticipation of seeing his beloved. There was a virulent form of influenza doing the rounds at university; they had cancelled lessons now as over half the school was sick. Fred hadn't been worried, being a large and robust sort of chap who'd never been ill a day in his life, but when his father had suggested he come home for a few days to avoid catching it, he'd not needed asking twice. Certainly not once he'd discovered his beloved was staying at Beverwyck for a few days.

"Fred?" The familiar voice made his already overexcited heart skip madly about in his chest.

Fred turned, breath snagging in his throat as he saw her, standing stock still, halfway down the magnificent staircase. Lord, but she tied him up in knots. Whilst she was not exactly beautiful, there was something compelling about her, something bright and quick that made his heart skip. It always had. Fred had loved her since they were children, fascinated by her and her outlook on life, which had seemed so very different from his own. They had fought like cat and dog at times, but never in his life had he known anyone so courageous, so clever and funny, so very loyal. Aggie had a mind like quicksilver. She was never still, always ready to do something new. To some people, she might seem rather stern, unfriendly, and even suspicious, but to the people she loved, she was full of mischief and the kindest person Fred had ever known. She was unlike any other girl he'd ever met, and he was going to marry her.

"Good morning, Aggie," he said, struggling to keep the grin from his face.

"Whatever are you doing here?" she cried, running across the entrance hall to him to take his hands in hers. "You've not been sent down? Oh, Fred, what did you do?"

"I didn't do anything!" he protested, laughing. "Everyone is sick and there are no lessons until Monday. Father said I might come home for a few days."

Her eyes widened with delight. "A few days!" she squealed, bouncing on her toes.

Fred knew she was restraining herself because the footman was still lingering like a bad smell, curse him. If they'd been alone, she would have thrown her arms around his neck and hugged him, or at least she would have done before he'd declared his feelings for her. Everything was different now. They weren't just friends any longer. She had said that she loved him, too. He knew the words she'd chosen to tell him off by heart, because the letter was in his coat pocket. It had been there since he'd received it two days ago, for it seemed too extraordinary to be true and he needed to read the words again and again to reassure himself.

> *Dearest Fred,*
>
> *How can such a clever fellow as you be such a big lummox?*
>
> *Of course I love you too.*

You daft ha'porth.

As love letters went, it wasn't exactly a sonnet, but Fred didn't care. It sounded exactly like Aggie and, when he read it, he heard her voice in his head. It was all he needed.

Fred gave the footman a speaking glance, and finally the man made himself scarce.

"I've missed you, Aggie," he said softly.

To his astonishment, colour rose in her cheeks.

"Are you blushing?" he demanded, entranced and delighted by this new turn of events.

"No!" she retorted, glaring at him and folding her arms. "Don't be ridiculous."

Fred smothered a grin and decided it was safer not to tease her over it.

"And stop looking so smug," she said crossly.

"Yes, Aggie," he said, almost choking himself as he struggled not to laugh.

She huffed and rolled her eyes and then her lips quirked. "I suppose I missed you too," she muttered.

Fred put a hand to his heart. "Oh, Aggie, you overwhelm me with your romantic words. I may swoon."

"Idiot."

"*Your* idiot," he said, grinning at her and bumping her with his shoulder.

Aggie bumped him back, glancing at him from under her lashes. From any other woman, it might have seemed a flirtatious glance, but Aggie didn't have the least clue how to flirt.

"Really?"

"Really," he agreed, reaching for her hand. He laced their fingers together and she let out a shaky breath. Fred knew how she felt. If her heart was anything like his, it was dancing a jig behind her ribs. "I'd suggest we go for a walk, but it's pouring with rain."

She gave a little snort, which delighted him, and shot him an amused glance. "Beverwyck is about ten miles wide and five miles deep. We can still go for a walk. Indoors."

"As the lady wishes, then," Fred replied, realising at once his ladylove was a genius. "How about a picnic?"

She darted him a glance, surprise and pleasure shining in the blue of her eyes. "Yes, please, Fred."

"Come along then, sweetheart," he said, bursting with happiness. "Let's see what Cook can make for us."

Chapter 14

Dearest Delia,

Please forgive me for not having written sooner. I know how worried you must have all been, but I hope you know me well enough to realise I am perfectly well and managing nicely.

If you want the truth, I am happy. No one here knows who I am, and for the first time in my life, I am grateful for how isolated my life has been. Please do not worry about my financial situation either. I took my jewellery with me and have sold a few pieces already which have set me up very nicely, but I have more hidden safely away should I require it. Even if I were not so content, I would still prefer it to marrying that disgusting old man.

After everything the duke has done, after all the petty cruelties, I still find it hard to believe that he planned such a fate for me. I know, as everyone knows, the Earl of Wendover beat his first wife so badly and so often, she killed herself to escape him, and he ruined his second wife in that awful crimcon. Now I know why, so he was free to marry me. My stomach roils at the villainy he is capable of. Yet my own grandfather would sell me to such a man. Well, I thwarted his plans. I shall let no man have dominion over me ever again, for they are all vile and untrustworthy, well except Wrexham, of course. But I shall live quietly and anonymously until the duke is cold in his grave.

Please send Aunt Lucy my love and embrace dear Rex for me. I worry for him more than anyone and wish I were there. I hope he can forgive me for deserting him, and understand why I did it. I truly felt it was life or death, or I would never have left you all with so much to deal with.

Be brave like those wicked pirates you so admire, Delia. I miss you all and love you so much.

Your own, Genevieve x

—Excerpt of a letter from The Lady Genevieve Hamilton to The Lady Cordelia Steyning.

18th February 1845, Cawston Hall, Cawston, Norfolk.

Rex sat at his desk, waiting for Emmeline to return with her maid. Not being a complete halfwit, he knew his wife was in the right. He had behaved badly this morning. Worse, he had behaved like the duke, shouting the odds and riding roughshod over anyone who didn't get out of his way quick enough. Emmeline had been right to take him to task, brave too, for Delia would not have dared and even Aunt Lucy steered clear when he lost his temper so utterly. He sighed and put his head in his hands, tugging at his hair, which would upset Lennox. He'd done enough of that this morning.

How he could have doubted Lennox even for a moment, when the man had been with him for so many years, he could not fathom. Lennox had run the bath while they were choosing Rex's outfit for the day. He'd gone back to turn off the water, but after that there had been plenty of time whilst they were in his dressing room, bickering over what waistcoat he ought to wear, for someone else to enter and execute their vile plan. Well, Rex would just have to apologise and hope Lennox didn't take his revenge by scalping him or dressing him in puce and orange. He shuddered at the idea.

What he did not want to think about, not for anything, was the contents of his bath.

He had known, the moment his toe had dipped into the water and bumped against unknown objects that were soft and round, that something was terribly wrong. How, he wasn't sure, but his instincts had told him to get the hell away and he had, moving too fast and subsequently slipping arse over apex. He'd cracked his head on the basin on the way down and very nearly done his father the service of doing away with himself. His head was still throbbing like the devil was using it as an anvil, and his stomach pitched every time his imagination conjured the bath, and those bedamned eyes staring up at him. He swallowed hard and told himself not to be such a baby, but the truth was the event had rattled him badly.

Living under his father's roof had been like living on a battleground. He'd not been able to let down his guard for a moment. Yet he'd got through it, and the main thing that had kept him going was the knowledge he would escape and come home to Cawston Hall, where he'd be safe.

Except he wasn't safe, and now there was Emmeline to consider. What if his selfishness the other night had already put a babe in her? What if the duke decided she, too, was in his way?

His blood chilled at the thought, and he sucked in a sharp breath. Emmeline was akin to a miracle, arriving in his life in his moment of need and, by some stroke of luck—or perhaps a lack of judgement on her part—she cared for him. No matter what happened to him, Emmeline must be kept safe.

He sat up at a knock on the door and smoothed down his hair.

"Come in."

"My lord, Janet has come to speak with you," Emmeline said, as he stood, inclining his head.

"Thank you, Janet," he said, bracing himself to add. "And I beg that you will not be afraid to speak plainly to me. I am aware I have been a little... overwrought at the events of the morning. I... apologise. I will also address the staff after this meeting to say the same to them."

"Lord Wrexham, there's no need to go apologising to the likes of me, I can assure you—"

He held out a hand to stop her and smiled. "My wife has told me in no uncertain terms that I behaved like an ignorant arse. Her words, not mine," he added ruefully. "If I were you, I should not wish to contradict her."

"No, my lord," Janet replied, though he heard the smile in her voice and relaxed somewhat.

"Tell me what you know, Janet."

"Well, my lord. It ain't much, truth be told. Mrs Tweedy was very kind to me when we arrived. My room was all ready and ever so pretty, and even Mr Bunting spoke politely to me. In the last house I worked the butler was a right piece of work. Oh, the stories I could tell—"

"Perhaps, for now, you might just tell us about the two men?" Emmeline suggested gently and Wrexham smiled. She was a managing creature, and he rather adored that about her.

"Sorry, my lady. I'm that nervous, and my tongue runs like a fiddle when I'm anxious. Well, the thing is, I was all settled in my room when I heard footsteps, someone running along the corridor outside. Well, being in a new place and all, I was a bit on edge, despite being ready to drop, so I looked out. There were two men at the end of the corridor, talking."

"Did you see them clearly?" Wrexham asked.

"No, my lord. It was dark, and they were in the shadows, but they saw me looking and they hurried off. About five minutes later, I heard voices outside though, so I cracked open my window. I'd swear it was the same two men, and they were laughing it up and…"

"It's all right, Janet. I know it's upsetting, but tell his lordship what you heard them say."

Janet's voice dropped to a whisper, so that Wrexham instinctively leaned in closer. "They said their master had some clever notions about how to make a fellow want to slit his own throat. They said… they said you'd be having nightmares about drowning in blood and guts and howling like a babe, wishing for the end afore the month was out."

Rex sucked in a breath, horrified. A moment later, he felt Emmeline's hand on his shoulder and reached up to grasp it, steadied by her nearness.

"Is there anything else you can tell us about them, Janet?"

"Yes, my lord. They weren't like the rest of your staff, leastways anyone I've spoken to yet."

"How so?" Emmeline asked.

"Well, the rest of the staff have been kinder than I expected, though it's awful difficult to understand them, for they don't half talk funny. They all got the local accent, like, but those two devils I heard, well, I understood every word. They were city folk. London born. Like me."

Once Janet had been dismissed to carry on with her day, Rex summoned Mrs Tweedy and Bunting. From them he discovered that they had hired two new underfootmen to replace two who had mysteriously upped and left about a month earlier.

"Their credentials were excellent, my lord," Bunting said, sounding mortified. "They'd worked for the Earl of Wendover, and everyone knows what a stickler he is. Also, I well understood why they might seek positions elsewhere after such a er... challenging situation."

"There's no need to be coy, Bunting. I am well aware of Wendover's tendency to instil obedience at the end of a crop, or a poker, or whatever else might come to hand."

He heard Emmeline gasp and wished he did not have to subject his wife to such unpleasantness. They ought to be honeymooning, for heaven's sake, not tracking down men hellbent on causing him harm.

"The two men who left so mysteriously, what do we know about them?" Emmeline asked, proving to him, as if he needed any further proof, that she did not shock easily and would not be distracted from her line of enquiry.

"Not a great deal," Bunting replied, but was interrupted by Mrs Tweedy, who gave a disgusted sniff.

"We know Melvin had pretensions. A right dandy he was, always looking at himself and preening. Thought he was better than the likes of us," she said, and Wrexham remembered the woman well enough to picture her disapproving expression.

"The sort of person who would be easy to seduce with the offer of a better position, perhaps?" Emmeline suggested.

"Exactly, my lady," Mrs Tweedy agreed. "Would have been no bother at all to lure them away and then set those two devils up in their place. I told you, did I not, Mr Bunting, that if those references were real, I'd eat my best Sunday hat."

"You did, Mrs Tweedy," Bunting agreed wearily. "And I had come to agree with you. The truth is, I'd been planning on dismissing them this morning."

"Why did you not tell me this at once?" Wrexham demanded.

There was a moment's hesitation, but Wrexham realised in that moment his wife had been correct. Bunting had asked to speak to him earlier and received short shrift because Wrexham was interviewing the upstairs staff. He had clearly not pressed the matter, as he had feared reprisals.

"Forgive me, my lord. I know I ought to have done at once, only—"

"Only I was behaving like a brute and you thought I might shoot the messenger," Wrexham said with a sigh.

"I am sorry, my lord. I did *try* to tell you," Bunting said, and Wrexham could hear his agitation.

"I believe you, Bunting, but I'm the one who is sorry. I hope you can both forgive me."

There were exclamations and assurances from his loyal butler and cook which only made him feel even more the ignorant arse Emmeline had accused him of being.

"Why did they do it, my lord?"

Wrexham had only ever told his sister Delia and Aunt Lucy of his father's plans for fear they would consider him paranoid, that they would believe it to be the first signs of madness and play into the duke's hands. Even they had thought him overwrought to begin with, disbelieving that the duke, as appalling as he was, would go so far. It had taken several incidents before they saw the reality of the situation he was living with.

Before he had time to gather his thoughts, Emmeline spoke.

"We believe his lordship is in danger, and I'm afraid to say we suspect Lord Cecil and the duke."

There were no gasps of shock or horror as Wrexham might have expected.

"Didn't I tell you?" Mrs Tweedy demanded, and Wrexham jumped a little, uncertain if she was addressing him or not. "Beg pardon, my lord, but I've feared that were the case this many years, but Mr Bunting told me I was too suspicious. Well, I know a bad 'un when I see one, and whenever your father is here…. But I ought not…."

"It's all right, Mrs Tweedy," Emmeline said, her voice soothing. "I promise you may speak freely. We are neither of us friends to the duke or Lord Cecil, and if you can help us, we would be grateful."

"My wife is quite right, Mrs Tweedy. I would appreciate your honesty, and any insight you may have."

"Well, I don't know how I can help but all I know is Lord Cecil has been jealous of Lord Wrexham since the day he was born, and that's mostly the duke's fault. He set the lad up against the marquess, which was cruel enough, when he's a scrawny thing with more hair than wit. I always thought it was because Lord Cecil was weak, and the duke knew he could control him when he could never get the better of Lord Wrexham. But that's just what I saw and I'm only a housekeeper."

"On the contrary, Mrs Tweedy, I think you are wiser than most," Emmeline said. "And now we face with the truth. Either the duke or Lord Cecil, or both, are set upon doing my husband harm."

"They'll not get another chance," Bunting said, his anger palpable. "I failed you once, my lord, it will not happen again. I will ensure the property is made safe, that no strangers come anywhere near. We will guard Cawston Hall every moment of the day and night. I swear you will not be troubled again."

"You failed no one, Bunting," Wrexham said. "You did not know the danger. Now you are aware, however, you do not know how grateful I am to be back home, among friends."

"We won't let any harm befall you, my lord," Mrs Tweedy said, determination ringing in her voice. "The nerve of them. The idea of that primped up little worm fancying himself Lord Wrexham, living here and putting on airs, the b—"

"That will be all, Mrs Tweedy!" Bunting said swiftly. "It is time we were about our business. I'll not have these upstarts interfere with the running of this house any more than they already have."

"Actually, Bunting, at the risk of causing further upheaval, might I request all the staff to gather in the great hall? I should like a word with them."

"As you wish, my lord. I will see to it at once."

Wrexham heard the door close and Emmeline moving towards him. She slid her arms around his neck.

"Well done," she said, pressing her cheek to his.

Wrexham shifted, reaching for her and smiling as she gave a squeal of protest. She landed in his lap with a frantic rustle of skirts and petticoats.

"My lord!" she exclaimed, before he smothered the words with his mouth, kissing her.

The tension left her body at once and her hands settled upon his chest. Wrexham settled one hand at the back of her head, holding her in place as he kissed her harder, deeper. Through all the disruption Emmeline had stood beside him, steady and unflinching, and a wave of emotion hit him hard, so fierce he hardly knew what to do with it.

It filled him up, chasing away thoughts of his father and half-brother, allowing him to forget the horror of the morning until there was only Emmeline and a strength of feeling that scared him to death as much as he welcomed it.

She broke the kiss with a gasp, pushing at his chest.

"You asked them to gather the staff!" she exclaimed.

"That will take a while," he murmured, finding her ankle beneath the layers of fabric and sliding his hand higher. Desire burned in his blood as his hand circled the slender limb, the feel of her stocking sliding beneath his palm tantalising.

"Not that long," she said breathlessly as his hand reached her thigh and warm, silken skin.

"But I want you," he murmured, nuzzling the sweetly scented skin of her neck.

"You do?" she asked, sounding so uncertain he raised his head, frowning.

"You doubt it?" he asked, astonished. "Surely you've had proof enough?"

His fingers found the slit in her drawers and the silken hair beneath as Emmeline sucked in a sharp breath.

"No," she said, the word faint. "Not enough."

Wrexham trailed his fingers back and forth through the feathery curls, parting the soft skin to find the little hidden place beneath. She gasped and buried her face against his neck.

Wrexham took her hand and pressed it against the placket of his trousers, his cock twitching under her palm. "How about now?" he asked, his voice low.

She gave an unsteady laugh, caressing him inexpertly but with enthusiasm, and his mind went black. The events of the morning had undermined his confidence, but over the past days Emmeline had consistently bolstered him, had made him feel invincible, as if he could do anything with her beside him. That some vile sneak had entered his home and so discomposed him had made him feel a fool again, though… somehow that hurt his pride far worse than any previous or more serious injury. He knew himself well enough to understand that was why he had behaved so badly. But now he was calm, and very much alive, and he wanted more than anything to prove that to himself and his wife.

Wrexham dipped his finger lower, his own breath snagging in his throat at the discovery that she wanted him too. The longing to sink into the wet heat surrounding his finger was so great his body ached with wanting. He groaned as he heard the staff gathering in the great hall beyond the door.

"Hell and damnation," he muttered.

Emmeline gave an unsteady laugh. "You'd best go."

"I should have told them to gather in an hour. Or two. Or this afternoon."

"But you didn't," she said, pushing at him when he tried to kiss her again.

"Very well," he grumbled. "But I'm not done with you, lady wife."

"I should think not," she said tartly as he released her, and he heard the swish of material as she rearranged her skirts. She stood up, but before he could do likewise, she pressed her mouth to his, kissing him hard and swift. "Later," she promised.

Wrexham smiled, more than happy to fulfil that request, and concentrated on ridding himself of a rather impressive cockstand before he addressed the staff.

Chapter 15

Dearest Ruth,

My heart is breaking. I know now how Lyall's ill-advised marriage must eat away at your heart. No matter how hard we wish perfect lives for our children, for the way to be smooth and free of the obstacles we faced in our time, we cannot live their lives for them. We cannot make their choices, for they are not us but themselves. Repeatedly, I wonder if I have given Catherine too much freedom, too much courage, yet I would not have her any other way. To see her so bereft though, is hard to bear. I believe it is worse for Lucian. He feels he has failed her, that he ought to have protected her, but how can one protect someone so young and headstrong when they run full tilt towards danger?

Cat believes Lord Kilbane to be redeemable. She believes if she is patient and kind that he will come to trust her, but I fear what it will cost her to make such an effort. I have never believed him the villain they purport him to be, but I cannot be easy in my mind. Yet it truly grieved him to be forced into marrying her, and in his own way he acted honourably.

Perhaps there is some shred of hope. I shall cling to it, for what else can I do?

—Excerpt of a letter from The Most Hon'ble Matilda Barrington, Marchioness of Montagu to her friend The Right Hon'ble Ruth Anderson, Countess of Morven.

18th February 1845, Cawston Hall, Cawston, Norfolk.

Emmeline stood beside her husband as he addressed his staff. Her heart swelled as he spoke, knowing how proud he was, how it irked him to apologise, but how gracious he was in doing so.

At first, the staff shifted uncomfortably, appearing uncertain and ill at ease at the master of the house lowering himself to apologise—they were probably wondering if he had an ulterior motive—but the longer Wrexham spoke, the easier the atmosphere became.

"I ought never to have doubted you, any of you," Wrexham carried on. "And I pray you will put it down to the stresses of the past days and the shock of the situation I found myself in this morning. I should have confided in you all before now, perhaps, but I have been too used to keeping my counsel. That ends today. I am putting my trust in you all from now on, and I am asking you to be discreet, for our sakes.

"You all know that my wife and I eloped, but we did so because we feared my father's interference. You here all remember Mr Thompson, who acted as my steward these past five years. He betrayed me to my father and sold the information about our elopement. The duke sent Lord Cecil in pursuit of us, hoping to delay us long enough so he could interfere and stop the marriage. I believe he means me harm, at the very least, to get me locked up in an asylum."

To Emmeline's relief, there were gasps of shock and angry murmurs at this revelation, and she knew she had been right to persuade Wrexham to do this.

"On what grounds?" demanded an indignant voice.

Wrexham gave a grim smile. "Those of you who have had experience of working in the duke's household will know his grace does not need grounds or proof. He wants me gone. He wants to take control of my finances and my lands and for Lord Cecil to take my place."

"Shame!" cried a woman's voice this time, the shout quickly taken up and echoed around the room. "Shame, shame on him!"

"We won't let them do you harm, my lord!" shouted one of the gardeners fiercely, an older man with thick, dark whiskers and a ruddy, weather worn countenance.

"Thank you, Greaves," Wrexham said, apparently recognising the voice. "That means a great deal to me."

Suddenly the room was filled with many more such comments, from a shy little kitchen maid who shouted, "God bless and keep you!" to the coachmen and grooms, who were louder and more raucous but no less sincere.

Emmeline's throat grew tight as she realised Wrexham was getting emotional. She doubted he had ever realised the regard with which his staff held him in. But she knew him now, knew he was gentle and kind and fair. He would have been a good employer, a generous one, and these people would know that. She moved closer to him and took his hand, unsurprised when he grasped it tightly.

"I think they've forgiven you," she said, smiling up at him.

He let out a breath, shaking his head. "Thanks to you, pet," he said. "Thank you for taking me to task. I did not mean to act the brute, it's just sometimes—"

"I know," she said, squeezing his hand. "There's no need to explain. Come along now. I think we've provided them with enough entertainment for one day."

It took forever to extricate themselves from the staff as everyone wanted to speak to them and Emmeline understood Wrexham did not wish to rush away, but gave them his time and attention, and made certain to thank everyone personally for their loyalty to him and Emmeline, and to Cawston Hall.

When they finally made their way back up the stairs, there was one thing that still nagged at Emmeline. "Where is Lord Cecil? He was apparently on our trail and the reason we had to keep moving, but if that is the case. Where is he?"

Wrexham considered this. "Biding his time and awaiting my father's arrival if I were to guess. Cecil is a bully, but only when he feels the odds are in his favour. Accosting me on the road with his hired thugs is one thing. Setting foot on my property where I have my staff at hand, that is another. I don't doubt his thugs will try to cause more trouble, though."

"You think he's nearby, then?" Emmeline asked, disturbed by the idea. "You think it was him who hired those men and put the eyeballs in your bath?" She shuddered again as she remembered, knowing she'd never forget the sight.

"Undoubtedly," Wrexham said. "The duke is a bull in a china shop, and he doesn't care who he hurts to get his own way, but he's not got a scrap of imagination. Cecil, though, he's petty, and he can be remarkably spiteful. He was the kind of boy who would torment small animals for the fun of it. I've punished him for such vile behaviour before now. The last time he was here was the worst. It must have been about five years ago, before things between us became openly hostile. Before that he always tried to toady up to me, but he attempted to importune one of the kitchen maids. I dread to think what might have happened if I hadn't come upon them. Poor girl, she was scared witless. I made good and sure he knew what that felt like before I kicked him out."

Emmeline wondered if it were possible to fall in love with him any harder. She kept thinking she had fallen quite hard and far enough, only to discover there was more. He was all she could think of, all she wanted, and she could well imagine why his loathsome half-brother resented him so badly. Wrexham was good and honourable, strong, and handsome and popular; all the things it appeared Cecil was not.

They walked in silence along the corridor, Wrexham finding his way with ease until he halted close to his bedroom door.

"You know, I had forgotten how kind and good the people are here, Emmeline. I have always loved this place. It has been my home since I was a boy, and I always loved it, but with everything that has happened to me, I think I forgot that much of what I love, that makes it home, are the people. Thank you for reminding me, love."

"You're welcome," she said, staring at him with a daft expression of adoration he would have found amusing had he been able to see her.

"Now then," he said. "I think we have some unfinished business, do we not?"

Emmeline blushed, remembering the brief interlude in his study. "It's the middle of the day. What if someone comes?"

"Then they will be told we are indisposed," he said with a suggestive grin, and hurried her through the door.

"You are terribly wicked, my lord," Emmeline said sometime later, sprawled over her husband's torso. He was breathing hard still, his skin damp as she trailed her fingers back and forth through the hair on his chest.

He grinned, looking exceedingly smug. She laughed and shook her head.

"Now I understand all those scandalous stories people whisper about you."

His face fell then, his expression darkening. "You heard such stories?" he asked, looking uncomfortable.

"Some, yes," she agreed, intrigued by his dismay. "I made some discreet enquiries after the first time I met you."

"And you didn't run a mile?" he asked, incredulous.

She laughed and kissed his chest. "I told you, the damage was done. I was infatuated."

"But I was appallingly rude to you," he said, looking so bewildered she could only snigger with amusement.

"Yes, you were, but you were also devastatingly handsome, and you made me laugh. I suppose I saw you as a challenge."

He let out a bark of laughter at that. "A challenge, by God. Well, that's true enough, I suppose."

Emmeline smiled and rested her head on his chest once more. She wondered what the future held for them. They would deal with the duke and the loathsome half-brother. She could not consider a world where her husband must live out his days in fear for his life. Yet, in all the drama and romance of the past days, there was one thing she had neglected to consider. Wrexham's past proved he was a passionate man who enjoyed the company of women. A lot of women. For the moment, he was content with her and this much reduced world because his confidence had been damaged, but she felt certain that would change. Soon enough, he would discover he was still the man he had always been in all the ways that mattered. And what would that mean for her? Would he go back to his old ways?

"Emmeline?"

The idea of Wrexham with another woman made her breath catch and her eyes sting. How could she bear it? And what if he never got over the idea of not having children? She had married him on the principle of it being a marriage in name only. No physical relationship, no children. She had hoped to change that and had partway succeeded, but what if he never gave her a child, what if he was unfaithful and she was left alone, and….

"Emmeline, what is it, love?"

Too late, she realised she had given herself away somehow.

"N-Nothing," she tried, doing her best to sound happy although her voice quavered.

He moved then, turning her onto her back, cupping her face with one hand. "What did I say? What is it? Emmeline?" He snatched his hand away, holding it out, his expression one of horror. "You're crying."

"I'm not!" she protested, swiping at her eyes. "Truly, I'm just being silly."

"Damn it, tell me what's wrong!"

"There's nothing wrong, it's just I wondered about the f-future."

His body grew tense immediately, and she hurried on, aware of what he would assume.

"I just wondered if you would g-grow tired of me and go back to your old ways, because I don't think I could bear it," she admitted.

There was a tense silence. Emmeline could hear nothing past her heart beating in her ears.

"You think I'd be unfaithful to you?"

She shrugged, unwilling to answer out loud.

He let out a harsh breath. "Silly goose," he said, shaking his head. "Come here."

Wrexham turned onto his back, holding out his arms to her and Emmeline lost no time in snuggling up, reassured by the way he held her close.

"You've no need to worry on that score, pet. I know how lucky I am, believe me. I always intended to give up my bad behaviour. I have never wished to emulate my father and add another generation of bastards to the family name. I wanted to settle down with someone one day, but after I lost my sight, I thought that was over. Ida—she's Lady Waring now—made it very clear I was no longer a fine catch. Title and fortune could not make up for the way society would pity her. She did not want to become a laughingstock by marrying a blind man, especially one who would eventually be dubbed 'the mad marquess.'"

"Oh!" Emmeline fumed, wondering how on earth the woman could look at Wrexham and see anything but a virile, handsome man with everything to live for. "I could shake her, the vile creature. Though I ought to thank her, for if she hadn't broken her engagement, I would never have married you and that…. Well, I can't even think of it," she said, holding him tighter still.

Wrexham bent and kissed the top of her head. "Me either, pet. I never dared to believe I could have anything resembling this, even before I lost my sight, but certainly not after. You're something of a miracle, Milly, love. I'll try your patience a dozen times a day, I don't doubt, but not in the way you feared. You can trust me. I swear it. Do you believe me?"

Emmeline nodded, her throat too tight to speak, but she forced the words out. "Yes, Rex."

He kissed her then, and though it seemed scandalous when he had only just made love to her, she wanted him again. Tugging at him, she urged him on top of her, wrapping her legs about his waist.

His chuckle was dark and sent shivers running down her spine. "And you said I was the wicked one," he murmured, nipping at her earlobe.

"You are, dreadfully wicked," she said.

"Then you only want a kiss?" he asked, all innocence.

"No!" she retorted.

He grinned, the boyish, impudent expression that made her brain melt and her heart override all good sense. "What then? Tell me."

"You know very well," she protested.

"Of course I do, but I want to hear you say it."

Frustrated, Emmeline reached down between them, curving her fingers around his arousal and stroking.

He groaned and rested his forehead against hers. "You don't play fair."

"This," she said, growing breathless. "This is what I want."

He made a sound that was half pain, half laughter and moved over her. "Anything for you, pet."

"Rex!" she cried as he thrust into her, stealing anything resembling thought as sensation surged through her.

He loved her until she was mindless and boneless and trembling, and then sent her spinning into the dark as the climax glittered through her, sparkling behind her eyelids. She held on to him, the one fixed point as everything else fell away. It was perfect and wonderful until he, too, found his release and withdrew from her body as he always did, spending across her stomach with a groan.

Emmeline bit her lip, holding her tongue. He had given her so much today: his trust in her judgement, his promise for the future.

There was time for everything else. It wasn't as if she wanted a child this minute. They had time.

The nagging reminder that Wrexham was certain he would not remain the man he was, that he would gradually descend into madness, was one she pushed away too. She would hope for the best for now, and she would make her own enquiries, too. In her opinion, too many of her husband's troubling ideas could be traced back to his loathsome father. If that were the case, she would do everything in her power to fight back.

Emmeline got up and went to the washstand, cleaning herself up and glancing outside to see the sun had come out and it was a bright afternoon. They had spent most of the day in bed, which seemed both decadent and wonderful. She hurried to join Wrexham, who had arranged the pillows in a heap behind him and was sitting back, looking like a cosseted pasha awaiting his harem.

He kissed her, welcoming her back, and Emmeline sighed with content.

"Did you like to read?" she asked, suddenly wondering about the things he must miss.

He nodded. "Yes, one of the many pleasures taken from me.

"Would you like me to read to you? I bought a book just before we left, and I think you would like it. It's called The Count of Monte Cristo. I'd love to share it with you… I mean if you'd like me to. What do you think?" she asked cautiously, wondering if she had been too enthusiastic. Perhaps he would consider being read to akin to being babied.

"I think you are the sweetest creature that ever walked the earth, pet. I should like that very much. Thank you for thinking of it."

Emmeline beamed, feeling pleased with herself, and then gasped as there was a knock at the door.

"My lord? I beg your pardon, but Lady Helena and Mr Gabriel Knight are here."

"Lud!" Emmeline squealed and leapt out of bed.

Chapter 16

My Lady,

Please allow me to introduce myself. I am Mr Gilbert Berrycloth, Lord Kilbane's private secretary. I believe Mr Bright has already been in contact with you and you should certainly refer to him regarding all financial matters. For anything else, however, please rest assured that I am entirely at your disposal.

If I might say so, I was delighted to hear of your recent nuptials to Lord Kilbane. If ever I can be of service to you, do not hesitate to contact me.

I also provide below the address where you may contact your husband and me for the following six weeks. I will ensure any change of address is forwarded to you in plenty of time.

—Excerpt of a letter from Mr Gilbert Berrycloth, private secretary to Lord Kilbane, to The Most Hon'ble Lady Catherine 'Cat' Kilbane (daughter of Lucian and Matilda Barrington, The

Most Hon'ble Marquess and Marchioness of Montagu).

18th February 1845, Cawston Hall, Cawston, Norfolk.

Gabe took out his pocket watch—yet again—tucked it back in his waistcoat pocket, and recommenced pacing.

"Oh, do sit down," Helena complained. "You promised me you would not murder anyone and you're acting like a caged tiger. It's hardly soothing."

"I said I wouldn't murder anyone," he grumbled, not breaking stride. "I said nothing about maiming. I could do with a bit of maiming right now. Where the devil are they?"

"For heaven's sake!" she said, and shot her husband a look of pure exasperation. "We've arrived unannounced, they're newlyweds, and it's the middle of the afternoon. Where the devil do you think they are?"

Gabe stilled, his expression darkening. "That didn't help."

Helena threw up her hands. "Gabriel Knight, you faced down the duke and told him if Emmeline had stood by Wrexham, it was because she judged him worthy, and that Emmeline was no fool. So stop acting like you don't believe it yourself."

"Did you really say that, Papa?"

Gabe swung around to see their daughter had entered the magnificent drawing room the butler had shown them into. It was so cavernous that the Queen's Guard could have walked in and gone unnoticed. The scale of Cawston Hall had quite staggered Helena, who had grown up at Beverwyck and was not easily impressed.

"Emmeline!"

Helena's eyes prickled as father and daughter flew across the room to embrace each other.

"I'm so sorry I worried you," Emmeline said, holding on tight.

Gabe closed his eyes and Helena saw much of the tension that had made him such a bear all morning dissipate now he could see his daughter for himself. He took Emmeline by the shoulders and stood back, studying her intently.

"You're well?"

Emmeline smiled at him, and with that smile Helena relaxed too, for it was joyful and excited, and everything that she could have wished for.

"Very well, Papa."

"And what about me?" Helena gave a little sniff. "Don't I merit a kiss?"

"Oh, Mama!" Emmeline hurried over and hugged her tightly, kissing her cheek. "I'm so happy to see you both."

"Are you quite sure about that?" she asked dryly, raising one eyebrow.

Emmeline blushed scarlet, which confirmed Helena's suspicions. "Quite sure," Emmeline replied with dignity. "But do come along. I'm dying for you to meet Wrexham, only... you won't be angry with him, will you?"

She turned to look at her father then, her expression stern.

"I won't have you upsetting him, Papa. He's been through enough these past days."

Gabe's eyebrows almost hit his hairline and Helena bit her lip. Well, something had happened since they'd eloped and no mistake, for Emmeline would never have spoken to her father in such a forthright way before now.

"And what about the upset he's caused me?" Gabe demanded indignantly.

"I said I was sorry, and there was no other choice," Emmeline said, putting her chin up. "We would have much preferred to marry with you and the rest of our friends and family to celebrate, but we could not. The duke and Lord Cecil are trying to harm Wrexham, maybe even kill him. We could not take the chance. As it was, Wrexham's steward betrayed him and told the duke of our plans. He got Lord Cecil to follow us the entire way, and then... well, this morning was horrific, too."

Gabe's dark eyebrows drew together, concern in his eyes now. "Go on," he said.

They listened as Emmeline explained the shocking events of the morning, which had obviously caused the entire household a good deal of upset. Yet as her daughter spoke, Helena found her concerns for Emmeline receding somewhat, for despite the situation with Wrexham's father and half-brother, there was something else their youngest child revealed as she spoke. She was in love with her husband.

Perhaps Gabe heard it too, for he hugged Emmeline again, and when he spoke, it was to reassure her. "We're here now, and you have my word I will do all in my power to thwart the duke or anyone else."

"I know that," Emmeline said, her voice quavering. "I never doubted that, not for a moment. I only hoped you wouldn't kill him yourself first," she added wryly.

Gabe snorted. "Well, as to that, the jury is still out, but let us see what the man has to say for himself, shall we? Then I'll let you know."

"Be nice, Papa," Emmeline scolded, her expression fierce, and so like her father's when he was in a temper that Helena could only laugh.

"Oh, do come along. I, for one, am dying to meet my new son-in-law."

Emmeline had left Wrexham waiting in his study, a room he knew like the back of his hand and one he could be at ease in, though he did not look entirely at ease as she entered with her parents. He stood, stiffly formal, by the fireplace, but in the circumstances that was only to be expected. She went to him, taking his arm as he moved further into the room to greet them.

"Lady Helena, Mr Knight, welcome to Cawston Hall."

Papa was still looking fierce, but Mama answered, easing the way before he could open his mouth. "Thank you, Lord Wrexham, and what a splendid place it is. I confess I knew little about it, and did not realise Cawston was so magnificent."

"Thank you, my lady. I remember well what exquisite taste you had, so I take that as a great compliment," Wrexham said, smiling.

"Yes, well, now the niceties are done with, what have you got to say for yourself, Wrexham? Or did you wish to comment on the weather first?"

"Papa!" Emmeline protested. "You promised."

"I did no such thing," Gabriel retorted, folding his arms.

Emmeline opened her mouth, but Wrexham placed his hand over hers. "No, pet. Your father is well within his rights. I have no doubt he'd be rolling up his sleeves if not for my indisposition. Though I still have a handy right hook if you prefer to go a few rounds, only you may need to keep still to allow me a fighting chance," he added, lips quirking.

"Don't tempt me," Papa said darkly. "What do you mean by involving my daughter in this business?"

"I ought never to have done it," Wrexham said, his voice low. "I know that. I knew it then, and if I had not felt so desperate, and if Emmeline had not been so very kind and brave, perhaps I would have resisted. But I don't regret it. It was the best decision I ever made, or ever will make. My only concern, besides not getting murdered or put in an asylum myself, is keeping her safe."

"We shall keep each other safe," Emmeline said, squeezing his arm. "And I shall never regret it."

"Hmph." Papa glowered. "That sounds most endearing, but I would rather have a plan of action, a lot of capable men and preferably some guard dogs thrown in there too, if you don't mind, Emmeline."

"Not at all, Papa."

Emmeline smiled, knowing that her father's bark was always far harsher than his bite. She suspected the worst was over, and that was not because of what Wrexham had said, but how he had said it. They must have heard, as she had heard, the tenderness in his voice, the adoration, perhaps even love. She had married him on faith, believing she knew the kind of man he was, that she could love him enough for both of them, and because he needed her. There was no denying she had always wanted a marriage like her parents had. It was not one where they never exchanged a cross word, far from it, but they adored each other, stood by each other, and always settled their differences because they admired and understood each other. Over the past days, Emmeline had caught glimpses of that future for herself, with Wrexham, and she would let nothing, and no one take it from her.

"Why don't we all sit down and discuss things like rational people?" Mama suggested.

"Forgive me, my lady. I am remiss. Please do, take a seat. Of course, you will stay at Cawston Hall for as long as you wish. My people are seeing to your belongings. I imagine you will wish to change for dinner, but for the moment, may I offer you a drink?"

"God, yes," Papa said fervently. "I'll take a glass of cognac."

"Of course. My lady, a sherry, perhaps?"

"Cognac," Mama said firmly. "It's been a trying day."

Wrexham's lips quirked, and he inclined his head. "Quite understandable."

Emmeline followed Wrexham to the tantalus. "May I help?" she asked softly.

He chuckled and shook his head. "Pouring myself a drink was one of the first things I learned to manage, though I should be obliged if you handed them around."

"Of course."

"And you, pet, what will you have?"

"I am a married lady and can do as I please in my own home, so I shall have cognac too, if you aren't too horribly shocked," she added with a smile.

"Oh, horribly," he added gravely.

Unable to stop herself, Emmeline leaned in and kissed his cheek.

"What was that for?" he asked, turning towards her.

"Just because," she said softly.

"Do it again," he whispered.

Emmeline glanced back at her parents, who were studiously looking elsewhere, before pressing a swift kiss to his lips.

"Much better," he said with a sigh, and carried on pouring the drinks.

By the time the cognac had gone, and refills had been supplied, the atmosphere had thawed considerably.

"I dislike the notion that your half-brother is lingering nearby, waiting for an opportunity to make trouble," Papa said, his expression one with which Emmeline was familiar. It usually ended with setting boardrooms into uproar.

"No more than I, let me assure you," Wrexham replied dryly. "But what is there to be done?"

"We draw him out," Gabe said. "Arrange circumstances so he believes he has the perfect opportunity for mischief and let him hoist himself with his own petard."

Wrexham sat up, alert. "I'm listening."

Papa pulled a face. "Give me a chance, I've not had time to think of how to do it, only that we ought to. It's always better to take control in these circumstances."

"Piffle," Mama said, laughing. "In your opinion it is always preferable to take control, no matter the circumstances."

Papa shrugged. "Well, obviously, but only because most people don't know their arse from their elbow."

"Papa!" Emmeline exclaimed, not because she was shocked— Papa had ever been rather candid in his speech—but because Wrexham wasn't used to him. Her husband was laughing, though, and she let out a breath of relief.

"I couldn't agree more, Mr Knight, and as one who has of late found more difficulty than most in deciphering the two, I'd welcome your opinion."

"Don't give me that flannel," her father said gruffly. "You've been dealt a harsh blow, and from what I can see, you've handled it admirably, despite everything your father has done to undermine you. You should be proud of yourself—eloping with my daughter notwithstanding—but all the same. Well done, lad."

Wrexham grew very still, colour cresting his cheeks. It occurred to Emmeline in that moment that he had never had a father who had said such a thing to him, had never had a man he might look up to praise him for everything he had achieved. Her father, too, was not a man given to idle flattery and Wrexham knew it. The words had been sincere, and they had meant a great deal to her husband, who appeared to be struggling to reply.

"You are quite correct, he has done admirably, Papa, but honestly, you don't know the half of it," she said quickly, giving Wrexham a moment to bring himself back under control.

"You're happy," Mama said, her eyes shining, for she too had understood the impact of Papa's words.

Emmeline nodded. "Terribly," she replied with a smile.

Papa met her eyes, and his expression softened. "I couldn't have settled for anything less," he said. "But whilst I am reassured that this is not the disastrous decision I had feared, there is a question that I must ask you, Wrexham."

"Gabe," Mama said, an unmistakable warning note to her voice.

Wrexham shook his head. "No, my lady. I don't wish to hide anything. Ask your question, Mr Knight."

"I have never been one to pay much mind to society gossip, mostly because half of it is usually tattling about me or one of my daughters," he said wryly. "But nonetheless, you know as well as I of the tales that are circulating about you. What can you tell me?"

"Nothing to contradict them," Wrexham said, his tone clipped. "I wish I could."

Before she could think better of it, Emmeline sprang to her feet, her temper getting the better of her. "Well, I can contradict them! I have not seen the least sign to suggest you are anything less than sane. Bearing in mind all the information about your uncle came to you via your father, who has done all in his power to undermine and harm you, I should say we need a far less biased opinion."

"That's my girl," Papa said, his expression at once both admiring and amused.

Emmeline blushed and busied herself with smoothing down her skirts. "Well," she said, rather embarrassed if pleased by her father's praise. "I just think it bears a good deal more investigation."

"Agreed," Papa said. "And I believe I know just the man to ask."

Chapter 17

Inigo,

You mentioned recently a doctor running an asylum of the sort you had never previously encountered, who'd had remarkable success dealing with insanity and unstable patients.

I urgently need your help in a matter that must remain entirely confidential. Please come to Cawston Hall, Norfolk, as quickly as you are able, and bring the doctor with you. I would also appreciate any and all information regarding the Duke of Sefton's brother. The one who so notoriously lost his mind. It may have some bearing on the help I require of you and the good doctor would do well to acquaint himself with the case. You may also assure him I am prepared to compensate him generously for his time.

—Excerpt of a letter from Mr Gabriel Knight to Mr Inigo DeBeauvoir.

18th February 1845, The Black Bull, The Port of Folkestone, Kent.

Kilbane looked up as his secretary hurried into the room. Gilbert Berrycloth was short and slender and looked as though he'd only just begun shaving, though he was actually older than Kilbane himself. His fragile looks were deceiving, however, and hid a formidable will, an iron constitution and—when given sufficient incentive—an arsenal of foul language that could rival any member of her majesty's navy on their best, or worst, day. Just as well, Kilbane thought with amusement, as working for him required all those skills, often at the same time.

"All is packed and ready, my lord. Unless, perhaps—"

"No."

"But only consider—"

"No."

"I just thought that—"

"No."

Berrycloth let out a despondent sigh. "I know it is not my place to say so, my lord."

Kilbane snorted. "When did that ever stop you?"

The man tugged at his waistcoat and pushed his spectacles back up his nose, a nervous tic to which Kilbane was well used.

"Well, I just can't imagine being in her position. A young bride, abandoned by her husband the moment he said, 'I do'." He adopted a mournful expression and shook his head. "And she's such a lovely thing."

"You ought to have said so sooner," Kilbane remarked, lip curling. "You could have married her."

Berrycloth narrowed his eyes. "You don't mean that. You know you don't."

"Devil take you, man," he snapped. "Do stop being so damned tedious. The chit chased a rat into a hole and then acted surprised when she got bitten. It's her own damned fault. For once, I am entirely blameless, and I'm sick and tired of everyone making out like I did something wrong!"

"I did not say that you did wrong in marrying her, or that it was your fault, only—"

"Enough!" Kilbane stood and stalked to the window. The sooner he was away from England, the better. There was nothing and no one keeping him here. The one man he'd considered a friend had made it clear he wanted no more to do with him and the only things that had ever given him any satisfaction had lost any lingering appeal, and God above, he was tired of it all. So damned tired.

"I beg your pardon, my lord," Berrycloth said, all stiff and formal, which meant Kilbane would suffer retribution by a thousand cuts over the coming week. "I shall leave you to finish your breakfast in peace. If it should be of any interest to you, there is a letter here. From your *wife*."

And after setting off that last, perfectly timed explosion, the man left him alone.

Kilbane swung around to see the door closing, and the offending letter on the table next to his coffee cup.

"A pox on the bloody interfering female!"

He glared at it, though why he should be so thoroughly overwrought by the sight of the thing, he did not know. She'd said she would write to him, and so she had. God knew he believed her now when she said she was going to do something. Experience had taught him that much. Never in his life had he met anyone so wilful and reckless. Marrying him was bad enough, but frankly, he was astonished she'd *lived* this long. He could only imagine the number of scrapes, holes, ponds, and cliffs she'd had to be dragged out of or away from since the moment she could walk.

Well, it didn't matter. He'd told her he wouldn't read it and he wasn't about to. He'd throw it on the fire. Just as he'd said he would.

He turned his back on the vexing article and stared out of the window at the comings and goings before him, the early morning world going about its day, but his mind was still fixed on the bedamned bloody letter. He would not give her the satisfaction of reading it. No doubt she would attempt to make him feel guilty for leaving her, but little did she know he was doing her a kindness. She was a silly child with notions about him that were entirely wrong-headed and downright insane, but such foolish naivety would end up hurting her. *He* would hurt her. By accident, or design if he was in an especially bleak mood. Staying away was a mercy, little did she know it. He knew the only people who would notice he'd gone would cheer about it. With good reason too, he thought with a bitter smile.

Kilbane turned away from the window and sat down again to finish his coffee, ignoring the letter. He'd put it on the fire in a moment. He pulled a face on discovering the coffee was cold, and cursed Berrycloth anew. Instead, he picked up the book he'd been reading, finding his place, and reading the same page three times before he gave up and threw the wretched thing down on the table in disgust.

"Bollocks," he muttered furiously, and picked up the letter.

19th February 1845, Cawston Hall, Cawston, Norfolk.

Emmeline closed the bedroom door and made her way to the stairs for breakfast, fully aware she was wearing a disgustingly smug smile and not caring a whit. Now, she understood the way Alana had gazed at Harry when they'd got married. Life would be entirely perfect if only the duke and Lord Cecil would go away. Well, and if she could stop worrying about the possibility of her husband losing his mind. Oh, and the fact he was too concerned about that to sire a child....

Her smile faded abruptly, and she gave herself a mental shake. *No.* The duke and Wrexham's vile half-brother would be dealt with, and she was by no means convinced about her husband's future. So, as far as she was concerned, everything would be perfect until she had incontrovertible proof she was wrong. There was no other way to carry on. With that little breakdown averted, Emmeline carried on her way, only to be stopped in her tracks as a deep *woof* echoed up the stairs from the great hall. Surely her father had only been joking about guard dogs?

Leaning over the minstrel's gallery to look at the entrance hall below, Emmeline saw an elegant woman with fiery red hair, dressed in a lush dark blue gown and pelerine. She seemed exceedingly familiar. Hurrying to the staircase, Emmeline gave a little cry of delight as the young woman looked up and she recognised her friend Cara and her husband, Lord Latimer.

"Cara!" she cried, hurrying down the stairs.

"Emmeline?" Cara stared at her with undisguised shock. "What on earth are you doing here?"

Emmeline hesitated as she reached the bottom of the stairs, blushing as she realised. "Oh. Of course, you don't know."

Cara hurried over and took her hands. "Don't know what?"

There was no gentle way of breaking the news in the circumstances. "I... well, I'm Lady Wrexham. We eloped."

Cara's hand flew to her mouth as she gasped, and her obvious distress upset the enormous beast that was her beloved Sultan. He stood, barking and staring at Cara with obvious anxiety, until Lord Latimer silenced him.

"Enough, Sultan. She's quite well," he said, stroking the dog's head affectionately. "Sit down."

The dog sat, gazing at his master with adoration.

"Eloped. With Lord Wrexham," Cara repeated faintly.

Emmeline nodded, offering her friend a tentative smile. "Perhaps you'd like to come and sit down? Have you had breakfast yet? I haven't and I'm famished. Come and join me and I'll explain everything."

Several cups of tea later, and Emmeline had outlined everything that had happened. Her parents had also joined them, and her father and Latimer seemed to get on like a house on fire.

"I'm so happy for you," Cara said, grinning broadly. "It's so romantic, well, apart from his loathsome half-brother and the duke, and the eyeballs. Ick. I shall struggle to forget that image," she added with a shudder.

"You're not alone," Emmeline said, feeling her breakfast churn in her stomach.

"But apart from all that, it *is* terribly romantic," Cara insisted, making Emmeline chuckle. "And you're happy. I can tell you are. You love him?"

Emmeline nodded. "I do."

Cara gave a happy sigh and pulled absently at Sultan's ears, the big dog having settled himself beside Cara hoping to be fed scraps from the table.

"But why are you here?" Emmeline asked. "Was Wrexham expecting you?"

"Oh, no." Cara shook her head. "We were visiting friends in Norwich, and we overheard someone talking about Wrexham and how he was back at Cawston Hall. Well, Wolf has had it in mind to visit and see if there was anything he could do for him. Wrexham got us out of the most awful fix with the duke, as you know, and we have always wanted to repay him, for he did not know Wolf was his nephew then. He was simply being kind."

"You give me too much credit, Lady Latimer," announced a deep and familiar voice from behind them. "I did it to vex my father. My motivation for a good many of my actions, I'm afraid."

Emmeline turned to see Wrexham with Humboldt, who was guiding him to the head of the table.

"Wrexham." Cara's husband stood and crossed the room.

"Lord Latimer," Humboldt said to her husband quietly, and took a step back as Wrexham held out his hand.

"Ah, my new nephew, though that still seems odd to me, as you are the elder of the two of us. However, this is a pleasant surprise, Latimer. You are most welcome."

"I hope so," Latimer said gruffly. "Though I would ask you to call me Wolf. I am still getting used to the title."

Wrexham inclined his head. "With pleasure. As we are family, you may address me as Uncle Rex." His lips quirked, and he held out his hand to Wolf, who shook it, his expression intent. Ignoring Wrexham's amusement at the family connection, he got straight to the point.

"I know what it is to have a devil for a father. I will do anything I can to help you. Just name it."

Wrexham looked quite taken aback by this and he frowned, shaking his head. "But you don't know me at all. I offered you a few words that got you out of a sticky situation, it cost me nothing to do so. This is entirely different. This means making an enemy of your grandfather and Lord Cecil. It may even be dangerous."

Wolf snorted and patted him on the shoulder. "You might want to take a bit of time to find out about my past, *Uncle*. You've had a lot on your plate, so I don't blame you for not knowing about it. Just rest assured, I'm on your side, and that's the only place anyone ever wants me to be."

"Latimer is rather well known in certain circles, Wrexham," her father added, looking amused. "Especially in Paris. There they knew him as *Le Loup Noir.*"

"The black wolf?" Wrexham translated, still looking perplexed. "Oh, wait. I have heard talk of... *Oh.* That's you?"

"For my sins," Wolf said with a wicked glint in his eyes. He leaned towards Wrexham. "There's a lot of those."

Wrexham gave a delighted bark of laughter. "Well, now things really are getting interesting."

The rest of the morning passed pleasantly, as far as Emmeline was concerned. Her parents were here, and her father seemed to warm to Wrexham as the day wore on. At first glance, the family connection between Wolf and Wrexham seemed unlikely, with Wrexham's golden beauty and Wolf's far harsher, darker looks in fierce contrast. But now and then there was something, a tilt of the head, a gesture or expression, and it made Emmeline smile.

"Wolf is so happy to have family to call his own," Cara said quietly. "It means a lot to him. He never said much about it, but he feared Wrexham would not recognise the connection."

"He's not like that," Emmeline said at once. "Wrexham is generous and kind and honourable, which is why it's so infuriating his father is such an obnoxious brute."

Cara nodded. "Indeed, though he seems to be bearing up," she added with a knowing smile. "He's besotted with you."

Emmeline perked up at this information. "What makes you say so?"

Cara laughed, shaking her head. "You goose! Don't tell me you doubted it? He lights up the moment he hears your voice."

"You really think so?" Emmeline asked, grinning like a lunatic and aware she was fishing.

"The poor man is head over ears for you, Emmeline, you daft creature."

The look on Emmeline's face must have been a picture, for Cara snorted with amusement, but their laughter faded as they realised the surrounding conversation had taken a sombre turn.

"So, we'll bait a trap, apparently leaving Wrexham alone and giving Cecil and the duke the perfect opportunity to grab him," her father said.

Emmeline's stomach lurched in horror.

"No!" she exclaimed. "No. We cannot risk the duke coming anywhere near him."

"It's all right, pet," Wrexham said, his voice soothing, but Emmeline was not soothed.

She got up and went to him, kneeling before him and taking his hand.

"It is certainly not all right. Not the least bit. I won't risk you. If they took you away, I…." She trailed off, aware she had an audience, and she was getting emotional.

"Emmeline, we won't put him in any danger. We said *apparently* leaving him alone. In reality, we won't do anything of the sort," her father said gently.

"I'll be with him, my lady," Wolf said, his expression grave. "I give you my word of honour, no one will harm him."

Emmeline frowned, hating the idea, but knowing she could not dismiss it without knowing more. So, she nodded and glanced back at her husband to see his expression was one that boded ill and immediately understood his pride was taking a blow.

"Rex," she whispered. "I know how this must gall you, but we all need the help of friends and family at difficult times. *This* is a difficult time, and I love you too dearly to take the slightest risk with your safety. Please, let Lord Latimer help you, for my sake."

He stilled at her words, the sensation that he was concentrating hard upon her difficult to ignore, but he nodded his agreement.

Emmeline let out a breath of relief. It was still a horrible idea, but at least he would not face it alone.

Chapter 18

My lord,

I hope you are well and have now settled comfortably in your accommodation in France. Are you staying with friends, or have you rented the property for your stay? Not that I expect you to answer, but it seems dull to carry on an entirely one-sided conversation so I shall pretend there is a chance you may answer me one day and carry on in the usual manner.

Did you receive my last two letters? I wish you would at least let me know if you read them or throw them in the fire as you promised. You do not know how much comfort it would give me to know that you read my words and perhaps think of me now and then. Even if it is only to mutter crossly about the annoying brat you married.

I promised myself I would not write again until the end of the week, but I find I am so excited I cannot help myself. Today I visited Connaught Place for the first time, and I have fallen in love! Of course, it is terribly gloomy and far too dark, and needs a good deal of refurbishing. Not that I mean to take issue with your taste, my lord. Everything is of the finest quality and most comfortable, only, well, to be frank, it looks like a pleasure house. Not that I've ever seen one, naturally, but if I should ever conjure the image, this is it. I don't have the slightest doubt you did it on purpose to vex everyone, for you have only ever displayed excellent taste in your wardrobe and it confounds me to discover the same man decorated this horror. I realise now I have taken issue with your taste, but only because I do not believe this is it. Anyway, I intend to save this beautiful house from your desire to offend everyone and make it everything that is elegant. You did say I could. You must inform me at once if you do not wish me to make changes and I shall, of course, desist. Only do hurry for I intend to begin at once.

If it eases your mind, I promise not to touch your study. I would not do so, as it is the only room in the house that does not seem to have been decorated with vengeance in mind. I feel this was your sanctuary, the place where you allowed yourself to be yourself. It still carries your scent.

I shall always write my letters to you here, where I may feel some small connection to the man I married and hope for better things in the future.

—Excerpt of a letter from The Most Hon'ble Lady Catherine 'Cat' St Just, Marchioness of Kilbane (daughter of The

Most Hon'ble Lucian and Matilda Barrington, Marquess and Marchioness of Montagu) to her husband, Ciarán St Just, Marquess of Kilbane.

23ʳᵈ February 1845, Cawston Hall, Cawston. Norfolk.

"I don't like it," Emmeline said for the fifth time that morning as Lennox tied Wrexham's cravat.

For the moment, Wrexham held his tongue. Lennox had only just forgiven him, and moving so much as an eyelash while the man was concentrating on the Osbaldiston knot would be seen as a direct affront to his valet's talents. He wasn't about to risk it.

Emmeline was fretting about the plan they were due to execute. Wrexham, however, was eager to get it done and get his blasted father and Cecil out of their lives, but he could not dismiss Emmeline's concerns, and that she was so anxious about him warmed him more than he could express.

"How do we know the duke's men won't outnumber yours?" she persisted. "How do we know your wretched brother won't be armed? How do we—"

"Leave us," Wrexham murmured to Lennox, once the delicate procedure was complete.

"Yes, my lord." Lennox removed himself with haste, leaving Wrexham to soothe his wife. He could hear her pacing, sense her agitation in the quick, clipped way she spoke. She was afraid for him because she loved him.

He wondered if she had the least idea of what those words had done to him? She had given them so casually, as though it were the most obvious and natural thing in the world, yet to Wrexham, they had exploded in his heart with the force of cannon-fire.

I love you too dearly to take the slightest risk.

Of course, she had been placating him because his pride was smarting. He wasn't a fool. He had known that much, and his brain had immediately told him that was the only reason she'd said it, she was simply trying to keep him calm by flattering him and playing the affectionate wife. Except he had believed nonsense about his wife before, when his instincts had told him otherwise. His instincts told him she had meant those words. They had been given too naturally, and with too much sincerity, to be mere flattery. He could not account for it, but his heart thudded in the oddest way, his breath snagging in his throat every time he remembered it, which was a dozen times an hour if he was being completely honest.

He had heard the words before. Before he'd lost his sight, women told him they loved him often enough, and yet he had never quite believed them. Love seemed to be a commodity that must be paid for with jewels and carriages and whatever else the lady wished for. Not that Wrexham had ever begrudged them, he had enjoyed their company and enjoyed pleasing them too, but he had never allowed himself to return the emotion or trust in their words, even though he had wanted to at times. He was uncertain why. There had certainly been little enough of it in his life, so he ought to have welcomed it.

His father had made his animosity clear from a young age, though Wrexham had never quite figured out why that was. He'd given up trying by the time he was twelve, resigned to being reviled by his sire. His mother had been a fleeting figure in his life and had died when he was barely five. Memories of her were vague and hard to grasp. Had she ever told him she loved him? If she had, he could not remember it. Delia and Genevieve had been his only sources of affection, he thought with a smile. They had been bright spots in his life, and he was only grateful that the duke had absolutely no interest in his female offspring... unless he could sell them to the highest bidder, of course. Wrexham had not known Genevieve until she was ten, and her parents had dumped her with the duke and then later died. But the duke had no time for his granddaughter, so she had come to Cawston Hall. His little sister, Delia, had been deposited at Cawston when she was barely three years old, and Wrexham had loved her at once. She had adored him too, and was likely the only person in his life who had loved him unconditionally and with no restraint.

Now, though, there was Emmeline. His heart did another odd thud in his chest as he heard his wife still pacing and talking earnestly about all the reasons he ought not to go along with her father's plan.

"—what if they know it's a trap? They may have other plans that we know nothing about and—"

"Emmeline."

"—and what if they hurt you? Oh, what should I do? I could not bear it! I will murder your father, for one, and—"

"Emmeline."

She paused, and he heard the rustle of her skirts as she grew closer.

"Yes?"

"Come here," he said, unable to keep the smile from his face.

"I am here," she said, sounding perplexed.

He shook his head. "No. Closer."

"Oh." She slid her arms about his waist and hugged him, laying her head on his shoulder.

Wrexham held her to him and closed his eyes, breathing in the scent of orange blossom. "One day we shall go to the Mediterranean. To Italy. I shall show you the sea. It is so blue, pet, you will adore it, and we shall visit every beautiful site and magnificent view, and sit beneath orange and lemon trees and picnic, and you will show me the world through your eyes, and I shall see it all anew."

"That sounds wonderful, but you hate travelling," she said, and he sensed her looking up at him.

Wrexham shook his head and raised his hand to stroke her hair. "Not with you. With you, everything is possible again. I don't want to live in a cage any longer, not even if it is tempting to do so with you. I won't keep you a prisoner as my father did me."

"I should never feel that way!" she exclaimed. "I should be content to live here with you for the rest of my days, Wrexham. So long as we are together, I am happy. This is enough," she said, and once again he heard the ring of truth behind the words and any hidden corner of his heart that had not been entirely hers, gave up the fight and surrendered on the spot.

He huffed out an exasperated breath and lowered his head, resting his cheek atop her head. "You are the most maddening creature," he protested, uncertain whether or not to laugh. "Every time I think I can do and say what I must without becoming entirely too sentimental, you do something to completely unravel me!"

"I don't understand," she said, sounding bewildered.

"Then let me make it plain for you, pet." He moved his hands carefully to frame her face, finding his throat suddenly tight. "I am yours, Emmeline. Entirely. You hold my heart in those delicate hands of yours. I love you, and I won't ever let anyone take me away from you or you from me. You have given me something to fight for, something to live for, and I shall never be able to show you how grateful I am to you for that. But I shall try, by loving you with all my heart, for as long as I may live."

There was a stunned silence and Wrexham was aware of his heart beating in his ears, of Emmeline's quickened breathing, the fine tremors running through her frame. Were those good signs? He wasn't certain, and he had never felt more exposed or vulnerable. For a man who had recently lost his sight, that was no small admission.

"Rex," she said at last, her voice quavering.

"Yes, pet?"

She said nothing else, just pressed her mouth hard to his, her arms wrapping around his neck and holding on so tight she was likely to throttle him. She would certainly ruin all Lennox's good work. He didn't give a damn.

Wrexham kissed her back, his arms pulling her against him, holding her as close as he could until she broke the kiss, breathing hard.

"I love you, too, Wrexham. I think I fell in love with you at my aunt's dinner party and I've been hopelessly smitten ever since."

His lips quirked, and she laughed. "Oh, you may well look smug, you dreadful man. I'm scared to death something will happen today, that it will go wrong and—"

He kissed her again, only releasing her when he was certain she would not speak again.

"You've made your feelings clear," he said gently. "But I need to do this. I'll have Wolf with me, and the plan is sound. You give my father and Cecil too much credit. They are merely bullies, and before I went blind, I ran rings around them. I won't let them get the better of me now. I swear it. I have only lost my sight, not my brain. Not yet, at least."

She drew in a sharp breath, and he knew he ought not to have said that last bit, but before she could fly up into the boughs, there was a knock at the door, followed by Bunting's voice.

"My lord, your guests have arrived."

"Thank you. I shall be down shortly," Wrexham called.

"Guests?" Emmeline asked. "What guests?"

"Your father's idea," he said, smiling at her. "I was not entirely happy with him at first, when he explained what he'd done, but, well... come along and let us see what you think."

Emmeline went with Wrexham down the grand double staircase that led to the entrance hall. On all sides, huge, framed portraits of his ancestors looked on as they passed, but Emmeline was in far too much of a dither to study them as she usually did. Wrexham loved her. She was in a daze, still struggling to comprehend his beautiful words. He loved her. A little bubble of giddy laughter escaped her, and Wrexham turned his head towards her.

"Did you say something?"

"No," she squeaked, biting her lip and thankful he could not see the stupid expression on her face as she gazed adoringly at him.

She must look like Sultan staring up at Cara or Wolf. Really, she must pull herself together before they met whoever it was her father had invited, but she was caught between hysterical laughter and sobbing. A sick sensation swirled beneath her joy as she considered the plan to trick Wrexham's father into exposing his subterfuge. She could not rid herself of the idea that, if something went wrong, the duke or Lord Cecil could harm or even kill her husband. They had come so far together in such a short time. The idea that those two awful men could possibly take it all from her was simply unbearable.

Bunting met them at the bottom of the stairs and led them to the drawing room. As they drew closer, Emmeline heard voices, her father's and... a man that sounded familiar.

They entered the room and moved to greet their guests.

"Mr DeBeauvoir," Emmeline said in surprise, welcoming the man with a smile. "How lovely to see you. I hope you and your family are well. How is Kathy?"

The man was tall and dark, his features rather hawk-like, his eyes bright and shining with intelligence. Hardly surprising when he was purported to have one of the finest minds in the country. A natural philosopher, occupied with all things scientific, Emmeline could not fathom what Inigo De Beauvoir could be doing here.

"Kathy is well, thank you and sends you much love, alongside a letter which is at least ten pages long, if the weight is anything to go on," he said with a smile. "We almost missed our train, as she insisted we wait for her to finish it."

Emmeline laughed. "I shall look forward to sitting down with the epic tale, but much as I am delighted to see you, I confess I cannot imagine why Papa invited you."

Mr DeBeauvoir turned to look at her father, one dark eyebrow raising. "You failed to explain to your daughter."

"She's become remarkably fierce of late, Inigo," her father said dryly. "I thought it prudent to wait."

"Wait for what? What is going on?" Emmeline demanded, unsettled now.

"I don't believe it is Mr DeBeauvoir whom your father needed to come, so much as the gentleman with him," Wrexham told her, and it was only then that Emmeline looked past DeBeauvoir to see a small, neat and rather serious looking man of perhaps five and sixty, dressed in the sombre attire of a medical man.

"Wrexham," she said, reaching for his hand and holding on. "Who is that?"

"That, my love, is Dr Boniface, and he has come to decide if I am a lunatic or not."

Chapter 19

My lady,

I hope this finds you in excellent health.

I recently received a letter from Mr Bright, who sounded delighted by the most ambitious plans you have outlined to renovate Connaught Place. To illustrate his obvious excitement, I must explain that I have never once received correspondence from him that was not devoted entirely to financial affairs. Men of business are, by nature, sober creatures, but the way he described your eye for colour and flair for design was most remarkable. I await more information about your progress with bated breath.

*Unfortunately, that is not the sole reason for this missive today. Lord Kilbane bid me contact you to 'demand you cease writing endless letters'. I have pointed out that as this is the crux of the agreement he made with you, he has no right to make such demands, and **you have no reason whatsoever** to do as he bids. However, as I am in his employ, I am duty bound to obey him in all things. Having done as he asks, I suggest you cast this scrap of paper onto the fire where it* *belongs and carry on, regardless. I am, of course, merely a lowly employee and in no position to advise either you or your husband.*

If there is the least thing I can do for you, please remember, I am at your disposal.

—Excerpt of a letter to The Most Hon'ble Lady Catherine 'Cat' St Just, Marchioness of Kilbane (daughter of The Most Hon'ble Lucian and Matilda Barrington, Marquess and Marchioness of Montagu) from her husband's private secretary, Mr Gilbert Berrycloth.

23ʳᵈ February 1845, Cawston Hall, Cawston. Norfolk.

Wrexham felt his wife's scowl. How, he was uncertain, but he had become attuned to her moods and knew immediately that she was vexed.

"Papa, you cannot be serious," she said, confirming his suspicions by her less than conciliatory tone.

"Why not?" her father replied, entirely unruffled. "If I wanted to build a bridge and someone opposed the plans on safety grounds, I would have reports done to show whether they were sound. Well, the duke has done his best to insinuate that Wrexham is mad. All I am doing is endeavouring to prove the opposite to counter his claims once and for all."

"I suppose that sounds reasonable," she said grudgingly. "But how do we know this man can be trusted? For all we know, he's in the duke's pocket."

"Emmeline!" her father said in shock, but Wrexham felt only a wave of adoration for this woman who would not even let her own father act unless she was certain it was in her husband's best interests.

"I beg your pardon, Dr Boniface," Emmeline said stiffly. "I mean no offence, but the duke has already turned my husband's steward of five years against him, and I do not know you at all."

"If I might speak," Mr DeBeauvoir said. "You *can* trust him, Emmeline. I give you my word. I know you have heard all the horrific tales of the way asylums are run and the poor devils who dwell within them, but Dr Boniface's establishment is nothing like—"

"He runs an asylum?" she exclaimed, and Wrexham jolted as she grabbed hold of his arm, clinging to him as if she feared they would drag him off before her eyes.

"Emmeline, you silly goose. Surely you do not believe your own father would do that to me?" he said, seeking her hand and covering it with his own.

"N-No," she said. "I don't, but that doesn't mean I trust *him*."
"Lady Wrexham," said an unfamiliar voice, who Wrexham assumed must be Boniface himself. "I should like to put your mind at rest. In the first place, I should never commit your husband unless he was a danger to himself or others, or wished to be committed, as many of our patients do. That is obviously not the case, and whilst I still need to interview Lord Wrexham, I can find no outward signs of lunacy in the very reasonable sounding man before me, and they are generally very easy to identify, so I beg you will not fear me or my methods."

"You do understand the idea is to prove he *is* sane, Emmeline," her father said, sounding a little exasperated.

"Obviously," she retorted, though she did not sound at all reassured.

"Do you doubt I can do it?" Wrexham asked with a wry smile. Emmeline hit him. Not hard, but it seemed to answer the question. He grinned. "Very well, doctor. Lead on and let us get this over with."

23rd February 1845, Beverwyck, London.

"Must you go?" Aggie said with a sigh.

Fred smiled at her, and her heart did a ridiculous lurch. Heavens, she was a ninny, but there was no help for it. She loved him, even to the point of asking stupid questions, because of course he must go. The university had reopened, and he was due to catch the train back to Oxford.

"I wish I could say no," he replied ruefully. "But the other fellows will be here shortly. We're all travelling to Paddington together."

Aggie nodded, making a mental note to be well out of the way before those idiots arrived. How Fred bore them she did not know, but apparently his friends weren't bad sorts, just 'a tad excitable' and 'occasionally reckless.' If Aggie had her way, she'd invite them to be reckless enough to jump out the nearest upper floor window, but she held her tongue on that point. Besides which, she couldn't think of anything at all when Fred took her in his arms.

"I'll miss you," he said, his eyes shining with everything he felt for her.

How he did it, she did not know. After that initial declaration, he had been the perfect beau. He simply said what he felt without a qualm, telling her how very much he loved her, of his plans for their future, and never missing an opportunity to compliment her beauty, or her cleverness. He was so much braver than she was, and so very good. Fred wore his heart on his sleeve and cared not a jot what anyone thought of it. Sometimes that frightened her. He was just so very perfect, and she… was not. Fred was entirely honourable, decent and loyal, and the very best friend. Except they were not just friends anymore.

"Might I kiss you goodbye, Aggie?"

She smiled, still amused that he would not do so without asking first, for surely he knew by now she would never refuse a kiss.

"If you go away without kissing me, I shall punish you by not writing," she said, attempting to look fierce.

"Oh, but that would be cruel, Agatha, when you know it would break my heart," he said, giving her big puppy dog eyes.

She snorted. "Call me Agatha again and I shall stomp all over it," she grumbled, though it was hard to keep a straight face when he pouted.

"Oh, stop it," she said, laughing. "You big lummox."

He grinned and then wiped the smile off her face by kissing her. Oh, and he was good at that, too. Perfect, in fact. His lips were soft and gentle, but not too gentle, firm enough to let her know there was more, but that he was behaving himself because he was a gentleman. He kissed her until she was giddy and clinging to him. When he let her go at last, she could hardly breathe, let alone speak.

"Oh," she managed, and by the time she had enough self-control to open her eyes, it was to see him looking pleased with himself. "Stop looking so smug."

"Can't," he said, preening.

"You are perfectly horrid," she said with a sigh.

"And you adore me."

"I do. It's hopeless."

The sound of wheels on gravel and the deep, booming voices of England's finest young men stirred Aggie from her little happy daze.

"You'd best go," she said, giving him a little push. "Or they'll come looking for you."

"Won't you come and speak to them?"

"No, thank you," she said politely, refraining from telling him she'd rather stick pins in her eyes than spend a moment with his awful friends.

"But I want to show you off. I'm a lucky devil, you see, and I want them all to know it."

"No," she said firmly. "Now, run along and be a clever fellow, and do it quickly so you can come home again."

"All right, then," he said, gazing at her. "You will write to me?"

"Yes."

"Every day?"

"Certainly not."

He pouted.

"Every other day is quite sufficient," she said, trying to look severe and failing miserably because he was adorable, and she was in a sorry way and no mistake.

"Very well, you cruel, cruel woman. But they had better be long letters, with lots of swooning and descriptions of how pitiful you are without me."

He stole another kiss and hurried out of the library. Aggie moved to the window and looked down to see the louts waiting for him outside. As Fred appeared, they gave a cheer that could have woken the dead, and Aggie cracked open the window to get a better look. There was a good deal of backslapping and friendly punching. She rolled her eyes. Men were odd creatures.

Two footmen hefted Fred's trunk out to the waiting carriage and fastened it in place with the others.

"Oh, devil take it. I forgot that blasted essay old Carter asked for. I was trying to finish it this morning," Fred cursed.

"Don't tell me you left it to the last minute? Not like you," remarked a big, burly fellow Aggie recognised as Mr Algernon Scrivener.

Fred shrugged, grinning. "I had other things on my mind. Anyway, I'd best run and grab it. Don't go without me."

Aggie shook her head affectionately as he bounded up the stairs to the front door, taking the steps three at a time. She was about to close the window and retreat when one of the other lads spoke.

"You know why he was distracted, don't you? It's that wretched girl. Miss *Smith*. She's been staying here. That's why he's all starry-eyed."

Aggie glowered at the speaker, who was scrawny and spotty and looked as if a strong breeze could knock him down. If she were a man, she would have knocked him down herself.

"No, she's Miss De Montluc now, and she's a pretty enough distraction," said another, wagging his eyebrows and making a leering expression that made Aggie want to go down there and punch him in the nose too.

"Yes, except he's not just dallying with the chit, he's courting her."

"No!" Exclamations of shock came from everyone but Scrivener. "You can't be serious?"

Scrivener assured his revolting acolytes it was true. "And if you know what's good for you, don't you say a word against her. He'll crucify you. Believe me, I know," he said, shaking his head.

"But Scrivs, she was born in the gutter. I know she's a prime article, and I don't blame him for having his fun with her, but he can't be thinking of *marrying* her? She's not the kind of creature a fellow *marries*, she's a nobody. It will *ruin* him. No one will even receive them."

Aggie stiffened, her breath catching at the cruel words.

"She's the Comte de Villen's daughter," Scrivener said, his tone sharp. "And if you say a word against her in *his* hearing, I'd lay odds on never seeing you again. Haven't you heard what they say about him?"

"Well, exactly. I mean, perhaps he *is* her natural father, but she's still a bastard and he's hardly respectable either, what with that business of the elopement. Besides which, she was raised in the Rookery. They say the comte picked her off the street when she was ten. I mean, imagine children with a mother like that. Bad blood, Scrivs. They'll probably all turn out to be a lot of pickpockets and murderers."

"Got to admit it, Scrivs. It's a terrible *mesalliance*. We ought to save him from himself and say something. Marriages like that never work, not when they're so unequal. He's the son of a duke, for the love of God. And not just any duke. *Bedwin!* He might not be the heir, but the way Blackstone is carrying on, he'll not live past five and thirty. Fred could marry anyone he chose, and she's nothing but a cheap doxy for all her fat dowry and fine clothes. He should let some common Cit marry her and find a real lady."

Aggie smothered her gasp, tears pricking at her eyes. She had known exactly what these men were, and what they thought of her, but to have it illustrated so vividly was more than she could bear.

"You do as you please," Scrivener said, his expression implacable. "But you say a word against her, and he'll murder you. Frampton tried to tell him something of the sort just before he came down here and he's spent most of the last week in the infirmary. Last term, Harrison made some innocent remark about her, and Fred broke his nose. So, you do as you please, but don't say I didn't warn you."

Aggie closed the window and staggered away, unable to listen to anything more. Her throat was tight, and her lungs felt squeezed in her chest. Fred had been fighting to defend her. *Her* Fred, who was the gentlest, kindest man she had ever known. Her heart thudded painfully as she saw the truth. His friends were right. It was a *mesalliance* and, if they persisted and married, Fred would spend the rest of his days fighting over her, defending her from disparaging comments. Since they were children, she had lost count of the times he had stepped in to protect her. A woman with her past would never be a wife he could take pride in, could take to events and parties without having to ignore spiteful whispers. It would make him wretched, and it would make her angry until she behaved in a manner no lady would, and ruined everything entirely.

It wouldn't work. It could never work. She thought perhaps she had always known it at heart, but she had not wanted to see it, nor to admit the truth. But those vile young men had spelled it out and, in a way, they had done her a kindness. They had protected Fred just as they had wished to do.

Perhaps one day he would be grateful for it, too.

23rd February 1845, Cawston Hall, Cawston, Norfolk.

Wrexham held his temper and answered every question Dr Boniface asked him with as much patience and good humour as he could manage. They'd been at it for over two hours, however, and he was ill used to having his faculties probed, or having to answer so many inane questions. As the morning wore on, his calm demeanour became increasing hard to hold on to when the doctor began repeating questions he'd already answered.

"And can you tell me, my lord, what is your usual morning routine? Talk me through an average day."

"I already did that and, surprisingly, the routine is still the same. I get up, bathe, eat breakfast, and then go about my business," he said evenly, wondering how much more of it he could stand.

"And have recent events given you an aversion to bathing?"

"Why? Do I smell? I can think of no other reason to ask me that three times over."

"Oh, no, my lord." The doctor chuckled. "At least, it is an altogether pleasant scent, reminiscent of an English garden. But such a disturbing event would unsettle the strongest of constitutions. Nightmares have not troubled you? Dark thoughts? Notions of doing yourself harm?"

"No," said Wrexham, though he might do the doctor an injury if this carried on much longer.

"Really? You've not thought of the events of that morning at all?"

"Well, obviously I've thought of it. I lost my sight, not my imagination. The image is a repulsive one, but it is not in my nature to dwell."

"So, you do not dwell upon it?"

"No. I do not."

"Not at all?"

"Not at all."

"Is there anything you do dwell upon?"

"For example?"

"You tell me."

"If I knew what you were asking me, I would not have demanded you clarify," Wrexham snapped as the last thread of his temper frayed. "For heaven's sake, I've had enough of this incessant questioning. You seem to have run out of ideas yourself, or you would not be repeating the same questions over again."

There was another soft chuckle, and the doctor sighed. "No, indeed, and I wondered how long it would take before you reached the end of your tether. You are a patient man, my lord, and I beg you will forgive me for having tried you so sorely."

Wrexham sat up, frowning. "You mean to say you were baiting me?"

"I'm afraid so."

"What the devil for?" he demanded.

"Because your sanity was not the only thing I was asked to verify."

Wrexham considered that. "Mr Knight," he grumbled.

"Quite so. This property is far removed from his own, and I confess Mr Knight strikes me as a doting and protective father. He wished to be reassured that his daughter was in safe hands, and not with a man who was easily provoked."

"I trust I passed?" Wrexham asked, though he could not fault her father for his concern. If he had to put Emmeline into another's keeping, he'd give the bastard the third degree, too.

"Undoubtedly, my lord. Indeed, I was hard pressed to decide which of us would break first. I was becoming thoroughly tired of my own voice."

"Hmph," Wrexham replied, somewhat mollified. "And as to the question of my sanity?"

"That was little in question before we entered the room," the doctor said, which meant the past two hours had been a colossal waste of time.

Yet, for all that, Wrexham felt a surge of relief, any irritation disappearing along with it.

"You are in fine fettle, my lord, and I should be happy to put that in writing should the need arise. I might also reassure you that Mr Knight has been very generous in becoming a benefactor to my little hospital and, more to the point, I despise bullies. You need not fear me being a man who would sell his principles for a bag of coin. I would rather die."

Wrexham nodded, pleased to hear it, and grateful to Mr Knight once more for thinking ahead. "Thank you, doctor. That *is* reassuring. However, might I ask your opinion?"

"Of course."

The doctor waited whilst Wrexham gathered his thoughts. Much as he needed to know, and as much as today's interview had been successful, the future was something he viewed with trepidation. Yet, if he was to follow in his uncle's footsteps, he must ensure that Emmeline was safe and cared for. "Did Mr Knight inform you of my uncle's situation?"

"He did indeed. Mr Knight also employed his considerable resources to furnish me with as much family history as he could lay his hands on."

"Did he, by God?" Wrexham was torn between indignation at the effrontery of the man and a deep-seated relief that the devil was on his side.

The doctor laughed. "Mr Knight does not strike me as a man accustomed to being told no," he said wryly. "However, in this instance it is all to the good. I believe you have been concerned that your blindness is linked to lunacy and that it is an inherited condition?"

"Yes," Wrexham replied, for there was no point in protesting the point.

"Well, your family tree is considerable and complex, to put it mildly, and with the time available to us, the information Mr Knight gathered was quite remarkable. From what I can tell, it seems that whilst there have been several cases of blindness within your bloodline, your uncle is the only one who displayed any signs of true lunatic behaviour."

"But Father said there were more. He cited aunts and—"

"If I might stop you. Erratic behaviour in those who have lost their sight is often attributed to mental deficiencies, when it has

243

been my observation that those patients are often disorientated for a multitude of reasons, not least the initial trauma of losing their sight. Especially if it was sudden. Also they have no way of distinguishing day and night. Perhaps you have experienced this yourself, waking in the night and thinking it is daytime, and getting up to discover the house is asleep. Now a man like you with an army of servants is less likely to make such a mistake, but a fellow who must see to himself might be observed to be up and dressed and eating breakfast in the middle of the night. Disabusing him of the notion he is in the wrong might cause him distress and confusion, and from these circumstances, assumptions of disturbed minds are easy to cling to."

Heat crawled up the back of Wrexham's neck as he remembered several such incidents in the first year after losing his sight. His father had been quick to tell him this was the first sign of him losing his mind, and he, already grieving the loss of the life he had known, had not questioned it.

Emmeline had.

"But my uncle," Wrexham persisted, too terrified to allow himself hope until he was certain.

"On having spoken to a nurse who tended to your uncle in his last days, I have come to certain conclusions, but I am afraid they are not happy observations."

"Go on," Wrexham said, his voice hoarse as his heart picked up speed.

"After hearing the nurse's firsthand experience, and reading the doctor's file associated with your uncle—and truly I do not wish to know how Mr Knight got his hands on that private document—it is my professional opinion that your uncle was driven to madness. He appears to have been an opium addict when the malady struck, a habit he was unable to give up. This habit, far from being curtailed as I would have insisted upon doing, was readily indulged in. This, combined with what I can only describe as consistent cruelty and mockery on the part of those in whose care he found himself, are at the root of his supposed madness. That is to say, my lord, I do not believe your unfortunate uncle's condition is anything you need to concern yourself with. You have nothing to fear."

Wrexham let out a sound he was mortified to note sounded horribly like a sob and covered his mouth with his hand. *Oh God. Oh God. Not mad. Not mad.* It took him several moments to compose himself as thoughts of a future he'd believe lost to him crowded in his mind and, at the centre of it all, was Emmeline.

"If you needed any further reassurance, please believe me when I tell you, I find nothing in your family history, or in yourself, that leads me to believe you are in the least danger of losing your faculties. No more or less than any other man, at least, for we none of us know what the future holds. But there is no reason yours ought not to be a bright and fulfilling one."

The doctor's voice was gentle, reassuring, and in that moment, Wrexham could have hugged him. As it was, he sat very still, struggling to compose himself.

"You cannot know—" Wrexham managed, shaking his head.

"My lord, I run an asylum. It is the kindest and most welcoming place I can make it for those troubled souls who find themselves at home there, but I promise you, I understand the fear you have lived with these past years. Now, you can let that go."

Wrexham laughed, a startled, breathless sound. "Thank you. I thank you from the bottom of my heart, and most of all, I must thank that overbearing, interfering father-in-law of mine. I fear he will be the bane of my existence, but that I have an existence to look forward to is, in no small part, thanks to him. So I will bear it with good grace."

"That sounds like the best course of action, my lord. Fighting Mr Knight strikes me as a wearying and futile endeavour."

"You are a wise man, Dr Boniface."

"I feel confident in returning the compliment. Now, if that is all?"

"No," Wrexham said, sitting forward, his hands grasping the chair arms, reassured by the strong English oak beneath his palms. He'd faced a good many truths over the past days, so he may as well face one more. "There's something else I'd like to know."

Chapter 20

Dear Mr Berrycloth,

I was so pleased to receive your letter this morning and to make the acquaintance of my husband's secretary. Have you held the position long? What a patient man you must be.

I shall not be coy about my situation, for I do not doubt you are aware of the details of my husband's private affairs, or else you would have little to occupy you. You are certainly aware of the deal I struck with Lord Kilbane concerning the letters.

I thank you kindly for forwarding his comment, but more so for your own. You cannot know how very much I appreciated your kind words. Dare I hope I have found an ally? If I might count you as such I shall be the most fortunate of women, for Mr Bright has been such a dear fellow. I confess it surprised me to read your description of him as a sober creature, for whilst he was terribly grave upon our first meeting, it took very little encouragement to involve him in my plans. Indeed, he has become quite indispensable to me. I cannot think what I should do without him. I have asked him and his wife to accompany me to the theatre this evening to thank him for all he has done. Shocking of me, I know, but if the Marchioness of Kilbane cannot be shocking, what is the point of the title?

Whilst I never burn correspondence – unless it is prudent to do so – I have mentally consigned your last letter to the fiery furnace, as you suggested. I will keep writing to my husband, as well as to you, for I feel we shall get along splendidly together.

You also asked me if there was the least thing you could do for me. There is. Please, could you discover if Lord Kilbane reads the letters I write to him, or if he casts them on the fire as he told me he would do? I know it will depress my spirits dreadfully if it is the latter, but I must face the truth, whatever it may be. I have never been of a mind to hide from reality, and I do not intend to begin now. So, tell me all, Mr Berrycloth.

Your friend and ally,

Lady K

—Excerpt of a letter from The Most Hon'ble Lady Catherine 'Cat' St Just, Marchioness of Kilbane (daughter of The Most Hon'ble Lucian and Matilda Barrington, Marquess and Marchioness of Montagu) to her husband's private secretary, Mr Gilbert Berrycloth.

23rd February 1845, Cawston Hall, Cawston, Norfolk.

Emmeline stared out of her bedroom window and forced herself not to turn back to the clock to check the time again. Wrexham had been talking with Dr Boniface for well over two hours and she was sick with anxiety. Not that she thought the doctor could find anything wrong with her husband's mind, but the entire day seemed to stretch before her, littered with pitfalls and dangers. Assuming Dr Boniface was satisfied—which he had better be or he would have her to reckon with—there was still the ordeal of executing her father's plan.

Before Wrexham had lost his sight, it had been his habit to visit his tenants on the last Saturday of the month. He had confided to Emmeline that riding out over his own land, seeing the crops growing and the landscape changing with the seasons, had been a profound pleasure, and he had felt its loss. However, he wished to return to doing as much as he could, and visiting his tenants would certainly fall under that heading. It also offered her father an opportunity to lay his trap.

In some regards, it appeared her husband had been a creature of habit. On returning from his visits, Wrexham would leave his horse at the stables and walk the short distance to the Buck's Arms with Humboldt for a drink. It was a popular pub and by early evening would be thronged with the locals; a good place to catch up with anyone he had not seen during his visits. Wrexham had usually arrived by five p.m. and, whilst the pub was quiet, would spend the next hour going over any issues with Humboldt. His duplicitous steward, Mr Thompson, would arrive later. Once business was done, Humboldt and Thompson would leave and Wrexham would stay, often until closing. Emmeline gathered from speaking to the staff at Cawston that this habit had endeared him to his tenants and the locals, who appreciated that they could approach his lordship directly. From everything she had heard, Wrexham was very warmly regarded and respected, and his accident and subsequent disappearance from their lives had been a heavy blow to everyone on and around the estate.

His staff had reacted with delight to the news that his lordship intended to revive this habit and so, naturally, the news had spread like wildfire. Which meant that the duke and Lord Cecil would know, too.

Emmeline's father had received information this morning that the duke was staying with a Mr Whittleton, a prosperous landowner and an old crony of the duke's, who lived in nearby Aylsham. She did not doubt that Lord Cecil was with him. So, their trap was set, and now they only needed to execute it... if Dr Boniface ever deigned to let her husband leave his blasted study.

Muted voices had Emmeline turning towards the door as it opened.

"Thank you, Humboldt. Yes, I can manage."

Wrexham entered the room, closing the door behind him.

"Wrexham," Emmeline said before she moved, so he was aware she was in the room. He turned towards her and smiled, and she lost no time in rushing over to hug him tightly.

"What's all this?" he said, laughing, closing his arms around her. "I wasn't gone that long."

"An eternity," she mumbled into his waistcoat, breathing in the scent of him with relief.

"Don't worry, pet. You're stuck with me for the foreseeable. According to Dr Boniface, I'm perfectly sane and he'll give me a signed letter to prove it. I may have it framed," he said, amusement in his voice.

"Oh, Rex, what else did he say?" Emmeline asked, too anxious to find her husband's flippancy the least bit amusing.

"He said," Wrexham began, cupping her face in his big warm hand and tilting it up to him, "that my wife is the wisest person I have ever met, and I ought to listen to her."

Emmeline's breath caught. "Why?"

"Because it was all a hum," he said, shaking his head. "It was just as you said, my father twisting the truth to suit his own ends. My uncle did go mad, but that was as much because of his opium addiction and some truly awful treatment at the hands of those supposed to care for him than to his blindness."

"Oh!" Emmeline said, pulling his head down so she could kiss him. "And may that be a lesson to you, vexing creature. I am always right!"

He laughed at that and lifted her into his arms, spinning her around. "Of course you are, Miss Milly. It was foolish of me to ever have doubted you. I shan't do so again."

He kissed her then, and for a long moment Emmeline could think of nothing at all. When he finally let her go, she gazed up at him, overwhelmed with happiness.

"We have a future," she said.

"We do, and it's all because of you, Emmeline. You've saved me, in more ways that you will ever know."

"No," she said, her voice thick. "You saved yourself, but I am so glad I was here to see you do it. You are the bravest person I know, my lord, and I love and admire you so much."

"Pack it in," he said gruffly, though his expression betrayed the pleasure he took in her words. "You'll unman me if you keep this up. I almost sobbed when Boniface gave me the news. Don't you set me off again."

"Then I shall sob for you," she said unsteadily.

Wrexham touched her face, wiping tears from her cheeks with his thumbs. "My dearest love," he said softly. "You are everything to me."

"Oh, stop it," she said, hiccoughing with laughter and tears. "I shall be in a puddle at your feet if you keep on, and that won't do at all. Not when we must leave shortly."

He nodded, and then frowned as his hands fell to her hips, his palms skimming the rich velvet. "Is that a riding habit?"

"Yes. It's new. A lovely fawn colour velvet, trimmed with brown satin. I'm very pleased with it."

"But why are you wearing it?" he asked.

"Because we are going to ride out together," she said, hoping he would not baulk at the plan she had conceived.

"But I cannot ride," he said. "Humboldt and I were going to take the dogcart and—"

"I know, but why can you not ride, Wrexham? Your limbs all still work, you are fit and strong, and your horse is not blind. He will guide you, and I will be with you, too. We shall stay close together and manage it all with ease. That is to say... if you wish to?"

Emmeline bit her lip, not having considered that he might not want to. She had only thought of how often he had ridden across his own land, and how it would chafe at his pride to have Humboldt drive him—and in the dog cart, of all things—but many of the tenant farms were unsuitable for visiting with a carriage, the roads too narrow or rough.

He said nothing for a long moment and Emmeline prayed she had not offended him.

"I had not considered," he said slowly. "It never even crossed my mind that I could still ride, but—"

He let out a breath and grasped her by the waist, bending to kiss her soundly.

"You are a marvel! And I'm an idiot for letting other people's perception of what I can and can't do influence me. Of course I can bloody ride. I bet I can still outride most anyone," he added defiantly.

Emmeline laughed, delighted by his enthusiasm. "I don't doubt it, but let us go slowly to begin with. It has been years since you've been in the saddle at all, and for my sake, you will be cautious, or I shall regret having said anything."

"I'll be good," he promised, before turning and stalking to the adjoining door that led to his dressing room. *"Lennox!"* he bellowed as he disappeared inside. "Lennox! I'm going riding. Get me ready. Dash it, where are you, man?"

Emmeline sat on the bed and let out a breath of laughter as she heard poor Lennox enter the room and hurry to do his master's bidding.

Emmeline bit her lip as Wrexham fidgeted in place, waiting for his horse to be brought to him. He had chosen a sweet-natured bay mare for her, and Emmeline stroked the beast's velvety nose as she sent a silent prayer to the Almighty that this go well for her husband. His excitement had become a tense, nervous energy as he waited with impatience for his mount. The sound of hooves upon cobbles had Wrexham all on alert and Emmeline held her breath as he greeted his favourite horse for the first time in three years. He'd not been here in all that time, too broken-hearted to visit when he'd believed he would never ride again.

A huge chestnut gelding stepped proudly into the yard, head tossing until he caught sight of Wrexham. With an excited whinny, he tore his lead rope from the astonished groom's hand and cantered up to Wrexham, skidding to a halt before him in the moment before Emmeline shouted to warn him. The horse bent his head and pushed at Wrexham's chest.

Wrexham staggered back a step and laughed, embracing his old friend. "Good afternoon, Jaeger, old fellow. Sorry it's been so long. Can you forgive me?"

The horse made a low, rumbling noise that, to Emmeline, sounded like part grumble, part acceptance, but Jaeger pushed his head into Wrexham's hands again, seeking another caress and Emmeline had to blink away tears. Looking around, she saw that she was not the only one so afflicted. Several of the groomsmen were surreptitiously wiping their eyes on their sleeves.

To her relief, Wrexham mounted with ease, but Jaeger looked back at him, turning his head to nibble at his boot. Emmeline watched as her husband gave the horse instruction to walk on, only for Jaeger to baulk, once again turning his head, this time pushing gently at Wrexham's leg.

"He knows," Emmeline said, her voice faint.

Wrexham's expression tightened for a moment, but he leant down and stroked Jaeger's neck.

"I'm just the same, old fellow," he murmured. "I need a little more help, but I'm just the same."

Jaeger whinnied, scratching at the cobbles with a hoof, before reluctantly walking on. Wrexham had a groom guide him to the outdoor menage, and with a little encouragement got Jaeger trotting in a circle. Soon, they were cantering, doing figures of eight, with Wrexham effortlessly guiding Jaeger into a flying change. The obvious connection between horse and rider was a pleasure to watch. As Wrexham brought his mount to a halt, Jaeger tossed his head, apparently eager to go now Wrexham had reassured him his rider was in no danger.

From that moment, the afternoon was an extraordinary success. The only problem from Emmeline's point of view was the desire to keep her husband from pushing too hard, too fast. That he had been a fantastic horseman was immediately apparent, as was the bond between him and Jaeger. With vast, flat expanses of land, it was an ideal environment for Wrexham to ride out and, with a horse he trusted so completely, it was not long before he was begging Emmeline to gallop across his favourite stretch of land.

"Can you see the windmill to the left?" he asked, such exhilaration in his voice she knew she could not deny him, no matter how hard her heart thudded with anxiety. "Which means Arnup's farm is over there, behind that little copse."

He pointed to a stand of trees on the far side of the great expanse of green before them.

"I see it." She turned back to stare at him and found it impossible to look away. He was breathtaking, his golden hair glinting in the winter sunshine like barley, broad shoulders highlighted by the beautifully cut riding coat, and his powerful thighs encased in soft buckskin trousers. Emmeline's heart swelled with love and pride. No man in the world could match him, and he belonged to her.

"It's our last stop before we go to the pub. Will you guide me?"

"Of course I will," she said, for she could refuse him nothing. She turned back to regard Humboldt behind them, atop a sturdy brown cob. He smiled reassuringly and moved to the far side of her husband, just to be safe. "Are you ready then, my lord?"

"I am," he said, grinning at her.

Emmeline urged her horse into a canter, waiting until Wrexham and Humboldt were level with her, and then with her heart thudding, she called out, "Now!"

They flew across the field, and she heard his shout of triumph and so she shouted too, and laughed and cried at once, as the wind buffeted her and the ground sped past in a blur of colour and motion.

Wrexham was still buzzing with exhilaration by the time they reached the Buck's Arms. The door creaked open and the familiar scent of beer and sawdust, of working men and well-polished wood, embraced him and wrapped him up with memories. He did not need to see it to remember the huge, scarred oak bar and the worn wooden stools. He could hear the fire crackling in the deep inglenook fireplace and smell the scent of something rich and meaty, which would fill empty bellies to the sound of laughter and conversation when the taproom filled up. He wished this was just a usual day, that he could have brought Emmeline and introduced her to the landlord, Mr Wells.

That was not the case, however. Gabriel Knight had posted lookouts all around the village and sent runners to keep Wrexham informed. They had seen the duke and Cecil at Ingworth, the neighbouring village. Wrexham did not doubt for a moment that they would appear.

Humboldt murmured in his ear that two of Knight's men were seated at the bar, and several of the footmen and gardeners from the hall were seated around the taproom. Wolf and the rest of Wrexham's available staff were hidden, waiting in the private parlour. Wrexham had spent the afternoon explaining why he had been absent for so long, and detailing his father's plans to his tenants. They had been hearteningly furious on his behalf, promising everything from taking up arms to cursing the duke's nether regions to blacken and shrivel like a rotten mushroom, an image Wrexham could have done without.

Instead, Wrexham had channelled their indignation into this afternoon's little theatrical display, and prayed he could both avoid a riot and thwart his father so thoroughly he would never dare show his face here again.

Humboldt guided him to his usual spot, and Wrexham smiled when he heard a familiar greeting.

"Bless me, if you're not a sight for sore eyes, my lord," exclaimed the jovial voice, swiftly followed by an awkward silence. "That is to say—I mean, it's good to have you here, is what I meant to—forgive me, my lord. Hardly got your foot in the door and I already put mine in my mouth."

Wrexham laughed and shook his head. "Good afternoon, Wells, and no offence taken. I beg you will treat me no differently to before. It has taken me a while to convince myself of the fact, but I'm just the same as ever I was."

"Well, I'm right glad to hear it," Wells said, clearly relieved. "You was our best customer."

"Good to know you missed me," Wrexham said with a bark of laughter. "Now bring us two pints of your finest before we die of thirst."

"With pleasure, Lord Wrexham, and to prove I'm a man of my word, these two are on the house."

The man bustled off and Wrexham became aware of Humboldt chuckling to himself.

"What?"

"He really meant that. I reckon that's the first free pint the fellow's ever given out in his life."

Wrexham grinned and hoped the landlord hurried back. A bit of liquid courage to settle his nerves would not go amiss. Much as it was good to discover his old life was just where he'd left it, he had a dragon to slay, and he'd just as soon get it over with.

Emmeline patted her horse's neck and tried to admire the lovely view of the house and the lake beyond, glittering in the dying rays of the afternoon sunshine. It would be dark soon and she really must go inside. Apart from anything else, she was frozen. She had been far too jittery to go back to the house and had chosen instead to walk her mare around the grounds. Cawston was vast and lovely, and she was so looking forward to exploring it and discovering its secrets. Today, however, the beauty of the place was lost on her; she chafed too much at being left behind. She ought to be with Wrexham, by his side, but between her husband and her father's protective instincts, all her efforts to be included in the coming confrontation had been soundly rebuffed.

Anxious and irritated, she made her way back to the stables to find her mother waiting for her.

"There you are!" Mama exclaimed, hands on her hips, looking remarkably fierce.

"I'm sorry. I didn't realise you were waiting for me," Emmeline said in surprise as she kicked her stirrup free and dismounted.

"Never mind that. Why the devil are you here when Wrexham is facing his father and that worm of a half-brother by himself?"

Emmeline frowned, handing her horse over to the care of the waiting groom. "He's not by himself. Papa and Lord Latimer and all the others are there, and—"

"And?" Mama asked, eyebrows raising.

"And they told me I wasn't to come! I tried to change their minds, but you know what Papa is. He said I must stay here," Emmeline said indignantly.

Mama threw up her hands. "Emmeline Knight, have you learned nothing from me, not to mention your sisters?"

Emmeline stared at her, wide-eyed as her heart leapt. "You think I should go?"

She watched as her mother tsked and then put her hand in the pocket of her pelerine and tugged out a little slip of paper.

"I picked up the book you've been reading, and this fell out," she said, waving it under Emmeline's nose. "Don't you think this is the perfect opportunity to fulfil it?"

Emmeline's heart skipped as she regarded the thin strip of paper, the one she had pulled out of the hat of dares. It seemed a lifetime ago. She took it from her mother's hand and unfolded it, staring at the writing, which suddenly seemed prophetic.

Defy convention and stand up to injustice.

"I rather thought I already had," Emmeline retorted. "I eloped with Wrexham to thwart his father, didn't I?"

"You did," Mama agreed, grinning. "And I was never prouder of you, but I do hate to see a job half done."

Emmeline considered the devilish glitter in her mother's green eyes for a moment and her lips twitched. "That is true," she said slowly "I suppose I ought to make certain the duke is quite thoroughly routed."

"You certainly ought." Mama nodded.

"Very well. In that case, I shall go." Emmeline began to turn away, but paused. She glanced nonchalantly over her shoulder. "Want to come with me?"

"Oh, Emmeline," Mama said with a huff. "I thought you'd never ask!"

When the door finally swung open and a tense silence filled the room, Wrexham discovered he was perfectly calm. Since his accident, he had lost his confidence, lost his belief in his own ability to manage his life after struggling so to perform the simplest of tasks by himself. But being blind and managing his life, or even his estate, was no different from riding Jaeger. Yes, sometimes he needed guidance from people he trusted, but he was still in control. It was still his judgement, the decisions he made, that counted.

Emmeline had made him face the truth, and proven to him the future was not the bleak, unwelcome prospect he had assumed it to be. She had given him back his life, and he wished suddenly that she was beside him. It had been wrong to leave her out of this when it would be *their* moment of triumph, not just his. For he would not be here without her. He no longer feared his father's power over him, not with so many people willing to take his part, but Emmeline had been the one who'd brought all these people together. Admittedly, she'd had help from the force of nature that was her father, but the apple had not fallen far from the tree.

"The duke has entered with your half-brother, my lord. There are four dangerous looking men, and what looks like a medical man with him."

"Is there, by Jove," Wrexham said, taking a sip from the pint he held before raising his voice to the room. "Good evening, your grace. How good of you to join us."

"Wrexham, my boy!" the duke said, and Wrexham heard the insincere note of relief in his exclamation. "I'm glad so glad to discover you are unharmed. We have been searching high and low for you?"

"Really? How strange. Surely Cecil knew where I was, as he's been following me like a little lamb since I left Holbrook House."

"I'm no lamb, Wrexham!" retorted an angry voice, and Wrexham only smiled, aware his title irked his half-brother enormously.

"No, more a snake in the grass, by my reckoning," Wrexham replied mildly, as a ripple of laughter moved through the room. Cecil was not popular in these parts. As a boy, he'd forever been getting the local lads into trouble by tattling on them, and no young woman was safe in his company. Not that the duke had ever taken him to task for his vile behaviour, and no one in the village could risk displeasing his father, but Wrexham had punished him more than once, and everyone here knew it.

"Now, I don't want you to make a scene, but it is past time you came home where there are people who can look after you as you ought to be cared for."

"You mean by leaving knives in unexpected places and moving furniture, or by leaving items for me to trip over at the top of the stairs? Are those your means of caring for your son, to arrange a fatal accident?"

Angry murmuring reached his ears, but Wrexham tuned it out, aware of movement around him.

"His men are moving to either side of us," Humboldt said in an undertone.

"You see, doctor?" his father said, his tone one of apparent regret. "I'm afraid his paranoia is worse than I feared, when all we have done is to try our utmost to keep him safe."

"Yes, yes. I do see. A tragic case," came a heavily accented voice.

"Doctor?" demanded a suspicious voice. "From where did you acquire your medical degree, sir?"

Wrexham frowned, leaning towards Humboldt. "Is that Dr Boniface?"

"Yes, my lord," Humboldt said. "When he discovered our plans for this afternoon, he insisted on playing his part in it."

"Well, bless the fellow," Wrexham said, quite taken aback.

This was turning out to be an entertaining afternoon. Folding his arms, he sat back to listen, and he was determined to enjoy every moment of it.

Chapter 21

Dear Lady K,

I have been your husband's secretary for almost seven years. Much as I would like to admit to being a patient fellow, it is not in the least true. I have, however, learned that walking briskly away from the house for a duration of at least ten minutes, and then screaming at the top of my lungs, is a useful and efficacious way of venting my frustration. Feel free to try it for yourself. It is most invigorating.

I am so delighted to be considered your ally, I have been in excellent humour all day. With this has come the added benefit that my cheerfully smiling countenance drove Lord Kilbane into an apoplexy, and he's taken himself off for a long ride. The house is blissfully quiet.

From the short correspondence we have shared, and the little I know of you, I do not find it the least bit surprising that Mr Bright is putty in your hands. Furthermore, I can think of no better use of the title of Marchioness of Kilbane than to scandalise society. After all, what is sauce for the goose is sauce for the gander, or vice-versa.

As for your letters, I sorely wish I could give you an answer, but the truth is, I do not know. I ensure to deliver your letters directly to your husband. So far, he has received them with everything from frigid glares to explosions of temper. However, I am always dismissed before he touches them, and I do not see them again. I cannot tell you more than this, but I will endeavour to discover the truth for you.

Your friend and ally,

G. Berrycloth.

—Excerpt of a letter from Lord Kilbane's private secretary, Mr Gilbert Berrycloth to The Most Hon'ble Lady Catherine 'Cat' St Just, Marchioness of Kilbane (daughter of The Most Hon'ble Lucian and Matilda Barrington, Marquess and Marchioness of Montagu)

23rd February 1845, Cawston Hall, Cawston. Norfolk.

Emmeline stalked past the gleaming carriage and the four elegant greys to the front door of the public house. It would be terribly shocking for ladies to enter the main room, especially unchaperoned.

"We'll cause the most awful scandal," she said to her mother as they stood on the steps.

"One can only hope," Mama said with a smirk.

On impulse, Emmeline hugged her mother tightly. "I adore you. I hope you know that."

"Of course I do," Mama said, patting her back affectionately. "I'm perfectly adorable. Now get in there and stand by your husband."

"Yes, Mama," Emmeline said dutifully, and tugged open the door.

A rush of warm air, heavily perfumed with wood smoke, cigars, and the sweet, earthy scent of beer surrounded them as they entered and gravitated towards the sound of voices. Emmeline cracked open the door to the taproom and peered inside.

The duke blocked much of her view, but she could see two large ruffians and a slight, overdressed young man in an eye-watering checked suit with matching cravat. That could only be Lord Cecil.

"Doctor? From where did you acquire your medical degree, sir?" enquired a polite voice that she recognised as belonging to Dr Boniface. Determined to discover what was going on, she opened the door and slipped inside. Mama followed her and they remained in the corner, unobserved for now, as all eyes were on the confrontation between the duke and Wrexham.

Emmeline's gaze settled on Rex greedily, and she drank in the sight of him with relief. He looked entirely calm, and even rather amused, and she let out the breath she'd been holding to discover he was still in good spirits. If the duke upset him, she would do the man an injury.

"That is none of your business, sir," replied a strangely accented voice.

"But it is entirely my business," Dr Boniface replied coolly. "If you are thinking of poaching my patient."

"Your patient!" the duke's man replied angrily, his accent shifting oddly from vaguely German to vaguely French via the

East End. "This man is not your patient, but mine, and he needs to return home to his grace's care, where he can be properly treated."

"Treated for what, exactly?" Dr Boniface asked with apparent interest.

"Ah... for insanity," the man said, tugging at his waistcoat, his expression grave.

"But he is not insane."

"Yes, he is," said the duke, Lord Cecil, and their doctor simultaneously.

Dr Boniface frowned. "I have conducted a thorough examination of Lord Wrexham and, far from being insane, he is one of the most sensible men it has been my good fortune to come across."

"Well, you would say that!" shouted Lord Cecil, pushing his way past his father. "Wrexham makes everyone do everything he wants them to do. He always has. It's not fair! Everyone always takes his side!"

Dr Boniface blinked and regarded Lord Cecil with interest. "Really?" he said, his voice soothing. "And why do you think that is?"

"Because he's got an excess of animal spirits," Cecil said eagerly. "That's right, ain't it, Pa? It's why women are always panting after him. It's not right."

"No, not when they ought to pant after you, hmmm?" Dr Boniface said, all sympathy.

Emmeline stifled a giggle.

"Well, yes," Lord Cecil said, and then snapped his mouth shut. "I mean, no. I mean... you made me say that."

"Did I? And how did I do that?" Boniface asked him.

"Enough of this. Take Wrexham now," commanded the duke.

Four large men moved at once, heading for Wrexham. There was a sudden scraping of chair legs as everyone in the room stood.

"I wouldn't do that if I were you, Grandfather," rumbled a deep voice.

Heads swivelled towards the fireplace, and next to it the open door to the private parlour, where Wolf stood, the firelight glinting off his harsh features and making him look even bigger and more intimidating than he did in daylight.

"What are you doing here, Latimer?" the duke demanded irritably. "This is none of your affair. I advise you to stay out of it."

"And I advise you to keep your ruffians away from my uncle," Wolf growled.

There was a glint in his eyes that left Emmeline in no doubt of where his name had sprung from.

"You would do well not to make an enemy of me, sir," the duke said, his voice cold and hard.

Wolf only chuckled. "Funny, that. I was about to say the same thing, only I'm uncertain what you think I have to fear from a bankrupt old man."

"Bankrupt!" the duke bellowed, turning an interesting shade of purple. "I'm the Duke of Sefton!"

"Yes. Bankrupt, you miserable swine."

Mama pushed past Emmeline at the sound of her husband's voice coming from behind the bar.

"I wondered where he got to," Mama whispered.

"Go to the devil!" the duke sneered at Papa. "I don't need some jumped up Cit spreading unfounded rumours. I'll take you to court!"

"No, you won't," Papa said in disgust. "Not when you haven't paid your own staff in two months. I have, by the by. They work for me now."

"What?" The duke was vibrating with rage at this point. "How dare you!"

"I suggest you four get lost," Wolf instructed the ruffians. "Because if he's not paid you upfront, you won't see a penny."

The men exchanged glances. Three of them shrugged and headed for the door.

"Come back!" the duke blustered, but the men kept moving. The remaining thug eyed the duke with a considering gaze. "Give me that stick pin, and I'll stay," he said, jerking his head to the large ruby glinting in the duke's cravat.

"Fine," the duke managed, through gritted teeth. "After you have Wrexham in the carriage."

The man nodded and Emmeline gasped as he headed towards her husband. Wrexham stood, his chair screeching on the flagstones as every man in the pub moved forward.

"Humboldt," Wrexham said, and Emmeline saw the man eyeing the thug approaching them. She thought he was holding his breath.

"Ten o'clock!" Humboldt yelled, startling everyone.

Wrexham's right fist struck out, connecting hard with the man's jaw and snapping his head back. The brute staggered back and then fell upon Wrexham, the two men crashing to the floor as a table overturned and glasses smashed, the powerful scent of beer filling the room. Emmeline screamed and pushed through the crowd gathered around two men, to discover her husband did not need to see his opponent, provided he could keep him in one place.

It was a short but comprehensive fight.

The duke's hired thug curled in upon himself, moaning softly as Wrexham got to his feet.

"Wrexham!" Emmeline rushed over to discover him investigating his cut lip and wincing.

"Emmeline?" He held his arms out, and she ran into them, holding on tight.

"Are you hurt? Oh, what did that brute do?"

Wrexham snorted. "I laid him out cold, did you not see?"

"Of course I saw. You were marvellous, but your poor lip...."

"You can kiss it better if you like," he said, sounding remarkably cheerful under the circumstances.

"We aren't alone!" she hissed, suddenly very aware of all the interested faces watching them.

"Ah, his lordship ain't changed none," quipped one wag. "Give her a kiss, lad. Poor lady is all a-tremble."

Much laughter ensued.

"I am not trembling," Emmeline retorted indignantly. "And no one is kissing anyone!"

"Pity," Wrexham murmured, which earned him another round of guffawing and ribald comments.

Emmeline shot him a look, which was pointless and only made her need to bite her tongue to stop from laughing, for the devil looked as if he was enjoying himself enormously. The duke, however, was making his escape unhindered and Emmeline wasn't about to let him get away with it. She needed to know they were free of him, for good.

"Excuse me, my lord," she said, leaving Wrexham and following his father. She made her way through the room, pausing as she noted Dr Boniface deep in conversation with Lord Cecil. He looked fascinated.

"But why is it fair if Wrexham gets everything? I ought to have it. Pa says I ought to have it. I'm just as good as he is," Cecil said, crossing his arms and pouting like a child of six, not a man full grown.

"And would you want it? Is that what you want? The running of that big house and dealing with all the tenants. Think of all the work that would go with it. Should you like that, and to live here, in Cawston?"

Cecil opened and closed his mouth. "Not really," he said frankly. "Only it ought to be mine. Pa says so."

"I see. And what about what you want, Cecil?"

"Oh." Cecil looked at the doctor as though he'd grown a second head. "What I want?"

"Yes."

"Nobody ever asked me that before," Cecil replied, looking a bit stunned.

"Well, why don't we go somewhere quiet and talk about it?" Dr Boniface suggested. "Perhaps that will help you decide what to do next."

Cecil considered this for a moment before giving a decisive nod. "I should like that."

Emmeline caught the doctor's eye and smiled, before hurrying after the duke.

"Duke," she called out, marching up to the man.

The duke glared at her with utter contempt. "Ah. The little ladybird that ran off with my son, I collect."

Emmeline's colour rose at the insult and the desire to slap the duke's face might have overwhelmed her, if not for the fact it would have meant touching him. His florid face sheened with sweat in the over-warm atmosphere of the taproom.

"I am Lady Wrexham," Emmeline returned icily. "And you might like to remember, I am my father's daughter. Come within ten miles of myself or my husband again, and I shall make you sorry."

"I'm all a-tremble," the man replied, lip curling.

"So I see. You look on the verge of an apoplexy to me. You've turned the most shocking colour. It cannot be healthy."

The duke's eyes glittered with malice, but Emmeline pressed on, for this man was not only a threat to Wrexham, but to all those who depended on him.

"Delia, Aunt Lucy, and Genevieve are Wrexham's responsibility now. I insist you leave them alone."

He snorted and shook his head. "Oh, no. Delia is my daughter, and I shall do as I please with her, as I will with Genevieve when I get my hands on the treacherous bitch. They at least ought to give me something in return for all the coin I've spent on them."

Emmeline started, shocked to hear him speak of his granddaughter so, even though she knew what manner of man he was.

"I'll drag you through every scandal sheet in society before I let you anywhere near them. Everyone will know of the things you've done, and all about your financial affairs. I'll get the details from my father," Emmeline said, her temper rising.

The duke sneered. "You don't frighten me, girl."

"Then you're a bigger fool than I credited you for," Wrexham said, and Emmeline relaxed a degree as her husband's large hand settled on the small of her back. "Lady Wrexham is a force to be reckoned with. She figured you out at once, and I still did not believe what she told me. No, I needed a doctor to tell me what she knew instinctively. There is *no* madness in our bloodline. That was just a convenient story you used to break me, or to try to. There is blindness, yes, but blindness is not a death sentence, and it does not diminish the other faculties, but heightens them."

Emmeline sought Wrexham's hand and curled her fingers about his, holding on tight.

"You wanted to send me mad, or at least to allow the world to believe me so. You were even prepared to allow me to break my damned neck, *accidentally,* of course. But you would have killed your own son, your heir, and all for what? For *money?* Why did you not ask me? Do you think it would have pleased me for the world to know my father was bankrupt? I would have helped, you miserable old sod. Not that you deserved it."

"Helped?" the duke growled in fury. *"Helped?* Your own father! How dare you? You think I would come cap in hand for a handout from you? That money is mine by right. I'm your sire. I am the *duke!"*

Wrexham stiffened and then let out a breath, shaking his head. "I don't give a damn about your blasted title. You've been no father to me, and that money is nothing to do with you. I inherited an estate barely making ends meet, and I turned it around. I invested every penny I could scrape together to invest in Mr Knight's railway company and the brilliant bastard turned it into gold. You had nothing to do with it, and I owe you nothing. Nonetheless, if you are in dire straits, I will give you an allowance to keep you from disgrace, providing I never hear from or see you ever again."

Emmeline could see the satisfaction Wrexham took in making the man such an offer, though it was a generous one in truth, for the duke was a spendthrift and too readily enjoyed the finer things in life.

Still, the duke was shaking with fury, clearly caught between the desire to tell his son to go to hell before everyone watching, and the knowledge that he was facing financial ruin.

"We shall discuss this in private," the duke said, the words clipped and angry.

"No. We won't," Wrexham said with a smile. "Humboldt will draw up the terms and send them to you. Accept them, or don't. I really don't care. However, I would like to finish my drink in peace, so do us all a favour and clear off. This is my land, and you're not welcome here."

There was a cheer from behind them at Wrexham's words and Emmeline turned to discover the room filled to bursting. Many of the staff from the Hall and all the tenants they had visited that afternoon were there, all of them supporting Lord Wrexham, because he was a good man and they all loved him.

Wrexham started in surprise, turning towards the sound.

"That's for you," Emmeline said, gazing up at his handsome face. "They're proud of you, Wrexham, and so happy to have you home."

He made a soft sound of surprise, his mouth quirking into a boyish smile.

"Kiss yer bride, man," yelled a voice from the crowd. "She's looking at you like you hung the moon, you silly bugger!"

Wrexham chuckled and turned to Emmeline, touching his fingers to her chin. "That true, pet?"

"Of course it's true, you vexing creature," she said with a sigh. "I told you. I'm quite disgustingly infatuated with you."

"Ah, well. You can't be blamed," he said. "What else is there to do but love me?"

"Nothing," Emmeline said, gazing up at him helplessly. "Not a thing."

"Well, so long as we're agreed," he said amicably, and kissed her.

Epilogue

Lord Frederick,

It pains me to write this letter to you, but I can keep the truth from you no longer.

Aggie is gone. It has been two days now. We do not know where, or why. I have men scouring the country for her, but my daughter knows well how to disappear, and it appears she does not wish to be found. My heart is breaking. I shall not rest until I find her. I know the esteem in which you hold my daughter, and that after the conversation we shared at our last meeting, this will be a dreadful blow to you, too.

Is there anything you can tell me, any reason you can think of that would have sent her running? Please understand, I am not accusing you of wrongdoing. I know you well enough to understand you would walk over hot coals for Agatha, and nothing would induce you to cause her harm. But is it possible she took fright? Did you speak of your future, of a proposal perhaps? Anything that may have overwhelmed her?

If there is the least clue to why she went or where she might go, I beg you will tell me at once. All I have is an empty wardrobe and a note with the words,

'Forgive me, I have no choice but to leave. I love you all.'

I will find her, Fred. I give you my word. I will not stop looking until she is safely back at home.

With regret,

Yrs, etc

—Excerpt of a letter from Louis César de Montluc, the Comte de Villen, to the Right Hon'ble Frederick Adolphus, (son of Their Graces, Robert and Prunella Adolphus, The Duke and Duchess of Bedwin).

Six months later...

19th August 1845, Positano, Italy.

Emmeline stared out at the view before her, overwhelmed by the beauty of it, though she had already seen it every day for the past week.

The villa perched high in the hills, surrounded by lush greenery. Their bedroom opened onto a private terrace. All around the house lemon and orange trees grew, the bright fruit vivid against the astonishing blue of the sea. They had picnicked beneath them more than once now, just as her husband had promised her.

"Come back to bed, pet," Wrexham grumbled.

Emmeline turned to look at him and found him reclining on the mattress, with only a sheet covering his bottom half, every bit as stunning as the view from the window. They had swum every day in a private cove, and his hair was an even brighter shade than its usual ripe barley, his skin tinged with gold. He shifted, one elbow bent behind his head, and she sighed, entranced by the way the muscles shifted in his chest and shoulders, the visible strength in his arms. Desire stirred in her blood, and she did not need him to ask her a second time.

She wandered back to him, shedding the sheer silk dressing gown as she went, revelling in the feel of her bare skin against his as she settled against his chest.

"Are you happy?" he asked, one hand toying with her hair.

She laughed at the absurd question. "I am in heaven," she said with a sigh.

He kissed the top of her head. "But you're still worried about your friend."

Emmeline nodded, unable to ignore the one flaw in her perfect world.

"At least she wrote to tell you she was well. Surely you can take comfort in that?"

"I do," she said with a sigh. "Aggie is an extraordinary young woman, and more than capable, but all the same. She is all alone in the world, and a woman alone is at risk, no matter how clever and brave she is."

"Was there no clue in the letter?" Wrexham asked, and Emmeline smiled, knowing he too would move heaven and earth to find Aggie if she asked him. But Aggie's father, the Comte de Villen and his brother were already tearing the world apart piece by piece, and Aggie did not wish to be found.

"It was postmarked from France. So, we know at least that she has left the country, but there was nothing more. Only a request not to come looking for her, assurances that she was safe and well, and that she would come home when she was ready. She has written to all her friends, all with the same instructions and reassurances, but giving nothing more away. Each letter was sent from a different town, in a different part of France, so there can be no way of knowing where she is."

"She has certainly taken a deal of trouble to cover her tracks," Wrexham observed.

Emmeline nodded sadly. "Yes. But why? That is what none of us understand, and poor Fred...." Her throat tightened with emotion as she remembered the last time she had seen him. "He's devastated. It's like the light has gone out of him."

"I can understand it," Wrexham said, his voice low. "I should not know how to go on if anything happened to you. I don't think I could do it. I wouldn't want to."

Emmeline blinked back tears and kissed him.

"No more," she said, shaking her head. "Aggie is safe. She is so resilient, and so clever and far more worldly wise than the rest of us. She will come back, and Fred will be happy again, and all will be well. It *will*."

"Because you say so," he said with a smile.

"Yes," she replied firmly. "Because it is how things must be. There is nothing else to believe in, and as for me, I'm going nowhere. You and I shall live marvellous lives and grow old and grey together."

He smiled at that, stroking her cheek with a gentle touch. "And how many children and grandchildren shall we have?"

Emmeline stilled. They had been so happy, and everything between them so perfect, that she had not raised the subject of their children again, wishing to give him time to reflect upon it.

"Children?" she whispered. "You want children? Since when?"

He nodded. "A while now, but I did not want you to think there was any hurry, that I wanted things to change, for I don't. Not yet, anyway. But, if they happen to come along... I should be very happy about that too."

"But what changed your mind?" she asked.

"Dr Boniface. The day that he told me I had nothing to fear. I asked him about the likelihood of our children being blind. He worked with Humboldt, looking into the family tree and it is clearly an inherited condition, but the incidences of it showing itself are very low when you consider the number of relatives who were not afflicted. In fact, according to their research, our particular branch of the family has very low odds. My uncle and myself are the only ones to have gone blind in over a hundred years, from what we can find in the records."

Emmeline sat up, gazing down at him, her heart skipping erratically. "You think it is safe for us?"

Wrexham shrugged. "A very wise woman once told me there are no guarantees in life. We never know what fate has in store for us, but it seems the chances our children will be unaffected are strong enough not to deny them their existence."

"You mean it?" she asked, emotion rising in her chest.

He nodded.

"And what if fate takes a hand? What if they are born blind or go blind? Will you hate yourself and blame yourself for it?"

He considered this. "I think there would certainly be a part of me that will carry the guilt of that with me, just as I will watch them grow with trepidation, wondering if something will go wrong. But, Emmeline, I love my life. Every day is a wonder to me. I am beyond blessed, and losing my sight has brought me so much that I never expected. It brought me you."

Emmeline pressed a hand to her mouth and blinked back tears.

"Any child we have will be blessed too, and if they end up like me, I will show them it is not the end of the world. It is certainly not the end of their lives. They will have every advantage, every opportunity, and parents that will ensure they live the most fulfilling lives they can." He smiled then, reaching for her. "Did I get that right, pet?"

"Yes," she said, sniffing and wiping her eyes. "Perfectly, wonderfully right."

"Well," he said gravely. "I am perfectly wonderful."

"Yes, you are," she said with a sigh.

"And handsome and rich, and clever and funny, and—"

She hit him with a snort. "Conceited devil."

He grinned, that boyish, carefree smile that did odd things to her heart. "And you are horribly infatuated with me."

"I am," she said with a sigh. "It's hopeless."

"Excellent," he said, tumbling her onto her back. "Now, tell me what you can see."

Emmeline smiled, for this was a game they played often, and both enjoyed. She turned her head to the open doors.

"I can see blue. Vivid blue. The whole world is blue with no break between the sea and the sky. And I can see the tops of the orange and lemon trees, and the white painted balustrade, and the open doors with the voile curtains fluttering in the breeze."

"What else?" he asked.

"I can see a beautiful bedroom, elegant and bright, with comfortable furnishings. The wallpaper is white with a pink trellis pattern and the bed is huge, though we have thrown all the covers in a heap on the floor. It's rather untidy."

Wrexham stroked the hair from her forehead, his expression intent. "What else?"

"I see you," she said, reaching up to touch his face. "My beautiful husband, my only love, and I see the love shining in your eyes for me."

"I see you too, Emmeline, my fierce Miss Milly, and the vision I hold of you is the only thing I will ever need to see. I love you."

He proved it to her then, as if she needed any further proof, but she was hardly about to complain, as her husband reminded her of all the ways their life was entirely perfect. Perhaps others would look at them—at him—and not see that perfection, but then, those people were blind in a far more profound way than Wrexham ever could be.

They were happy, the future was bright, and that was everything.

And next in the exciting Daring Daughter series:

Truth or Dare
Daring Daughters Book 18

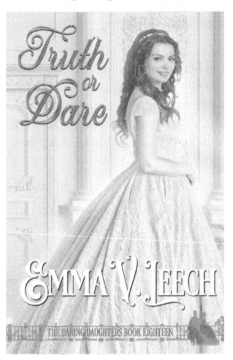

Not a daring daughter...

Agatha de Montluc's life is a fairy story.

Born in the rookery and alone in a dangerous world, the day she picked the Comte de Villen's pocket might have seen her transported, or even hanged. But the beautiful comte's past was dark too, and he sees himself in the grubby urchin he determines to save.

Now, Aggie is a lady, the Comte de Villen, her adopted father, and she is living in the lap of luxury, with a family that loves her, and the best friends a girl could ask for.

And then there is Fred.

Not a wicked son…

Lord Frederick Adolphus is the kindest, most honourable man in the world. A younger son of the Duke of Bedwin, he is titled, handsome, rich and popular, and hopelessly in love with his childhood sweetheart.

So when Aggie disappears without a trace, leaving only a brief note explaining that she had to go, she destroys his world and his happiness.

The greatest sacrifice…

Leaving Fred and the people she loves is the hardest thing Aggie has ever done, but too late, she realises her fairytale cannot come true. Too late she discovers Fred has been fighting his friends, because of her, because of the things they say about her, because she will never be a lady. A girl born in squalor can never marry the son of a duke.

The world will never let them be together.

A surprising alliance…

When she runs away to France to start a new life, hidden far from her beloved and those that care for her, Aggie does not expect to cross paths with her best friend's estranged husband, Lord Kilbane. For five long years, an uneasy entente exists between them as they both do their best to forget England, and avoid a world they can no longer bear to live in.

So when the Marquess of Kilbane gets himself into the kind of trouble that might finally ruin him for good, Aggie determines to help him, for his wife's sake. An adventure ensues that sends Aggie to England, and crashing headlong back into Fred's life.

And no matter how hard Aggie tries to escape, this time Fred is not letting her out of his sight.

Pre Order here: Truth or Dare

The Peculiar Ladies who started it all…

Girls Who Dare—The exciting series from Emma V Leech, the multi-award-winning, Amazon Top 10 romance writer behind the Rogues & Gentlemen series.

Inside every wallflower is the beating heart of a lioness, a passionate individual willing to risk all for their dream, if only they can find the courage to begin. When these overlooked girls make a pact to change their lives, anything can happen.

Twelve girls—Twelve dares in a hat. Twelve stories of passion. Who will dare to risk it all?

To Dare a Duke
Girls Who Dare Book 1

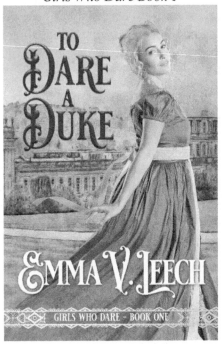

Dreams of true love and happy ever afters

Dreams of love are all well and good, but all Prunella Chuffington-Smythe wants is to publish her novel. Marriage at the price of her independence is something she will not consider. Having tasted success writing under a false name in The Lady's Weekly Review, her alter ego is attaining notoriety and fame and Prue rather likes it.

A Duty that must be endured

Robert Adolphus, The Duke of Bedwin, is in no hurry to marry, he's done it once and repeating that disaster is the last thing he desires. Yet, an heir is a necessary evil for a duke and one he cannot shirk. A dark reputation precedes him though, his first wife may have died young, but the scandals the beautiful, vivacious and spiteful creature supplied the ton have not. A wife must be found. A wife who is neither beautiful nor vivacious but sweet and dull, and certain to stay out of trouble.

Dared to do something drastic.

The sudden interest of a certain dastardly duke is as bewildering as it is unwelcome. She'll not throw her ambitions aside to marry a scoundrel just as her plans for self-sufficiency and freedom are coming to fruition. Surely showing the man she's not actually the meek little wallflower he is looking for should be enough to put paid to his intentions? When Prue is dared by her friends to do something drastic, it seems the perfect opportunity to kill two birds.

However, Prue cannot help being intrigued by the rogue who has inspired so many of her romances. Ordinarily, he plays the part of handsome rake, set on destroying her plucky heroine. But is he really the villain of the piece this time, or could he be the hero?

Finding out will be dangerous, but it just might inspire her greatest story yet.

To Dare a Duke

Also check out Emma's regency romance series, Rogues & Gentlemen. Available now!

The Rogue
Rogues & Gentlemen Book 1

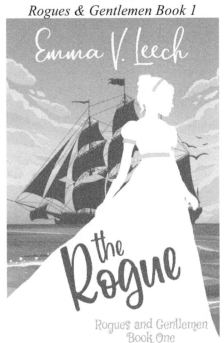

The notorious Rogue that began it all.

Set in Cornwall, 1815. Wild, untamed and isolated.

Lawlessness is the order of the day and smuggling is rife.

Henrietta always felt most at home in the wilds of the outdoors but even she had no idea how the mysterious and untamed would sweep her away in a moment.

Bewitched by his wicked blue eyes.

Henrietta Morton knows to look the other way when the free trading 'gentlemen' are at work.
Yet when a notorious pirate bursts into her local village shop, she

can avert her eyes no more. Bewitched by his wicked blue eyes, a moment of insanity follows as Henrietta hides the handsome fugitive from the Militia.

Her reward is a kiss, lingering and unforgettable.

In his haste to flee, the handsome pirate drops a letter, a letter that lays bare a tale of betrayal. When Henrietta's father gives her hand in marriage to a wealthy and villainous nobleman in return for the payment of his debts, she becomes desperate.

Blackmailing a pirate may be her only hope for freedom.

**** **Warning**: This book contains the most notorious rogue of all of Cornwall and, on occasion, is highly likely to include some mild sweating or descriptive sex scenes. ****

Free to read on *Kindle Unlimited*: The Rogue

Interested in a Regency Romance with a twist?

A Dog in a Doublet

The Regency Romance Mysteries Book 2

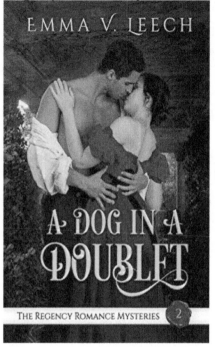

A man with a past

Harry Browning was a motherless guttersnipe, and the morning he came across the elderly Alexander Preston, The Viscount Stamford, clinging to a sheer rock face he didn't believe in fate. But the fates have plans for Harry whether he believes or not, and he's not entirely sure he likes them.

As a reward for his bravery, and in an unusual moment of charity, miserly Lord Stamford takes him on. He is taught to read, to manage the vast and crumbling estate, and to behave like a gentleman, but Harry knows that is something he will never truly be.

Already running from a dark past, his future is becoming increasingly complex as he finds himself caught in a tangled web of jealousy and revenge.

A feisty young maiden

Temptation, in the form of the lovely Miss Clarinda Bow, is a constant threat to his peace of mind, enticing him to be something he isn't. But when the old man dies his will makes a surprising demand, and the fates might just give Harry the chance to have everything he ever desired, including Clara, if only he dares.

And as those close to the Preston family begin to die, Harry may not have any choice.

Order your copy here. *A Dog in a Doublet*

Lose yourself in Emma's paranormal world with The French Vampire Legend series…..

The Key to Erebus
The French Vampire Legend Book 1

The truth can kill you.

Taken away as a small child, from a life where vampires, the Fae, and other mythical creatures are real and treacherous, the beautiful young witch, Jéhenne Corbeaux is totally unprepared when she returns to rural France to live with her eccentric Grandmother.

Thrown headlong into a world she knows nothing about she seeks to learn the truth about herself, uncovering secrets more shocking than anything she could ever have imagined and finding that she is by no means powerless to protect the ones she loves.

Despite her Gran's dire warnings, she is inexorably drawn to the dark and terrifying figure of Corvus, an ancient vampire and master of the vast Albinus family.

Jéhenne is about to find her answers and discover that, not only is Corvus far more dangerous than she could ever imagine, but that he holds much more than the key to her heart…

Now available at your favourite retailer.

The Key to Erebus

Check out Emma's exciting fantasy series with hailed by Kirkus Reviews as "An enchanting fantasy with a likable heroine, romantic intrigue, and clever narrative flourishes."

The Dark Prince
The French Fae Legend Book 1

Two Fae Princes
One Human Woman
And a world ready to tear them all apart.

Laen Braed is Prince of the Dark fae, with a temper and reputation to match his black eyes, and a heart that despises the human race. When he is sent back through the forbidden gates between realms to retrieve an ancient fae artifact, he returns home with far more than he bargained for.

Corin Albrecht, the most powerful Elven Prince ever born. His golden eyes are rumoured to be a gift from the gods, and destiny is calling him. With a love for the human world that runs deep, his friendship with Laen is being torn apart by his prejudices.

Océane DeBeauvoir is an artist and bookbinder who has always relied on her lively imagination to get her through an unhappy and uneventful life. A jewelled dagger put on display at a nearby museum hits the headlines with speculation of another race, the Fae. But the discovery also inspires Océane to create an extraordinary piece of art that cannot be confined to the pages of a book.

With two powerful men vying for her attention and their friendship stretched to the breaking point, the only question that remains…who is truly The Dark Prince.

The man of your dreams is coming…or is it your nightmares he visits? Find out in Book One of The French Fae Legend.

Available now to read at your favorite retailer.

The Dark Prince

Want more Emma?

If you enjoyed this book, please support this indie author and take a moment to leave a few words in a review. *Thank you!*

To be kept informed of special offers and free deals (which I do regularly) follow me on *https://www.bookbub.com/authors/emma-v-leech*

To find out more and to get news and sneak peeks of the first chapter of upcoming works, go to my website and sign up for the newsletter.
http://www.emmavleech.com/

Come and join the fans in my Facebook group for news, info and exciting discussion...

Emmas Book Club

Or Follow me here...

http://viewauthor.at/EmmaVLeechAmazon
Facebook
Instagram
Emma's Twitter page
TikTok

Can't get your fill of Historical Romance? Do you crave stories with passion and red hot chemistry?

If the answer is yes, have I got the group for you!

Come join myself and other awesome authors in our Facebook group.

Historical Harlots

Be the first to know about exclusive giveaways, chat with amazing HistRom authors, lots of raunchy shenanigans and more!

Historical Harlots Facebook Group

Made in the USA
Monee, IL
20 June 2023

36410390R00177